Melanchthon Fennessy Libby, William Wordsworth

Select Poems of William Wordswith

Melanchthon Fennessy Libby, William Wordsworth

Select Poems of William Wordswith

ISBN/EAN: 9783744711913

Printed in Europe, USA, Canada, Australia, Japan

Cover: Foto ©Andreas Hilbeck / pixelio.de

More available books at **www.hansebooks.com**

Select Poems

OF

WILLIAM WORDSWORTH

EDITED, WITH N

BY

M. F. LIBBY,

English Master of the Jameson Aven

> 'Come out into the light of things—
> Let Nature be your teacher."
>
> —Wordsworth

TORONTO
THE COPP, CLARK COMPANY, Limited
1892

At school I enjoyed the inestimable advantage of a very sensible, though at the same time a very severe master, the Reverend James Bowyer......At the same time that we were studying the Greek tragic poets, he made us read Shakespeare and Milton as lessons : and they were the lessons, too, which required most time and trouble to "bring up," so as to escape his censure. I learned from him that poetry, even that of the loftiest and, seemingly, that of the wildest odes, had a logic of its own, as severe as that of science ; and more difficult, because more subtle, more complex, and dependent upon more, and more fugitive causes. "In the truly great poets " he would say, "there is a reason assignable, not only for every word, but for the position of every word."

—Coleridge's " Biographia Literaria."

•

PREFACE.

At first sight the extreme simplicity of the greater number of these selections from Wordsworth may appear to make editing and annotating almost superfluous, but a closer view will reveal the truth that the poet's simplicity is not the direct method of childhood, but rather of a profound (however successful) manhood guided by both instinctive and acquired rules of art.

Classes in our schools may be expected to understand the thoughts and feelings of the simpler poems here more readily than they would understand the average work of poets like Coleridge and Byron ; while the more difficult poems here can hardly prove so obscure as the most difficult poems of other great poets.

Indeed the simplicity of these poems is likely to be the chief stumbling-block to those who study them.   It is in storm, passion, and excess, that the untrained find most to interest them whether in picture, play, or real life.   So in poetry, the warlike lines of Scott, the straining and heaving cadences of Byron, and the morbid, tear-starting beauty of parts of Longfellow and Tennyson, seize upon the young student with power and stir him into feeling.   But these poets are to Wordsworth as wine to water, as a scene of revelry to a homely evening, as a Christmas dinner to a frugal meal. .

Is it the nature of boys and girls to prefer the plain, wholesome, healthful thoughts and feelings of this poet, thoughts that never err from the line of truth and good sense, and feelings that never stirs the heart to undue activity, is it their nature to prefer these to the tumult and excitement of more

popular writers? Is it possible to make them love the frugal
and Puritan diet of Wordsworth without first making them as
simple, as wise, and as passionless? However one may reply to
these questions one will not deny that the reverence, and
modesty, and love of all good and beauty found in this poét's
works are qualities that every right-minded pupil may be led
to respect, and that a study of these verses cannot fail to do
good in a land where reverence for the Wordsworthian virtues
is said by the thoughtful to be far from conspicuous.

to not a few. To tenth-rate critics and compilers, for whom any violent shock to the public taste would be a temerity not to be risked, it is still quite permissible to speak of Words-worth's poetry, not only with ignorance, but with impertinence. On the Continent he is almost unknown.

I cannot think, then, that Wordsworth has, up to this time, at all obtained his deserts. " Glory," said M. Renan the other day, " glory after all is the thing which has the best chance of not being altogether vanity." Wordsworth was a homely man, and himself would certainly never have thought of talking of glory as that which, after all, has the best chance of not being altogether vanity. Yet we may well allow that few things are less vain than *real* glory. Let us conceive of the whole group of civilised nations as being, for intellectual and spiritual purposes, one great confederation, bound to a joint action and working towards a common result; a confederation whose members have a due knowledge both of the past, out of which they all proceed, and of one another. This was the ideal of Goethe, and it is an ideal which will impose itself upon the thoughts of our modern societies more and more. Then to be recognised by the verdict of such a confederation as a master, or even as a seriously and eminently worthy workman, in one's own line of intellectual or spiritual activity, is indeed glory ; a glory which it would be difficult to rate too highly. For what could be more beneficent, more salutary ? The world is for-warded by having its attention fixed on the best things ; and here is a tribunal, free from all suspicion of national and pro-vincial partiality, putting a stamp on the best things, and recommending them for general honour and acceptance. A nation, again, is furthered by recognition of its real gifts and successes ; it is encouraged to develop them further. And here is an honest verdict, telling us which of our supposed successes are really, in the judgment of the great impartial world, and not in our own private judgment only, successes, and which are not.

It is so easy to feel pride and satisfaction in one's own things, so hard to make sure that one is right in feeling it! We have a great empire. But so had Nebuchadnezzar. We extol the "unrivalled happiness" of our national civilisation. But then comes a candid friend, and remarks that our upper class is materialised, our middle class vulgarized, and our lower class brutalised. We are proud of our painting, our music. But we find that in the judgment of other people our painting is questionable, and our music non-existent. We are proud of our men of science. And here it turns out that the world is with us ; we find that in the judgment of other people, too, Newton among the dead, and Mr. Darwin among the living, hold as high a place as they hold in our national opinion.

Finally, we are proud of our poets and poetry. Now poetry is nothing less than the most perfect speech of man, that in which he comes nearest to being able to utter the truth. It is no small thing, therefore, to succeed eminently in poetry. And so much is required for duly estimating success here, that about poetry it is perhaps hardest to arrive at a sure general verdict, and takes longest. Meanwhile, our own conviction of the superiority of our national poets is not decisive, is almost certain to be mingled, as we see constantly in English eulogy of Shakspeare, with much of provincial infatuation. And we know what was the opinion current amongst our neighbours the French, people of taste, acuteness, and quick literary tact, not a hundred years ago, about our great poets. The old *Biographie Universelle* notices the pretension of the English to a place for their poets among the chief poets of the world, and says that this is a pretension which to no one but an Englishman can ever seem admissable. And the scornful, disparaging things said by foreigners about Shakspeare and Milton, and about our national over-estimate of them, have been often quoted, and will be in every one's remembrance.

A great change has taken place, and Shakspeare is now

generally recognized, even in France, as one of the greatest of
poets. Yes, some anti-Gallican cynic will say, the French
rank him with Corneille and with Victor Hugo ! But let me
have the pleasure of quoting a sentence about Shakspeare,
which I met with by accident not long ago in the *Correspond-
ant*, a French review which not a dozen English people, I
suppose, look at. The writer is praising Shakspeare's prose.
.With Shakspeare, he says, "prose comes in whenever the
subject, being more familiar, is unsuited to the majestic English iambic." And he goes on : "Shakspeare is the king of
poetic rhythm and style, as well as the king of the realm of
thought ; along with his dazzling prose, Shakspeare has suc-
ceeded in giving us the most varied, the most harmonious
verse which has ever sounded upon the human ear since the
verse of the Greeks." M. Henry Cochin, the writer of this
sentence, deserves our gratitude for it ; it would not be easy to
praise Shakspeare, in a single sentence, more justly. And
when a foreigner and a Frenchman writes thus of Shakspeare,
and when Goethe says of Milton, in whom there was so much
to repel Goethe rather than to attract him, that "nothing has
ever been done so entirely in the sense of the Greeks as *Sam-
son Agonistes*," and that "Milton is in very truth a poet whom
we must treat with all reverence," then we understand what.
constitutes a European recognition of poets and poetry as con-
tradistinguished from a merely national recognition, and that
in favour both of Milton and of Shakspeare the judgment of
the high court of appeal has finally gone.

I come back to M. Renan's praise of glory, from which I
started. Yes, real glory is a most serious thing, glory authenti-
cated by the Amphictyonic Court of final appeal, definitive
glory. And even for poets and poetry, long and difficult as
may be the process of arriving at the right award, the right
award comes at last, the definitive glory rests where it is
deserved. Every establishment of such a real glory is good

and wholesome for mankind at large, good and wholesome for the nation which produced the poet crowned with it. To the poet himself it can seldom do harm, for he, poor man, is in his grave, probably, long before his glory crowns him.

Wordsworth has been in his grave for some thirty years, and certainly his lovers and admirers cannot flatter themselves that this great and steady light of glory as yet shines over him. He is not fully recognized at home; he is not recognised at all. abroad. Yet I firmly believe that the poetical performance of Wordsworth is, after that of Shakspeare and Milton, of which all the world now recognises the worth, undoubtedly the most considerable in our language from the Elizabethan age to the present time. Chaucer is anterior; and on other grounds, too, he cannot well be brought into the comparison. But taking the roll of our chief poetical names, besides Shakspeare and Milton, from the age of Elizabeth downwards, and going through it,—Spenser, Dryden, Pope, Gray, Goldsmith, Cowper, Burns, Coleridge, Scott, Campbell, Moore, Byron, Shelley, Keats (I mention those only who are dead),—I think it certain that Wordsworth's name deserves to stand, and will finally stand, above them all. Several of the poets named have gifts and excellences which Wordsworth has not. But taking the performance of each as a whole, I say that Wordsworth seems to me to have left a body of poetical work superior in power, in interest, in the qualities which give enduring freshness, to that which any one of the others has left.

But this is not enough to say. I think it certain, further, that if we take the chief poetical names of the Continent since the death of Molière, and, omitting Goethe, confront the remaining names with that of Wordsworth, the result is the same. Let us take Klopstock, Lessing, Schiller, Uhland, Rückert, and Heine for Germany; Filicaia, Alfieri, Manzoni, and Leopardi for Italy; Racine, Boileau, Voltaire, André Chenier, Béranger, Lamartine, Musset, M. Victor Hugo (he

has been so long celebrated that although he still lives I may
be permitted to name him) for France. Several of these, again,
have evidently gifts and excellences to which Wordsworth can
make no pretension. But in real poetical achievement it
seems to me indubitable that to Wordsworth, here again,
belongs the palm. It seems to me that Wordsworth has left
behind him a body of poetical work which wears, and will
wear, better on the whole than the performance of any one of
these personages, so far more brilliant and celebrated, most of
them than the homely poet of Rydal. Wordsworth's performance in poetry is on the whole, in power, in interest, in the
qualities which give enduring freshness, superior to theirs.

This is a high claim to make for Wordsworth. But if it is
a just claim, if Wordsworth's place among the poets who have
appeared in the last two or three centuries is after Shakspeare,
Molière, Milton, Goethe, indeed, but before all the rest, then
in time Wordsworth will have his due. We shall recognise
him in his place, as we recognise Shakspeare and Milton; and
not only we ourselves shall recognise him, but he will be
recognised by Europe also. Meanwhile, those who recognise
him already may do well, perhaps, to ask themselves whether
there are not in the case of Wordsworth certain special
obstacles which hinder or delay his due recognition by others,
and whether these obstacles are not in some measure remova-
able.

The *Excursion* and the *Prelude*, his poems of greatest bulk,
are by no means Wordsworth's best work. His best work is
in his shorter pieces, and many indeed are there of these which
are of first-rate excellence. But in his seven volumes the pieces
of high merit are mingled with a mass of pieces very inferior
to them; so inferior to them that it seems wonderful how the
same poet should have produced both. Shakspeare frequently
has lines and passages in a strain quite false, and which are
entirely unworthy of him. But one can imagine his smiling if

one could meet him in the Elysian Fields and tell him so; smiling and replying that he knew it perfectly well himself, and what did it matter? But with Wordsworth the case is different. Work altogether inferior, work quite uninspired, flat and dull, is produced by him with evident unconsciousness of its defects, and he presents it to us with the same faith and seriousness as his best work. Now a drama or an epic fill the mind, and one does not look beyond them; but in a collection of short pieces the impression made by one piece requires to be continued and sustained by the piece following. In reading Wordsworth the impression made by one of his fine pieces is too often dulled and spoiled by a very inferior piece coming after it.

Wordsworth composed verses during a space of some sixty years; and it is no exaggeration to say that within one single decade of those years, between 1798 and 1808, almost all his really first-rate work was produced. A mass of inferior work remains, work done before and after this golden prime, imbedding the first-rate work and clogging it, obstructing our approach to it, chilling, not unfrequently, the high-wrought mood with which we leave it. To be recognized far and wide as a great poet, to be possible and receivable as a classic, Wordsworth needs to be relieved of a great deal of the poetical baggage which now encumbers him. To administer this relief is indispensable, unless he is to continue to be a poet for the few only, a poet valued far below his real worth by the world.

There is another thing. Wordsworth classified his poems not according to any commonly received plan of arrangement, but according to a scheme of mental physiology. He has poems of the fancy, poems of the imagination, poems of sentiment and reflection, and so on. His categories are ingenious but far-fetched, and the result of his employment of them unsatisfactory. Poems are separated one from another which possess a kinship of subject or of treatment far more vital and deep than the supposed unity of mental origin which was Wordsworth's reason for joining them with others.

The tact of the Greeks in matters of this kind was infallible. We may rely upon it that we shall not improve upon the classification adopted by the Greeks for kinds of poetry; that their categories of epic, dramatic, lyric, and so forth, have a natural propriety, and should be adhered to. It may sometimes seem doubtful to which of two categories a poem belongs; whether this or that poem is to be called for instance, narrative or lyric, lyric or elegiac. But there is to be found in every good poem a strain, a predominant note, which determines the poem as belonging to one of these kinds rather than the other; and here is the best proof of the value of the classification, and of the advantage of adhering to it. Wordsworth's poems will never produce their due effect until they are freed from their present artificial arrangement, and grouped more naturally.

Disengaged from the quantity of inferior work which now obscures them, the best poems of Wordsworth, I hear many people say, would indeed stand out in great beauty, but they would prove to be very few in number, scarcely more than half-a-dozen. I maintain, on the other hand, that what strikes me with admiration, what establishes in my opinion Wordsworth's superiority, is the great and ample body of powerful work which remains to him, even after all his inferior work has been cleared away. He gives us so much to rest upon, so much which communicates his spirit and engages ours!

This is of very great importance. If it were a comparison of single pieces, or of three or four pieces, by each poet, I do not say that Wordsworth would stand decisively above Grey, or Burns, or Coleridge, or Keats, or Manzoni, or Heine. It is in his ampler body of powerful work that I find his superiority. His good work itself, his work which counts, is not all of it, of course, of equal value. Some kinds of poetry are in themselves lower kinds than others. The ballad kind is a lower kind;

2

the didactic kind, still more, is a lower kind. Poetry of this latter sort, counts, too, sometimes, by its biographical interest partly, not by its poetical interest pure and simple ; but then this can only be when the poet producing it has the power and importance of Wordsworth, a power and importance which he assuredly did not establish by such didactic poetry alone. Altogether, it is, I say, by the great body of powerful and significant work which remains to him, after every reduction and deduction has been made, that Wordsworth's superiority is proved.

To exhibit this body of Wordsworth's best work, to clear away obstructions from around it, and to let it speak for itself, is what every lover of Wordsworth should desire. Until this has been done, Wordsworth, whom we, to whom he is dear, all of us know and feel to be so great a poet, has not had a fair chance before the world. When once it has been done, he will make his way best not by our advocacy of him, but by his own worth and power. We may safely leave him to make his way thus, we who believe that a superior worth and power in poetry finds in mankind a sense responsive to it and disposed at last to recognize it. Yet at the outset, before he has been duly known and recognized, we may do Wordsworth a service, perhaps, in indicating in what his superior power and worth will be found to consist, and in what it will not.

Long ago, in speaking of Homer, I said that the noble and profound application of ideas to life is the most essential part of poetic greatness. I said that a great poet receives his distinctive character of superiority from his application, under the conditions immutably fixed by the laws of poetic beauty and poetic truth, from his application, I say, to his subject, whatever it may be, of the ideas

"On man, on nature, and on human life,"

which he has acquired for himself. The line quoted is Words-

worth's own ; and his superiority arises from his powerful use,
in his best pieces, his powerful application to his subject, of
ideas " on man, on nature, and on human life."

Voltaire, with his signal acuteness, most truly remarked that
" no nation has treated in poetry moral ideas with more energy
and depth than the English nation." And he adds : " There,
it seems to me, is the great merit of the English poets." Voltaire does not mean, by " treating in poetry moral ideas," the
composing moral and didactic poems :—that brings us but a very
little way in poetry. He means just the same thing as was
meant when I spoke above " of the noble and profound application of ideas to life ; " and he means the application of these
ideas under the conditions fixed for us by the laws of poetic
beauty and poetic truth. If it is said that to call these ideas
moral ideas it is to introduce a strong and injurious limitation,
I answer that it is to do nothing of the kind, because moral
ideas are really so main a part of human life. The question,
how to live, is itself a moral idea ; and it is the question which
most interests every man, and with which, in some way or
other, he is perpetually occupied. A large sense is of course
to be given to the term *moral*. Whatever bears upon the
question, " how to live," comes under it.

> " Nor love thy life, nor hate ; but, what thou liv'st,
> Live well ; how long or short, permit to heaven."

In those few lines, Milton utters, as every one at once perceives, a moral idea. Yes, but so too, when Keats consoles the
forward-bending lover on the Grecian Urn, the lover arrested
and presented in immortal relief by the sculptor's hand before
he can kiss, with the line,

> " For ever wilt thou love, and she be fair "—

he utters a moral idea. When Shakespeare says, that

> " We are such stuff
> As dreams are made of, and our little life
> Is rounded with a sleep,"

he utters a moral idea.

Voltaire was right in thinking that the energetic and profound treatment of moral ideas, in this large sense, is what distinguishes the English poetry. He sincerely meant praise, not dispraise or hint of limitation ; and they err who suppose that poetic limitation is a necessary consequence of the fact, the fact being granted as Voltaire states it. If what distinguishes the greatest poets is their powerful and profound application of ideas to life, which surely no good critic will deny, then to prefix to the term ideas here the term moral makes hardly any difference, because human life itself is in so preponderating a degree moral.

It is important, therefore, to hold fast to this : that poetry is at bottom a criticism of life ; that the greatness of a poet lies in a powerful and beautiful application of ideas to life, — to the question : How to live. Morals are often treated in a narrow and false fashion, they are bound up with systems of thought and belief which have had their day, they are fallen into the hands of pedants and professional dealers, they grow tiresome to some of us. We find attraction, at times, even in a poetry of revolt against them ; in a poetry which might take for its motto Omar Kheyam's words : " Let us make up in the tavern for the time which we have wasted in the mosque." Or we find attractions in a poetry indifferent to them, in a poetry where the contents may be what they will, but where the form is studied and exquisite. We delude ourselves in either case ; and the best cure for our delusion is to let our minds rest upon that great and inexhaustible word *life*, until we learn to enter into its meaning. A poetry of revolt against moral ideas is a poetry of revolt against *life ;* a poetry of indifference towards moral ideas is a poetry of indifference towards *life*

Epictetus had a happy figure for things like the play of the
senses, or literary form and finish, or argumentative ingenuity,
in comparison with " the best and master thing " for us, as he
called it, the concern, how to live. Some people were afraid of
them, he said, or they disliked and undervalued them. Such
people were wrong ; they were unthankful or cowardly. But
the things might also be over-prized, and treated as final when
they are not. They bear to life the relation which inns bear to
home. " As if a man, journeying home, and finding a nice inn
on the road, and liking it, were to stay for ever at the inn !
Man, thou hast forgotten thine object ; thy journey was not *to*
this but *through* this. ' But this inn is taking.' And how
many other inns, too, are taking, and how many fields and
meadows ! but as places of passage merely. You have an
object, which is this : to get home, to do your duty to your
family, friends, and fellow-countrymen, to attain inward freedom, serenity, happiness, contentment. Style takes your fancy,
arguing takes your fancy, and you forget your home and want
to make your abode with them and to stay with them, on the
plea that they are taking. Who denies that they are taking ?
but as places of passage, as inns. And when I say this, you
suppose me to be attacking the care for style, the care for argument. I am not ; I attack the resting in them, the not looking
to the end which is beyond them."

Now, when we come across a poet like Théophile Gautier,
we have a poet who has taken up his abode at an inn, and never
got farther. There may be inducements to this or that one of
us, at this or that moment, to find delight in him, to cleave to
him ; but after all, we do not change the truth about him,—we
only stay ourselves in his inn along with him. And when we
come across a poet like Wordsworth, who sings,

> " Of truth, of grandeur, beauty, love and hope,
> And melancholy fear subdued by faith,
> Of blessed consolations in distress,

Of moral strength and intellectual power,
Of joy in widest commonalty spread "—

then we have a poet intent on "the best and master thing,"
and who prosecutes his journey home. We say, for brevity's
sake, that he deals with *life*, because he deals with that in
which life really consists. This is what Voltaire means to
praise in the English poets,—this dealing with what is really
life. But always it is the mark of the greatest poets that they
deal with it; and to say that the English poets are remarkable
for dealing with it, is only another way of saying, what is true,
that in poetry the English genius has especially shown its
power.

Wordsworth deals with it, and his greatness lies in his dealing with it so powerfully. I have named a number of celebrated poets above all of whom he, in my opinion, deserves to
be placed. He is to be placed above poets like Voltaire, Dryden, Pope, Lessing, Schiller, because these famous personages,
with a thousand gifts and merits, never, or scarcely ever, attain
the distinctive accent and utterance of the high and genuine
poets—

"Quique pii vates et Phœbo digna locuti,"

at all. Burns, Keats, Heine, not to speak of others in our
list, have this accent ;—who can doubt it ? And at the same
time they have treasures of humour, felicity, passion, for which
in Wordsworth we shall look in vain. Where, then, is Wordsworth's superiority ? It is here ; he deals with more of *life*
than they do ; he deals with *life*, as a whole, more powerfully.

No Wordsworthian will doubt this. Nay, the fervent
Wordsworthian will add, as Mr. Leslie Stephen does, that
Wordsworth's poetry is precious because his philosophy is
sound ; that his "ethical system is as distinctive and capable of
exposition as Bishop Butler's ; " that his poetry is informed by

ideas which "fall spontaneously into a scientific system of thought." But we must be on our guard against the Words-worthians, if we want to secure for Wordsworth his due rank as a poet. The Wordsworthians are apt to praise him for the wrong things, and to lay far too much stress upon what they call his philosophy. His poetry is the reality, his philosophy,— so far, at least, as it may put on the form and habit of "a scientific system of thought," and the more that it puts them on,—is the illusion. Perhaps we shall one day learn to make this proposition general, and to say : Poetry is the reality, philosophy the illusion. But in Wordsworth's case, at any rate, we cannot do him justice until we dismiss his formal poilosophy.

The *Excursion* abounds with philosophy, and therefore the *Excursion* is to the Wordsworthian what it never can be to the disinterested lover of poetry,—a satisfactory work, "Duty exists," says Wordsworth, in the *Excursion ;* and then he proceeds thus :—

> . . . . "Immutably survive,
> For our support, the measures and the forms,
> Which an abstract Intelligence supplies,
> Whose kingdom is, where time and space are not."

And the Wordsworthian is delighted, and thinks that here is a sweet union of philosophy and poetry. But the disinterested lover of poetry will feel that the lines carry us really not a step farther than the proposition which they would interpret ; that they are a tissue of elevated but abstract verbiage, alien to the very nature of poetry.

Or let us come direct to the centre of Wordsworth's philosophy, as "an ethical system, as distinctive and capable of systematic exposition as Bishop Butler's " :—

> . . . . . "One adequate support
> For the calamities of mortal life
> Exists, one only ;—an assured belief
> That the procession of our fate, howe'er
> Sad or disturbed, is ordered by a Being
> Of infinite benevolence and power ;
> Whose everlasting purposes embrace
> All accidents, converting them to good."

That is doctrine such as we hear in church too, religious and philosophic doctrine; and the attached Wordsworthian loves passages of such doctrine, and brings them forward in proof of his poet's excellence.   But however true the doctrine may be, it has, as here presented, none of the characters of *poetic* truth, the kind of truth which we require from a poet, and in which Wordsworth is really strong.

Even the "intimations" of the famous Ode, those corner-stones of the supposed philosophic system of Wordsworth,—the idea of the high instincts and affections coming out in childhood, testifying of a divine home recently left, and fading away as our life proceeds,—this idea, of undeniable beauty as a play of fancy, has itself not the character of poetic truth of the best kind; it has no real solidity.   The instinct of delight in Nature and her beauty had no doubt extraordinary strength in Wordsworth himself as a child.   But to say that universally this instinct is mighty in childhood, and tends to die away afterwards, is to say what is extremely doubtful.   In many people, perphaps with the majority of educated persons, the love of nature is nearly imperceptible at ten years old, but strong and operative at thirty.   In general we may say of these high instincts of early childhood, the base of the alleged systematic philosophy of Wordsworth, what Thucydides says of the early achievements of the Greek race :—" It is impossible to speak with certainty of what is so remote; but from all that we can really investigate, I should say that they were no very great things."

Finally the "scientific system of thought" in Wordsworth gives us at least such poetry as this, which the devout Wordsworthian accepts :—

> "O for the coming of that glorious time
> When, prizing knowledge as her noblest wealth
> And best protection, this Imperial Realm,
> While she exacts allegiance, shall admit
> An obligation, on her part, to *teach*
> Them who are born to serve her and obey ;
> Binding herself by statute to secure,
> For all the children whom her soil maintains,
> The rudiments of letters, and inform
> The mind with moral and religious truth."

Wordsworth calls Voltaire dull, and surely the production of these un-Voltairian lines must have been imposed on him as a judgment ! One can hear them being quoted at a Social Science Congress ; one can call up the whole scene. A great room in one of our dismal provincial towns ; dusty air and jaded afternoon daylight ; benches full of men with bald heads and women in spectacles ; an orator lifting up his face from a manuscript written within and without to declaim these lines of Wordsworth ; and in the soul of any poor child of nature who may have wandered in thither, an unutterable sense of lamentation, and mourning, and woe !

"But turn we," as Wordsworth says, "from these bold, bad men," the haunters of Social Science Congresses. And let us be on our guard, too, against the exhibitors and extollers of a "scientific system of thought" in Wordsworth's poetry. The poetry will never be seen aright while they thus exhibit it. The cause of its greatness is simple, and may be told quite simply. Wordsworth's poetry is great because of the extraordinary power with which Wordsworth feels the joy offered to us in nature, the joy offered to us in the simple primary affections and duties ; and because of the extraordinary power

with which, in case after case, he shows us this joy, and
renders it so as to make us share it.

The source of joy from which he thus draws is the truest
and most unfailing source of joy accessible to man.   It is also
accessible universally.   Wordsworth brings us word, therefore,
according to his own strong and characteristic line, he brings
us his word

> "Of joy in widest commonalty spread."

Here is an immense advantage for a poet.   Wordsworth tells
of what all seek, and tells of it at its truest and best source,
and yet a source where all may go and draw for it.

Nevertheless, we are not to suppose that everything is
precious which Wordsworth, standing even at this perennial
and beautiful source, may give us.   Wordsworthians are apt
to talk as if it must be.   They will speak with the same
reverence of *The Sailor's Mother*, for example, as of *Lucy Gray*.
They do their master harm by such lack of discrimination.
Lucy Gray is a beautiful success; *The Sailor's Mother* is a
failure.   To give aright what he wishes to give, to interpret
and render successfully, is not always within Wordsworth's
own command.   It is within no poet's command; here is the
part of the Muse, the inspiration, the God, the "not ourselves."
In Wordworth's case, the accident, for so it may almost be
called, of inspiration, is of peculiar importance.   No poet,
perhaps, is so evidently filled with a new and sacred energy
when the inspiration is upon him; no poet, when it fails him,
is so left "weak as is a breaking wave."   I remember hearing
him say that "Goethe's poetry was not inevitable enough."
The remark is striking and true; no line in Goethe, as Goethe
said himself, but its maker knew well how it came there.
Wordsworth is right, Goethe's poetry is not inevitable; not
inevitable enough.   But Wordsworth's poetry, when he is at
his best, is inevitable, as inevitable as Nature herself.   It

might seem that Nature not only gave him the matter for his poem, but wrote his poem for him. He has no style. He was too conversant with Milton not to catch at times his master's manner, and he has fine Miltonic lines; but he has no assured poetic style of his own, like Milton. When he seeks to have a style he falls into ponderosity and pomposity. In the *Excursion* we have his style, as an artistic product of his own creation; and although Jeffrey completely failed to recognise Wordsworth's real greatness, he was yet not wrong in saying of the *Excursion*, as a work of poetic style: "This will never do." And yet magical as is that power, which Wordsworth has not, of assured and possessed poetic style, he has something which is an equivalent for it.

Every one who has any sense for these things feels the subtle turn, the heightening, which is given to a poet's verse by his genius for style. We can feel it in the

> "After life's fitful fever, he sleeps well"—

of Shakespeare; in the

> . . . . . . "though fall'n on evil days,
> On evil days though fall'n, and evil tongues"—

of Milton. It is the incomparable charm of Milton's power of poetic style which gives such worth to *Paradise Regained*, and makes a great poem of a work in which Milton's imagination does not soar high. Wordsworth has in constant possession, and at command, no style of this kind; but he had too poetic a nature, and had read the great poets too well, not to catch, as I have already remarked, something of it occasionally. We find it not only in his Miltonic lines; we find it in such a phrase as this, where the manner is his own, not Milton's—

> . . . . "the fierce confederate storm
> Of sorrow barricadoed evermore
> Within the walls of cities;"

although even here, perhaps, the power of style, which is
undeniable, is more properly that of eloquent prose than the
subtle heightening and change wrought by genuine poetic
style.   It is style, again, and the elevation given by style,
which chiefly makes the effectiveness of *Laodameia*.   Still the
right sort of verse to choose from Wordsworth, if we are to
seize his true and most characteristic form of expression, is a
line like this from *Michael* :—

> "And never lifted up a single stone."

There is nothing subtle in it, no heightening, nor study of
poetic style, strictly so called, at all; yet it is expression of the
highest and most truly expressive kind.

Wordsworth owed much to Burns, and a style of perfect
plainness, relying for effect solely on the weight and force of
that which with entire fidelity it utters, Burns could show him.

> "The poor inhabitant below
> Was quick to learn and wise to know,
> And keenly felt the friendly glow
>   And softer flame ;
> But thoughtless follies laid him low
>   And stain'd his name."

Every one will be conscious of a likeness here to Wordsworth ;
and if Wordsworth did great things with this nobly plain
manner, we must remember, what indeed he himself would
always have been forward to acknowledge, that Burns used it
before him.

Still· Wordsworth's use of it has something unique and
unmatchable.   Nature herself seems, I say, to take the pen
out of his hand, and to write for him with her own bare, sheer,
penetrating power.   This arises from two causes; from the
profound sincereness with which Wordsworth feels his subject,
and also from the profoundly sincere and natural character of

his subject itself. He can and will treat such a subject with nothing but the most plain, first-hand, almost austere naturalness. His expression may often be called bald, as, for instance, in the poem of *Resolution and Independence;* but it is bald as the bare mountain tops are bald, with a baldness which is full of grandeur.

Wherever we meet with the successful balance, in Words-worth, of profound truth of subject with profound truth of execution, he is unique. His best poems are those which most perfectly exhibit this balance. I have a warm admiration for *Laodameia* and for the great *Ode;* but if I am to tell the very truth, I find *Laodameia* not wholly free from something artifical, and the great *Ode* not wholly free from something declamatory. If I had to pick out poems of a kind most perfectly to show Wordsworth's unique power, I should rather choose poems such as *Michael, The Fountain, The High'and Reaper.* And poems with the peculiar and unique beauty which distinguishes these, Wordsworth produced in considerable number; besides very many other poems of which the worth, although not so rare as the worth of these, is still exceedingly high.

On the whole, then, as I said at the beginning. not only is Wordsworth eminent by reason of the goodness of his best work, but he is eminent also by reason of the great body of good work which he has left to us. With the ancients I will not compare him. In many respects the ancients are far above us, and yet there is something that we demand which they can never give. Leaving the ancients, let us come to the poets and poetry of Christendom. Dante, Shakespeare, Molière, Milton, Goethe, are altogether larger and more splendid luminaries in the poetical heaven than Wordsworth. But I know not where else, among the moderns, we are to find his superiors.

To disengage the poems which show his power, and to present them to the English-speaking public and to the world, is the object of this volume. I by no means say that it contains all which in Wordsworth's poems is interesting. Except in the case of *Margaret,* a story composed separately from the rest of the *Excursion,* and which belongs to a different part of England, I have not ventured on detaching portions of poems, or on giving any piece otherwise than as Wordsworth himself gave it. But, under the conditions imposed by this reserve, the volume contains, I think, everything, or nearly everything, which may best serve him with the majority of lovers of poetry, nothing which may disserve him.

I have spoken lightly of Wordsworthians: and if we are to get Wordsworth recognised by the public and by the world, we must recommend him not in the spirit of a clique, but in the spirit of disinterested lovers of poetry. But I am a Wordsworthian myself. I can read with pleasure and edification *Peter Bell,* and the whole series of *Ecclesiastical Sonnets,* and the address to Mr. Wilkinson's spade, and even the *Thanksgiving Ode ;*—everything of Wordsworth, I think, except *Vaudracour and Julia.* It is not for nothing that one has been brought up in the veneration of a man so truly worthy of homage; that one has seen him and heard him, lived in his neighbourhood and been familiar with his country. No Wordsworthian has a tenderer affection for this pure and sage master than I, or is less really offended by his defects. But Wordsworth is something more than the pure and sage master of a small band of devoted followers, and we ought not to rest satisfied until he is seen to be what he is. He is one of the very chief glories of English Poetry ; and by nothing is England so glorious as by her poetry. Let us lay aside every weight which hinders our getting him recognised as this, and let our one study be to bring to pass, as widely as possible and as truly as possible, his own word concerning his poems :—"They will co-operate with the benign tendencies in human nature and society, and will, in their degree, be efficacious in making men wiser, better, and happier."

POEMS OF BALLAD FORM

" 'Tis all men's office to speak patience
To those that wring under the load of sorrow."
—Much Ado about Nothing.

SELECTIONS.

THE REVERIE OF POOR SUSAN.

At the corner of Wood Street, when daylight appears,
Hangs a Thrush that sings loud, it has sung for three years :
Poor Susan has passed by the spot, and has heard
In the silence of morning the song of the Bird.   5

'Tis a note of enchantment ; what ails her? She sees
A mountain ascending, a vision of trees ;
Bright volumes of vapour through Lothbury glide, *imagine a*
And a river flows on through the vale of Cheapside.

Green pastures she views in the midst of the dale,   10
Down which she so often has tripped with her pail ;
And a single small Cottage, a nest like a dove's,
The one only dwelling on earth that she loves.

She looks, and her heart is in heaven : but they fade,
The mist and the river, the hill and the shade :   15
The stream will not flow, and the hill will not rise,
And the colours have all passed away from her eyes.

WE ARE SEVEN.

———A simple child,
That lightly draws its breath,
And feels its life in every limb,
What should it know of death?   5

3

I met a little cottage girl :
She was eight years old, she said ;
Her hair was thick with many a curl
That clustered round her head.

She had a rustic, woodland air,
And she was wildly clad :
Her eyes were fair, and very fair
—Her beauty made me glad.

"Sisters and brothers, little Maid,
How many may you be ?"
"How many ?   Seven in all," she said,
And wondering looked at me.

"And where are they ?   I pray you tell."
She answered, "Seven are we ;
And two of us at Conway dwell,
And two are gone to sea.

"Two of us in the churchyard lie,
My sister and my brother ;
And, in the churchyard cottage, I
Dwell near them with my mother."

"You say that two at Conway dwell,
And two are gone to sea,
Yet ye are seven !—I pray you tell,
Sweet Maid, how this may be."

Then did the little Maid reply,
"Seven boys and girls are we ;
Two of us in the churchyard lie,
Beneath the churchyard tree."

" You run about, my little Maid,
  Your limbs they are alive ;
  If two are in the churchyard laid,
  Then ye are only five."

" Their graves are green, they may be seen," *The*
  The little Maid replied,
"Twelve steps or more from my mother's door,   40
  And they are side by side.

" My stockings there I often knit,
  My kerchief there I hem ;
  And there upon the ground I sit—
  I sit and sing to them.   45

" And often after sunset, Sir,
  When it is light and fair,
  I take my little porringer,
  And eat my supper there.

" The first that died was little Jane ;   50
  In bed she moaning lay,
  Till God released her of her pain ;
  And then she went away.

" So in the churchyard she was laid ;
  And, when the grass was dry,   55
  Together round her grave we played,
  My brother John and I.

"And when the ground was white with snow,
  And I could run and slide,
  My brother John was forced to go,   60
  And he lies by her side."

" How many are you, then," said I.
" If they two are in Heaven ? "
　The little Maiden did reply,
" O Master! we are seven."　　　　　　　　　65

" But they are dead; those two are dead !
　Their spirits are in Heaven ! "
'Twas throwing words away : for still
The little Maid would have her will,
And said, " Nay, we are seven ! "　　　　　70

LUCY GRAY,

OR, SOLITUDE.

OFT I had heard of Lucy Gray:
And, when I crossed the wild,
I chanced to see at break of day　　　　　5
The solitary Child.

No mate, no comrade Lucy knew;
She dwelt on a wide moor,
—The sweetest thing that ever grew
Beside a human door!　　　　　　　　　10

You yet may spy the fawn at play,
The hare upon the green;
But the sweet face of Lucy Gray
Will never more be seen.

" To-night will be a stormy night—　　　15
You to the town must go;
And take a lantern, Child, to light
Your mother through the snow."

" That, Father! will I gladly do :
'Tis scarcely afternoon –   20
The Minster-clock has just struck two,
And yonder is the Moon."

At this the Father raised his hook,
And snapped a faggot-band ;
He plied his work ;—and Lucy took   25
The lantern in her hand.

Not blither is the mountain roe :
With many a wanton stroke
Her feet disperse the powdery snow,
That rises up like smoke.   30

The snow came on before its time :
She wandered up and down ;
And many a hill did Lucy climb ;
But never reached the town.

The wretched parents all that night   35
Went shouting far and wide ;
But there was neither sound nor sight
To serve them for a guide.

At day-break on a hill they stood
That overlooked the moor ;   40
And thence they saw the bridge of wood,
A furlong from their door.

They wept—and, turning homeward, cried,
" In Heaven we all shall meet : "
—When in the snow the mother spied   45
The print of Lucy's feet.

Half breathless from the steep hill's edge
They tracked the footmarks small ;
And through the broken hawthorn-hedge,
And by the long stone-wall ;   · 50

And then an open field they crossed :
The marks were still the same ;
They tracked them on, nor ever lost ;
And to the Bridge they came.

They followed from the snowy bank   55
Those footmarks, one by one,
Into the middle of the plank ;
And further there were none !

—Yet some maintain that to this day
She is a living child ;   60
That you may see sweet Lucy Gray
Upon the lonesome wild.

O'er rough and smooth she trips along
And never looks behind ;
And sings a solitary song   65
That whistles in the wind.

NARRATIVE POEMS.

"*A verse may find him who a sermon flies,*
And turn delight into a sacrifice."
—George Herbert, 1593-1632.

MICHAEL.

A PASTORAL POEM.

IF from the public way you turn your steps
Up the tumultuous brook of Green-head Ghyll,
You will suppose that with an upright path   5
Your feet must struggle; in such bold ascent
The pastoral mountains front you, face to face.
But, courage! for around that boisterous Brook
The mountains have all opened out themselves,
And made a hidden valley of their own.   10
No habitation can be seen; but they
Who journey hither find themselves alone
With a few sheep, with rocks and stones, and kites
That overhead are sailing in the sky.
It is in truth an utter solitude;   15
Nor should I have made mention of this Dell
But for one object which you might pass by,
Might see and notice not.   Beside the brook
Appears a straggling heap of unhewn stones!
And to that place a story appertains,   20
Which, though it be ungarnished with events,
Is not unfit, I deem, for the fireside,
Or for the summer shade.   It was the first
Of those domestic tales that spake to me
Of Shepherds, dwellers in the valleys, men   25
Whom I already loved;—not verily
For their own sakes, but for the fields and hills
Where was their occupation and abode.
And hence this tale, while I was yet a Boy
Careless of books, yet having felt the power   30

Of Nature, by the gentle agency
Of natural objects led me on to feel
For passions that were not my own, and think
(At random and imperfectly indeed) .
On man, the heart of man, and human life.   35
Therefore, although it be a history
Homely and rude, I will relate the same
For the delight of a few natural hearts;
And, with yet fonder feeling, for the sake
Of youthful Poets, who among these Hills   40
Will be my second self when I am gone.

Upon the Forest-side in Grasmere Vale
There dwelt a Shepherd, Michael was his name;
An old man, stout of heart, and strong of limb.
His bodily frame had been from youth to age   45
Of an unusual strength : his mind was keen,
Intense, and frugal, apt for all affairs,
And in his Shepherd's calling he was prompt
And watchful more than ordinary men.
Hence had he learned the meaning of all winds,   50
Of blasts of every tone; and, oftentimes,
When others heeded not, he heard the South
Make subterraneous music, like the noise
Of Bagpipers, on distant Highland hills.
The shepherd, at such warning, of his flock   55
Bethought him, and he to himself would say,
" The winds are now devising work for me ! "
And, truly, at all times, the storm—that drives
The traveller to a shelter—summoned him
Up to the mountains : he had been alone   60
Amid the heart of many thousand mists,
That came to him and left him on the heights.
So lived he till his eightieth year was past.

And grossly that man errs, who should suppose
That the green Valleys, and the Streams and Rocks,⠀⠀⠀65
Were things indifferent to the Shepherd's thoughts.
Fields, where with cheerful spirits he had breathed
The common air; the hills, which he so oft
Had climbed with vigorous steps; which had impressed
So many incidents upon his mind⠀⠀⠀70
Of hardship, skill or courage, joy or fear;
Which, like a book, preserved the memory
Of the dumb animals, whom he had saved,
Had fed or sheltered, linking to such acts,
The certainty of honourable gain,⠀⠀⠀75
Those fields, those hills—what could they less? had laid
Strong hold on his affections, were to him
A pleasurable feeling of blind love,
The pleasure which there is in life itself.

His days had not been passed in singleness.⠀⠀⠀80
His Helpmate was a comely Matron, old—
Though younger than himself full twenty years.
She was a woman of a stirring life,
Whose heart was in her house: two wheels she had
Of antique form, this large for spinning wool,⠀⠀⠀85
That small for flax; and if one wheel had rest,
It was because the other was at work.
The pair had but one inmate in their house,
An only Child, who had been born to them
When Michael, telling o'er his years, began⠀⠀⠀90
To deem that he was old,—in Shepherd's phrase,
With one foot in the grave. This only Son
With two brave Sheep-dogs tried in many a storm,
The one of an inestimable worth,
Made all their household. I may truly say,⠀⠀⠀95
That they were as a proverb in the vale

For endless industry.   When day was gone,
And from their occupations out of doors
The Son and Father were come home, even then
Their labour did not cease; unless when all   100
Turned to their cleanly supper-board, and there,
Each with a mess of pottage and skimmed milk,
Sat round their basket piled with oaten cakes,
And their plain home-made cheese.   Yet when their meal
Was ended, LUKE (for so the Son was named)   105
And his old father both betook themselves
To such convenient work as might employ
Their hands by the fireside; perhaps to card
Wool for the Housewife's spindle, or repair
Some injury done to sickle, flail, or scythe,   110
Or other implement of house or field.

    Down from the ceiling by the chimney's edge,
That in our ancient uncouth country style
Did with a huge projection overbrow
Large space beneath, as duly as the light   115
Of day grew dim the Housewife hung a Lamp;
An aged utensil, which had performed
Service beyond all others of its kind.
Early at evening did it burn and late,
Surviving comrade of uncounted Hours,   120
Which, going by from year to year, had found,
And left the couple neither gay perhaps
Nor cheerful, yet with objects and with hopes,
Living a life of eager industry.
And now, when LUKE had reached his eighteenth year 125
There by the light of this old lamp they sat,
Father and Son, while late into the night
The Housewife plied her own peculiar work,
Making the cottage through the silent hours

Murmur as with the sound of summer flies.   130
This Light was famous in its neighbourhood,
And was a public symbol of the life
That thrifty Pair had lived.   For, as it chanced,
Their Cottage on a plot of rising ground
Stood single, with large prospect, North and South,   135
High into Easedale, up to Dunmail-Raise,
And westward to the village near the Lake;
And from this constant light, so regular
And so far seen, the House itself, by all
Who dwelt within the limits of the vale,   140
Both old and young, was named THE EVENING STAR.

    Thus living on through such a length of years,
The Shepherd, if he loved himself, must needs
Have loved his Helpmate; but to Michael's heart
This Son of his old age was yet more dear—   145
Less from instinctive tenderness, the same
Blind spirit, which is in the blood of all—
Than that a child more than all other gifts,
Brings hope with it, and forward-looking thoughts,
And stirrings of inquietude, when they   150
By tendency of nature needs must fail.
Exceeding was the love he bare to him,
His Heart, and his Heart's joy !   For oftentimes
Old Michael, while he was a babe in arms,
Had done him female service, not alone   155
For pastime and delight, as is the use
Of fathers, but with patient mind enforced
To acts of tenderness ; and he had rocked
His cradle with a woman's gentle hand.

    And, in a later time, ere yet the Boy   160
Had put on boy's attire, did Michael love,
Albeit of a stern unbending mind,

To have the Young-one in his sight, when he
Had work by his own door, or when he sat
With sheep before him on his Shepherd's stool,   165
Beneath that large old Oak, which near their door
Stood,--and, from its enormous breadth of shade
Chosen for the shearer's covert from the sun,
Thence in our rustic dialect was called
The CLIPPING TREE,* a name which yet it bears. 170
There, while they two were sitting in the shade,
With others round them, earnest all and blithe,
Would Michael exercise his heart with looks
Of fond correction and reproof bestowed
Upon the Child, if he disturbed the sheep   175
By catching at their legs, or with his shouts
Scared them, while they lay still beneath the shears.

 And when by Heaven's good grace the Boy grew up
A healthy lad, and carried in his cheek
Two steady roses that were five years old,   180
Then Michael from a winter coppice cut
With his own hand a sapling, which he hooped
With iron, making it throughout in all
Due requisites a perfect shepherd's Staff,
And gave it to the Boy ; wherewith equipt 185
He as a watchman oftentimes was placed
At gate or gap, to stem or turn the flock ;
And, to his office prematurely called,
There stood the Urchin, as you will divine,
Something between a hinderance and a help ; 190
And for this cause not always, I believe,
Receiving from his Father hire of praise ;
Though nought was left undone which staff, or voice,
Or looks, or threatening gestures, could perform.

---

* Clipping is the word used in the North of England for shearing.

But soon as Luke, full ten years old, could stand   195
Against the mountain blasts ; and to the heights,
Not fearing toil, nor length of weary ways,
He with his Father daily went, and they
Were as companions, why should I relate
That objects which the Shepherd loved before   200
We're dearer now! that from the Boy there came
Feelings and emanations—things which were
Light to the sun and music to the wind ;
And that the Old Man's heart seemed born again!

Thus in his Father's sight the boy grew up :   205
And now, when he had reached his eighteenth year,
He was his comfort and his daily hope.

While in this sort the simple Household lived
From day to day, to Michael's ear there came
Distressful tidings.   Long before the time   210
Of which I speak, the Shepherd had been bound
In surety for his Brother's Son, a man
Of an industrious life, and ample means,—
But unforseen misfortunes suddenly
Had prest upon him,—and old Michael now   215
Was summoned to discharge the forfeiture,
A grievous penalty, but little less
Than half his substance.   This unlooked-for claim,
At the first hearing, for a moment took
More hope out of his life than he supposed   220
That any old man ever could have lost.
As soon as he had gathered so much strength
That he could look his trouble in the face,
It seemed that his sole refuge was to sell
A portion of his patrimonial fields.   225
Such was his first resolve ; he thought again,

And his heart failed him. " Isabel," said he,
Two evenings after he had heard the news,
"I have been toiling more than seventy years,
And in the open sunshine of God's love　　　　　230
Have we all lived ; yet if these fields of ours
Should pass into a stranger's hand, I think
That I could not lie quiet in my grave.
Our lot is a hard lot ; the sun himself
Has scarcely been more diligent than I ;　　　　235
And I have lived to be a fool at last
To my own family.　An evil Man
That was, and made an evil choice, if he
Were false to us ; and if he were not false,
There are ten thousand to whom loss like this　240
Had been no sorrow.　I forgive him—but
'Twere better to be dumb than to talk thus.
When I began, my purpose was to speak
Of remedies, and of a cheerful hope.
Our Luke shall leave us, Isabel ; the land　　　245
Shall not go from us; and it shall be free ;
He shall possess it, free as is the wind
That passes over it.　We have, thou know'st,
Another Kinsman—he will be our friend
In this distress.　He is a prosperous man　　　250
Thriving in trade—and Luke to him shall go,
And with his Kinsman's help and his own thrift
He quickly will repair this loss, and then
May come again to us.　If here he stay,
What can be done?　Where every one is poor,　255
What can be gained?"　At this the Old man paused,
And Isabel sat silent, for her mind
Was busy, looking back into past times.
There's Richard Bateman, thought she to herself,
He was a Parish-boy—at the Church-door　　　260

They made a gathering for him, shillings, pence,
And halfpennies, wherewith the neighbours bought
A basket, which they filled with pedlar's wares;
And, with this basket on his arm, the Lad
Went up to London, found a Master there,   265
Who, out of many, chose the trusty Boy
To go and overlook his merchandise
Beyond the seas: where he grew wondrous rich,
And left estates and monies to the poor,
And, at his birth-place, built a Chapel floored   270
With marble, which he sent from foreign lands.
These thoughts, and many others of like sort,
Passed quickly through the mind of Isabel,
And her face brightened. The Old Man was glad,
And thus resumed:—"Well, Isabel! this scheme,   275
These two days, has been meat and drink to me.
Far more than we have lost is left us yet.
We have enough—I wish indeed that I
Were younger,—but this hope is a good hope.
—Make ready Luke's best garments, of the best   280
Buy for him more, and let us send him forth
To-morrow, or the next day, or to-night:
—If he *could* go, the Boy should go to-night."
Here Michael ceased, and to the fields went forth
With a light heart. The Housewife for five days   285
Was restless morn and night, and all day long
Wrought on with her best fingers to prepare
Things needful for the journey of her son.
But Isabel was glad when Sunday came
To stop her in her work: for when she lay   290
By Michael's side, she through the two last nights
Heard him, how he was troubled in his sleep:
And when they rose at morning she could see
That all his hopes were gone. That day at noon

4

She said to Luke, while they two by themselves   295
Were sitting at the door, "Thou must not go :
We have no other Child but thee to lose,
None to remember—do not go away,
For if thou leave thy Father he will die."
The youth made answer with a jocund voice ;   300
And Isabel, when she had told her fears,
Recovered heart.   That evening her best fare
Did she bring forth, and all together sat
Like happy people round a Christmas fire.

    With daylight Isabel resumed her work ;   305
And all the ensuing week the house appeared
As cheerful as a grove in Spring : at length
The expected letter from their Kinsman came,
With kind assurances that he would do
His utmost for the welfare of the Boy ;   310
To which, requests were added, that forthwith
He might be sent to him.   Ten times or more
The letter was read over ; Isabel
Went forth to show it to the neighbours round ;
Nor was there at that time on English land   315
A prouder heart than Luke's.   When Isabel
Had to her house returned, the Old Man said,
"He shall depart to-morrow."   To this word
The Housewife answered, talking much of things
Which, if at such short notice he should go,   320
Would surely be forgotten.   But at length
She gave consent, and Michael was at ease.

    Near the tumultuous brook of Green-head Ghyll,
In that deep Valley, Michael had designed
To build a Sheep-fold ; and, before he heard   325
The tidings of his melancholy loss,

For this same purpose he had gathered up
A heap of stones, which by the Streamlet's edge
Lay thrown together, ready for the work.
With Luke that evening thitherward he walked ; 330
And soon as they had reached the place he stopped
And thus the Old Man spake to him :—" My Son,
To-morrow thou wilt leave me : with full heart
I look upon thee, for thou art the same
That wert a promise to me ere thy birth, 335
And all thy life hast been my daily joy.
I will relate to thee some little part
Of our two histories ; 'twill do thee good
When thou art from me, even if I should speak
Of things thou canst not know of.——After thou 340
First camest into the world—as oft befalls
To new-born infants—thou didst sleep away
Two days, and blessings from thy Father's tongue
Then fell upon thee.   Day by day passed on,
And still I loved thee with increasing love. 345
Never to living ear came sweeter sounds
Than when I heard thee by our own fireside
First uttering, without words, a natural tune ;
When thou, a feeding babe, didst in thy joy
Sing at thy Mother's breast.   Month followed month, 350
And in the open fields my life was passed
And on the mountains ; else I think that thou
Hadst been brought up upon thy Father's knees.
But we were playmates, Luke : among these hills,
As well thou knowest, in us the old and young 355
Have played together, nor with me didst thou
Lack any pleasure which a boy can know."
Luke had a manly heart ; but at these words
He sobbed aloud.   The Old Man grasped his hand,
And said, " Nay, do not take it so—I see 360

That these are things of which I need not speak.
— Even to the utmost I have been to thee
A kind and a good Father: and herein
I but repay a gift which I myself
Received at others' hands; for, though now old   365
Beyond the common life of man, I still
Remember them who loved me in my youth.
Both of them sleep together: here they lived,
As all their Forefathers had done; and when
At length their time was come, they were not loth   370
To give their bodies to the family mould.
I wished that thou shouldst live the life they lived
But, 'tis a long time to look back, my Son,
And see so little gain from threescore years.
These fields were burthened when they came to me;   375
Till I was forty years of age, not more
Than half of my inheritance was mine.
I toiled and toiled; God blessed me in my work,
And till these three weeks past the land was free.
—It looks as if it never could endure   380
Another Master. Heaven forgive me, Luke,
If I judge ill for thee, but it seems good
That thou shouldst go."   At this the Old Man paused;
Then, pointing to the Stones near which they stood,
Thus, after a short silence, he resumed: 385
"This was a work for us; and now, my Son,
It is a work for me. But, lay one stone—
Here, lay it for me, Luke, with thine own hands,
Nay, Boy, be of good hope;—we both may live ·
To see a better day. At eighty-four   390
I still am strong and hale;—do thou thy part;
I will do mine.—I will begin again
With many tasks that were resigned to thee:
Up to the heights, and in among the storms,

AT WASTDALE HEAD.

Will I without thee go again, and do   395
All works which I was wont to do alone,
Before I knew thy face.   Heaven bless thee, Boy !
Thy heart these two weeks has been beating fast
With many hopes.—It should be so—Yes—yes—
I knew that thou couldst never have a wish   400
To leave me, Luke; thou hast been bound to me
Only by links of love: when thou art gone
What will be left to us !—But, I forget
My purposes.   Lay now the corner-stone,
As I requested; and hereafter, Luke,   405
When thou art gone away, should evil men
Be thy companions, think of me, my Son,
And of this moment; hither turn thy thoughts,
And God will strengthen thee : amid all fear
And all temptation, Luke, I pray that thou   410
Mayst bear in mind the life thy Fathers lived,
Who, being innocent, did for that cause
Bestir them in good deeds.   Now, fare thee well—
When thou returnest, thou in this place wilt see
A work which is not here : a covenant   415
'Twill be between us—But, whatever fate
Befall thee, I shall love thee to the last,
And bear thy memory with me to the grave."

    The Shepherd ended here ; and Luke stooped down,
And, as his Father had requested, laid   420
The first stone of the Sheep-fold.   At the sight
The Old Man's grief broke from him ; to his heart
He pressed his son, he kisséd him and wept;
And to the house together they returned.
—Hushed was that House in peace, or seeming peace,   425
Ere the night fell :—with morrow's dawn the Boy
Began his journey, and when he had reached

The public way, he put on a bold face ;
And all the neighbours, as he passed their doors,
Came forth with wishes and with farewell prayers,   430
That followed him till he was out of sight.

   A good report did from their Kinsman come,
Of Luke and his well-doing : and the Boy
Wrote loving letters, full of wondrous news,
Which, as the Housewife phrased it, were throughout   435
"The prettiest letters that were ever seen."
Both parents read them with rejoicing hearts.
So, many months passed on : and once again
The Shepherd went about his daily work
With confident and cheerful thoughts ; and now   440
Sometimes when he could find a leisure hour
He to that valley took his way, and there
Wrought at the Sheep-fold.   Meantime Luke began
To slacken in his duty ; and, at length
He in the dissolute city gave himself   445
To evil courses : ignominy and shame
Fell on him, so that he was driven at last
To seek a hiding-place beyond the seas.

   There is a comfort in the strength of love ;
'Twill make a thing endurable, which else   450
Would overset the brain, or break the heart,
I have conversed with more than one who well
Remember the Old Man, and what he was
Years after he had heard this heavy news.
His bodily frame had been from youth to age   455
Of an unusual strength.   Among the rocks
He went, and still looked up towards the sun,
And listened to the wind ; and, as before,
Performed all kinds of labour for his Sheep,

And for the land his small inheritance.   460
And to that hollow Dell from time to time
Did he repair, to build the Fold of which
His flock had need.   'Tis not forgotten yet
The pity which was then in every heart
For the Old Man—and 'tis believed by all   465
That many and many a day he thither went,
And never lifted up a single stone.

    There, by the Sheep-fold, sometimes was he seen
Sitting alone, with that his faithful Dog,
Then old, beside him, lying at his feet.   470
The length of full seven years, from time to time,
He at the building of this Sheep-fold wrought,
And left the work unfinished when he died.
Three years, or little more, did Isabel
Survive her Husband : at her death the estate   475
Was sold, and went into a stranger's hand.
The Cottage which was named the EVENING STAR
Is gone—the ploughshare has been through the ground
On which it stood ; great changes have been wrought
In all the neighbourhood :—yet the Oak is left   4S0
That grew beside their door ; and the remains
Of the unfinished Sheep-fold may be seen
Beside the boisterous brook of Green-head Ghyll.

HART-LEAP WELL.

Hart-Leap Well is a small spring of water, about five miles from Richmond in York-
shire, and near the side of the road that leads from Richmond to Askrigg.   Its name
is derived from a remarkable Chase, the memory of which is preserved by the monuments spoken of in the second Part of the following Poem, which monuments do
now exist as I have there described them.

THE Knight had ridden down from Wensley Moor
With the slow motion of a summer's cloud ;
He turned aside towards a vassal's door,
And "Bring another horse !" he cried aloud.   5

"Another horse !"—That shout the vassal heard
And saddled his best steed, a comely gray ;
Sir Walter mounted him ; he was the third
Which he had mounted on that glorious day.

Joy sparkled in the prancing courser's eyes ;   10
The Horse and Horseman are a happy pair ;
But, though Sir Walter like a falcon flies,
There is a doleful silence in the air.

A rout this morning left Sir Walter's Hall,
That as they galloped made the echoes roar ;   '   15
But horse and man are vanished, one and all ;
Such race, I think, was never seen before.

Sir Walter, restless as a veering wind,
Calls to the few tired dogs that yet remain :
Blanch, Swift, and Music, noblest of their kind,   20
Follow, and up the weary mountain strain.

The Knight hallooed, he cheered and chid them on
With suppliant gestures and upbraidings stern ;
But breath and eyesight fail ; and, one by one,
The dogs are stretched among the mountain fern.   25

Where is the throng, the tumult of the race ?
The bugles that so joyfully were blown ?
—This Chase it looks not like an earthly Chase ;
Sir Walter and the Hart are left alone.

The poor Hart toils along the mountain side ;   30
I will not stop to tell how far he fled,
Nor will I mention by what death he died ;
But now the Knight beholds him lying dead.

Dismounting, then, he leaned against a thorn ;
He had no follower, Dog, nor Man, nor Boy :   35
He neither cracked his whip, nor blew his horn,
But gazed upon the spoil with silent joy.

Close to the thorn on which Sir Walter leaned,
Stood his dumb partner in this glorious feat ;
Weak as a lamb the hour that it is yeaned ;   40
And white with foam as if with cleaving sleet.

Upon his side the Hart was lying stretched :
His nostril touched a spring beneath a hill.
And with the last deep groan his breath had fetched
The waters of the spring were trembling still.   45

And now, too happy for repose or rest,
(Never had living man such joyful lot !)
Sir Walter walked all round, north, south, and west,
And gazed and gazed upon that darling spot.

And climbing up the hill—(it was at least   50
Nine rods of sheer ascent) Sir Walter found
Three several hoof-marks which the hunted Beast
Had left imprinted on the grassy ground.

Sir Walter wiped his face, and cried, " Till now
Such sight was never seen by living eyes :   55
Three leaps have borne him from this lofty brow,
Down to the very fountain where he lies.

" I'll build a Pleasure-house upon this spot,
And a small Arbour, made for rural joy ;
'Twill be the traveller's shed, the pilgrim's cot,   60
A place of love for damsels that are coy.

" A cunning artist will I have to frame
A basin for that Fountain in the dell !
And they who do make mention of the same,
From this day forth, shall call it HART-LEAP WELL.   65

" And, gallant Stag ! to make thy praises known,
Another monument shall here be raised ;
Three several Pillars, each a rough-hewn stone,
And planted where thy hoofs the turf have grazed.

" And, in the summer-time when days are long,   70
I will come hither with my Paramour ;
And with the dancers and the minstrel's song
We will make merry in that pleasant Bower.

" Till the foundations of the mountains fail
My Mansion with its Arbour shall endure ;—   75
The joy of them who till the fields of Swale,
And them who dwell among the woods of Ure !"

Then home he went, and left the Hart, stone-dead,
With breathless nostrils stretched above the spring.
— Soon did the Knight perform what he had said,   80
And far and wide the fame thereof did ring.

Ere thrice the Moon into her port had steered,
A Cup of stone received the living Well ;
Three Pillars of rude stone Sir Walter reared,
And built a House of Pleasure in the dell.   85

And near the Fountain, flowers of stature tall
With trailing plants and trees were intertwined,—
Which soon composed a little sylvan Hall,
A leafy shelter from the sun and wind.

And thither, when the summer days were long,   90
Sir Walter led his wondering Paramour ;
And with the dancers and the minstrel's song
Made merriment within that pleasant Bower.

The Knight, Sir Walter, died in course of time,
And his bones lie in his paternal vale.—   95
But there is matter for a second rhyme,
And I to this would add another tale.

PART SECOND.

THE moving accident is not my trade :
To freeze the blood I have no ready arts :   100
'Tis my delight, alone in summer shade,
To pipe a simple song for thinking hearts. *Who* .   *and*

As I from Hawes to Richmond did repair,
It chanced that I saw standing in a dell
Three Aspens at three corners of a square ;   105
And one, not four yards distant, near a Well.

What this imported I could ill divine :
And, pulling now the rein my horse to stop,
I saw three Pillars standing in a line,
The last stone-Pillar on a dark hill-top.   110

The trees were gray, with neither arms nor head ;
Half-wasted the square Mound of tawny green ;
So that you just might say, as then I said,
" Here in old time the hand of man hath been."

I looked upon the hill both far and near,   115
More doleful place did never eye survey ;
It seemed as if the spring-time came not here,
And Nature here were willing to decay.

I stood in various thoughts and fancies lost,
When one, who was in shepherd's garb attired,   120
Came up the hollow :—Him did I accost,
And what this place might be I then inquired.

The Shepherd stopped, and that same story told
Which in my former rhyme I have rehearsed.
" A jolly place," said he, " in times of old !   125
But something ails it now ; the spot is curst.

" You see these lifeless stumps of aspen wood—
Some say that they are beeches, others elms—
These were the Bower ; and here a Mansion stood,
The finest palace of a hundred realms !   130

" The Arbour does its own condition tell ;
You see the Stones, the Fountain, and the Stream ;
But as to the great Lodge ! you might as well
Hunt half a day for a forgotten dream.

" There's neither dog nor heifer, horse nor sheep,   135
Will wet his lip within that Cup of stone ;
And oftentimes, when all are fast asleep,
This water doth send forth a dolorous groan.

" Some say that here a murder has been done,
And blood cries out for blood : but, for my part, 140
I've guessed, when I've been sitting in the sun,
That it was all for that unhappy Hart.

" What thoughts must through the Creature's brain have past
Even from the topmost stone, upon the steep,
Are but three bounds—and look, Sir, at this last— 145
—O Master ! it has been a cruel leap.

" For thirteen hours he ran a desperate race ;
And in my simple mind we cannot tell
What cause the Hart might have to love this place,
And come and make his deathbed near the Well. 150

" Here on the grass perhaps asleep he sank,
Lulled by the Fountain in the summer-tide ;
This water was perhaps the first he drank
When he had wandered from his mother's side.

" In April here beneath the scented thorn 155
He heard the birds their morning carols sing ;
And he, perhaps, for aught we know, was born
Not half a furlong from that self-same spring.

" Now, here is neither grass nor pleasant shade ;
The sun on drearier hollow never shone ; 160
So will it be, as I have often said,
Till Trees, and Stones, and Fountain, all are gone."

" Gray-headed Shepherd, thou hast spoken well ;
Small difference lies between thy creed and mine :
This Beast not unobserved by Nature fell ; 165
His death was mourned by sympathy divine.

" The Being, that is in the clouds and air,
  That is in the green leaves among the groves,
  Maintains a deep and reverential care
  For the unoffending creatures whom he loves.   170

" The Pleasure-house is dust :—behind, before,
  This is no common waste, no common gloom ;
  But Nature, in due course of time, once more
  Shall here put on her beauty and her bloom.

" She leaves these objects to a slow decay,   175
  That what we are, and have been, may be known ;
  But, at the coming of the milder day,
  These monuments shall all be overgrown.

" One lesson, Shepherd, let us two divide,
  Taught both by what she shows, and what conceals,   180
  Never to blend our pleasure or our pride
  With sorrow of the meanest thing that feels."

FIDELITY.

A BARKING sound the Shepherd hears,
A cry as of a dog or fox ;
He halts—and searches with his eyes
Among the scattered rocks ;   5
And now at distance can discern
A stirring in a brake of fern ;
And instantly a dog is seen,
Glancing through that covert green.

The Dog is not of mountain breed ;   10
Its motions, too, are wild and shy ;
With something, as the Shepherd thinks,
Unusual in its cry :
Nor is there any one in sight
All round, in hollow or on height ;   15
Nor shout, nor whistle strikes his ear ;
What is the Creature doing here ?

It was a cove, a huge recess,
That keeps, till June, December's snow ;
A lofty precipice in front,   20
A silent tarn* below !
Far in the bosom of Helvellyn,
Remote from public road or dwelling
Pathway, or cultivated land ; ·
From trace of human foot or hand.   25

There sometimes doth a leaping fish
Send through the tarn a lonely cheer ; a
The crags repeat the raven's croak,
In symphony austere ;
Thither the rainbow comes—the cloud—   30
And mists that spread the flying shroud ;
And sunbeams ; and the sounding blast,
That, if it could, would hurry past ;
But that enormous barrier binds it fast.

Not free from boding thoughts, a while   35
The Shepherd stood : then makes his way
Towards the Dog, o'er rocks and stones,
As quickly as he may ;

---

* Tarn is a *small* Mere or Lake, mostly high up in the mountains.

Nor far had gone before he found
A human skeleton on the ground;   40
The appalled discoverer with a sigh
Looks round, to learn the history.

From those abrupt and perilous rocks
The Man had fallen, that place of fear!
At length upon the Shepherd's mind   45
It breaks, and all is clear:
He instantly recalled the name,
And who he was, and whence he came;
Remembered, too, the very day
On which the traveller passed this way.   50

But hear a wonder, for whose sake
This lamentable tale I tell!
A lasting monument of words
This wonder merits well.
The Dog, which still was hovering nigh,   55
Repeating the same timid cry,
This Dog, had been through three months' space
A dweller in that savage place.

Yes, proof was plain that, since the day
When this ill-fated traveller died,   60
The Dog had watched about the spot,
Or by his Master's side:
How nourished here through such long time
He knows, who gave that love sublime;
And gave that strength of feeling, great   65
Above all human estimate.

THE LEECH-GATHERER;

OR,

RESOLUTION AND INDEPENDENCE.

THERE was a roaring in the wind all night;
The rain came heavily and fell in floods ;   5
But now the sun is rising calm and bright;
The birds are singing in the distant woods ;
Over his own sweet voice the Stock-dove broods ;
The Jay makes answer as the Magpie chatters;
And all the air is filled with pleasant noise of waters.•   10

All things that love the sun are out of doors ;
The sky rejoices in the morning's birth ;
The grass is bright with rain-drops ;—on the moors
The Hare is running races in her mirth ;
And with her feet she from the plashy earth   15
Raises a mist ; that, glittering in the sun,
Runs with her all the way, wherever she doth run.

I was a traveller then upon the moor ;
I saw the Hare that raced about with joy ;
I heard the woods and distant waters roar ;   20
Or heard them not, as happy as a boy :
The pleasant season did my heart employ :
My old remembrances went from me wholly ;
And all the ways of men, so vain and melancholy !

But, as it sometimes chanceth, from the might   25
Of joy in minds that can no further go,
As high as we have mounted in delight
In our dejection do we sink as low,
To me that morning did it happen so;
And fears and fancies thick upon me came ;   30
Dim sadness—and blind thoughts, I know not, nor could name.

I heard the Sky-lark warbling in the sky ;
And I bethought me of the playful Hare :
Even such a happy child of earth am I ;
Even as these blissful creatures do I fare ;   35
Far from the world I walk, and from all care ;
But there may come another day to me—
Solitude, pain of heart, distress, and poverty.

My whole life I have lived in pleasant thought,
As if life's business were a summer mood :   40
As if all needful things would come unsought
To genial faith, still rich in genial good :
But how can He expect that others should
Build for him, sow for him, and at his call
Love him, who for himself will take no heed at all ?   45

I thought of Chatterton, the marvellous Boy,
The sleepless Soul that perished in his pride ;
Of Him who walked in glory and in joy
Following his plow, along the mountain-side :
By our own spirits are we deified ;   50
We Poets in our youth begin in gladness ;
But thereof comes in the end despondency and madness.

Now, whether it were by peculiar grace,
A leading from above, a something given,
Yet it befel, that, in this lonely place,   55
When I with these untoward thoughts had striven,
Beside a pool bare to the eye of heaven
I saw a Man before me unawares :
The oldest man he seemed that ever wore grey hairs.

As a huge Stone is sometimes seen to lie   60
Couched on the bald top of an eminence ;
Wonder to all who do the same espy,

By what means it could thither come, and whence;
So that it seems a thing endued with sense:
Like a Sea-beast crawled forth, that on a shelf   65
Of rock or sand reposeth, there to sun itself;

Such seemed this Man, not all alive nor dead,
Nor all asleep—in his extreme old age:
His body was bent double, feet and head
Coming together in life's pilgrimage;   70
As if some dire constraint of pain, or rage
Of sickness felt by him in times long past,
A more than human weight upon his frame had cast.

Himself he propped, his body, limbs, and face,
Upon a long grey Staff of shaven wood: 75
And, still as I drew near with gentle pace,
Upon the margin of that moorish flood
Motionless as a Cloud the Old-man stood;
That heareth not the loud winds when they call:
And moveth all together, if it move at all.   80

At length, himself unsettling, he the Pond
Stirred with his Staff, and fixedly did look
Upon the muddy waters, which he conned,
As if he had been reading in a book:
And now a stranger's privilege I took: 85
And, drawing to his side, to him did say,
"This morning gives us promise of a glorious day."

A gentle answer did the Old-man make,
In courteous speech which forth he slowly drew:
And him with further words I thus bespake,   90
" What occupation do you there pursue?
This is a lonesome place for one like you."
He answered, while a flash of mild surprise
Broke from the sable orbs of his yet vivid eyes.

His words came feebly, from a feeble chest,   95
But each in solemn order followed each,
With something of a lofty utterance drest—
Choice word and measured phrase, above the reach
Of ordinary men : a stately speech ;
Such as grave livers do in Scotland use,   100
Religious men, who give to God and Man their dues.

He told, that to these waters he had come
To gather Leeches, being old and poor :
Employment hazardous and wearisome !
And he had many hardships to endure ;   105
From pond to pond he roamed, from moor to moor ;
Housing, with God's good help, by choice or chance ;
And in this way he gained an honest maintenance.

The Old-man still stood talking by my side;
But now his voice to me was like a stream   110
Scarce heard ; nor word from word could I divide ;
And the whole Body of the Man did seem
Like one whom I had met with in a dream ;
Or like a man from some far region sent,
To give me human strength, by apt admonishment.   115

My former thoughts returned : the fear that kills ;
And hope that is unwilling to be fed ;
Cold, pain, and labour, and all fleshly ills ;
And mighty Poets in their misery dead.
—Perplexed, and longing to be comforted,   120
My question eagerly did I renew,
" How is it that you live, and what is it you do ? "

He with a smile did then his words repeat ;
And said, that, gathering Leeches, far and wide
He travelled; stirring thus about his feet   125

The waters of the Pools where they abide.
" Once I could meet with them on every side ;
But they have dwindled long by slow decay ;
Yet still I persevere, and find them where I may."

While he was talking thus, the lonely place,   130
The Old-man's shape, and speech, all troubled me :
In my mind's eye I seemed to see him pace
About the weary moors continually,
Wandering about alone and silently.
While I these thoughts within myself pursued,   135
He, having made a pause, the same discourse renewed.

And soon with this he other matter blended,
Cheerfully uttered, with demeanour kind,
But stately in the main ; and when he ended,
I could have laughed myself to scorn to find   140
In that decrepit Man so firm a mind.
" God," said I, " be my help and stay secure ;
I'll think of the Leech-gatherer on the lonely moor ! "

LYRICAL POEMS.

—

"Higher still and higher,
From the earth thou springest,
Like a cloud of fire;
The blue deep thou wingest,
And singing still dost soar, and soaring ever singest."
—Shelley.

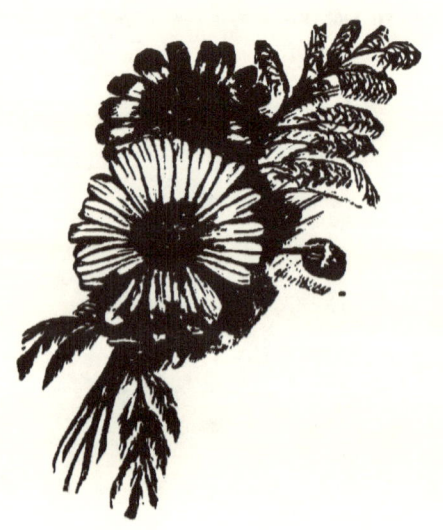

TO THE DAISY.

In youth from rock to rock I went,
From hill to hill in discontent
Of pleasure high and turbulent,
    Most pleased when most uneasy;   5
But now my own delights I make,—
My thirst at every rill can slake,
And gladly Nature's love partake
    Of thee, sweet Daisy!

Thee Winter in the garland wears   10
That thinly decks his few grey hairs;
Spring parts the clouds with softest airs,
    That she may sun thee;
Whole summer-fields are thine by right;
And Autumn, melancholy wight!   15
Doth in thy crimson head delight
    When rains are on thee.

In shoals and bands, a morrice train,
Thou greet'st the traveller in the lane,
Pleased at his greeting thee again;   20
    Yet nothing daunted,
Nor grieved, if thou be set at nought:
And oft alone in nooks remote
We meet thee, like a pleasant thought,
    When such are wanted.   25

Be violets in their secret mews
The flowers the wanton Zephyrs choose;
Proud be the rose, with rains and dews

Her head impearling.
Thou liv'st with less ambitious aim,   30
Yet hast not gone without thy fame;
Thou art indeed by many a claim
    The Poet's darling.

If to a rock from rains he fly,
Or, some bright day of April sky,   35
Imprisoned by hot sunshine lie
    Near the green holly,
And wearily at length should fare;
He needs but look about, and there
Thou art!—a friend at hand, to scare   40
    His melancholy.

A hundred times, by rock or bower,
Ere thus I have lain crouched an hour,
Have I derived from thy sweet power
    Some apprehension;   45
Some steady love; some brief delight;
Some memory that had taken flight;
Some chime of fancy wrong or right;
    Or stray invention.

If stately passions in me burn,   50
And one chance look to Thee should turn,
I drink out of an humbler urn
    A lowlier pleasure;
The homely sympathy that heeds
The common life our nature breeds;   55
A wisdom fitted to the needs
    Of hearts at leisure.

Fresh smitten by the morning ray,
When thou art up, alert and gay,
Then, cheerful Flower! my spirits play   60

With kindred gladness :
And when, at dusk, by dews opprest
Thou sink'st, the image of thy rest
Hath often eased my pensive breast
    Of careful sadness.   65

And all day long I number yet,
All seasons through, another debt,
Which I, wherever thou art met,
    To thee am owing ;
An instinct call it, a blind sense ;   70
A happy, genial influence,
Coming one knows not how, nor whence,
    Nor whither going.

Child of the Year ! that round dost run
Thy course, bold lover of the sun,   75
And cheerful when the day's begun
    As lark or leveret,
Thy long-lost praise* thou shalt regain ;
Nor be less dear to future men
Than in old times ;—thou not in vain   80
    Art Nature's favourite.

TO THE SAME.

Bright flower, whose home is everywhere !
A Pilgrim bold in Nature's care,
And oft, the long year through, the heir
    Of joy or sorrow ;   5
Methinks that there abides in thee
Some concord with humanity,
Given to no other flower I see
    The forest through !

---

* See, in Chaucer and the elder Poets, the honours formerly paid to this flower.

And wherefore?   Man is soon deprest;   10
A thoughtless Thing! who, once unblest,
Does little on his memory rest,
    Or on his reason;
But Thou would'st teach him how to find
A Shelter under every wind,   15
A hope for times that are unkind
    And every season.

TO A HIGHLAND GIRL.

(AT INVERSNEYDE, UPON LOCH LOMOND.)

SWEET Highland Girl, a very shower
Of beauty is thy earthly dower!
Twice seven consenting years have shed   5
Their utmost bounty on thy head:
And these grey Rocks; this household Lawn;
These Trees, a veil just half withdrawn;
This fall of water, that doth make
A murmur near the silent Lake;   10
This little Bay, a quiet road
That holds in shelter thy abode;
In truth together do ye seem
Like something fashioned in a dream;
Such forms as from their coverts peep   15
When earthly cares are laid asleep!
Yet, dream and vision as thou art,
I bless thee with a human heart:
God shield thee to thy latest years!
Thee neither know I nor thy peers;   20
And yet my eyes are filled with tears.

With earnest feeling I shall pray
For thee when I am far away :
For never saw I mien, or face,
In which more plainly I could trace　　　25
Benignity and home-bred sense
Ripening in perfect innocence.
Here scattered like a random seed,
Remote from men, Thou dost not need
The embarrassed look of shy distress,　　　30
And maidenly shamefacedness :
Thou wear'st upon thy forehead clear
The freedom of a Mountaineer :
A face with gladness overspread !
Soft smiles, by human kindness bred !　　　35
And seemliness complete, that sways
Thy courtesies, about thee plays ;
With no restraint, but such as springs　　　·
From quick and eager visitings
Of thoughts that lie beyond the reach　　　40
Of thy few words of English speech :　•
A bondage sweetly brooked, a strife
That gives thy gestures grace and life !
So have I, not unmoved in mind,
Seen birds of tempest-loving kind,　　　45
Thus beating up against the wind.

What hand but would a garland cull
For thee who art so beautiful ?
O happy pleasure ! here to dwell
Beside thee in some heathy dell ;　　　50
Adopt your homely ways, and dress,
A Shepherd, thou a Shepherdess !
But I could frame a wish for thee
More like a grave reality :

Thou art to me but as a wave   55
Of the wild sea : and I would have
Some claim upon thee, if I could,
Though but of common neighbourhood.
What joy to hear thee, and to see !
Thy elder Brother I would be,   60
Thy Father, any thing to thee !

   Now thanks to Heaven ! that of its grace
Hath led me to this lonely place.
Joy have I had ; and going hence
I bear away my recompense.   65
In spots like these it is we prize
Our Memory, feel that she hath eyes :
Then, why should I be loth to stir ?
I feel this place was made for her ; ⌒
To give new pleasure like the past,   70
Continued long as life shall last.
Nor am I loth, though pleased at heart,
Sweet Highland Girl ! from Thee to part ;
For I, methinks, till I grow old,
As fair before me shall behold,   75
As I do now, the Cabin small,
The Lake, the Bay, the Waterfall ;
And Thee, the Spirit of them all !

STEPPING WESTWARD.

While my Fellow-traveller and I were walking by the side of Loch Katrine, one fine
evening after sunset, in our road to a Hut where in the course of our Tour we had
been hospitably entertained some weeks before, we met, in one of the loneliest parts
of that solitary region, two well-dressed Women, one of whom said to us, by way of
greeting, " What, you are stepping westward ?"

" *What, you are stepping westward ?*"—" *Yea.*"
—'Twould be a *wildish* destiny,

THE SOLITARY REAPER.

If we, who thus together roam
In a strange land, and far from home,   5
Were in this place the guests of Chance:
Yet who would stop, or fear to advance,
Though home or shelter he had none,
With such a Sky to lead him on?

The dewy ground was dark and cold;   10
Behind, all gloomy to behold;
And stepping westward seemed to be
A kind of *heavenly* destiny:
I liked the greeting; 'twas a sound
Of something without place or bound;   15
And seemed to give me spiritual right
To travel through that region bright.

The voice was soft, and she who spake
Was walking by her native Lake:
The salutation had to me   20
The very sound of courtesy:
Its power was felt; and while my eye
Was fixed upon the glowing sky,
The echo of the voice enwrought
A human sweetness with the thought   25
Of travelling through the world that lay
Before me in my endless way.

THE SOLITARY REAPER.

Behold her, single in the field,
You solitary Highland Lass!
Reaping and singing by herself;
Stop here, or gently pass!   5

Alone she cuts, and binds the grain,
And sings a melancholy strain ;
O listen ! for the Vale profound
Is overflowing with the sound.

No Nightingale did ever chant   10
So sweetly to reposing bands
Of Travellers in some shady haunt,
Among Arabian sands :
A voice so thrilling ne'er was heard
In spring-time from the Cuckoo-bird,   15
Breaking the silence of the seas
Among the farthest Hebrides.

Will no one tell me what she sings ?
Perhaps the plaintive numbers flow
For old, unhappy, far-off things,   20
And battles long ago :
Or is it some more humble lay,
Familiar matter of to-day ?
Some natural sorrow, loss, or pain,
That has been, and may be again !   25

What'er the theme, the Maiden sang
As if her song could have no ending ;
I saw her singing at her work,
And o'er the sickle bending ;—
I listened till I had my fill,   30
And when I mounted up the hill,
The music in my heart I bore,
Long after it was heard no more.

AT THE GRAVE OF BURNS,

1803.

SEVEN YEARS AFTER HIS DEATH.

I SHIVER, Spirit fierce and bold,
At thought of what I now behold :   5
As vapours breathed from dungeons cold
    Strike pleasure dead,
So sadness comes from out the mould
    Where Burns is laid.

And have I then thy bones so near,   10
And thou forbidden to appear?
As if it were thyself that's here
    I shrink with pain ;
And both my wishes and my fear
    Alike are vain.   15

Off weight—nor press on weight !—away
Dark thoughts !—they came, but not to stay ;
With chastened feelings would I pay
    The tribute due
To him, and aught that hides his clay   20
    From mortal view.

Fresh as the flower, whose modest worth
He sang, his genius "glinted" forth,
Rose like a star that touching earth,
    For so it seems,   25
Doth glorify its humble birth
    With matchless beams.

The piercing eye, the thoughtful brow,
The struggling heart, where be they now?—
Full soon the Aspirant of the plough,   30
    The prompt, the brave,
Slept, with the obscurest, in the low
    And silent grave.

Well might I mourn that He was gone,
Whose light I hail'd when first it shone,   35
When, breaking forth as nature's own,
    It showed my youth
How Verse may build a princely throne
    On humble truth.

Alas! where'er the current tends,   40
Regret pursues and with it blends,—
Huge Criffel's hoary top ascends
    By Skiddaw seen,—
Neighbours we were, and loving friends
    We might have been: 45

True friends though diversely inclined;
But heart with heart, and mind with mind,
Where the main fibres are entwined,
    Through Nature's skill,
May even by contraries be joined   50
    More closely still.

The tear will start, and let it flow;
Thou "poor Inhabitant below,"
At this dread moment—even so—
    Might we together   55
Have sate and talked where gowans blow,
    Or on wild heather.

What treasures would have then been placed
Within my reach ; of knowledge graced
By fancy what a rich repast !   60
    But why go on !—
Oh ! spare to sweep, thou mournful blast,
    His grave grass-grown.

There, too, a Son, his joy and pride,
(Not three weeks past the Stripling died,)   65
Lies gathered to his Father's side,
    Soul-moving sight !
Yet one to which is not denied
    Some sad delight.

For *he* is safe, a quiet bed   70
Hath early found among the dead,
Harboured where none can be misled,
    Wronged, or distrest ;
And surely here it may be said
    That such are blest.   75

And oh for Thee, by pitying grace
Checked oft-times in a devious race,
May He, who halloweth the place
    Where Man is laid,
Receive thy Spirit in the embrace   80
    For which it prayed !

Sighing I turned away ; but ere
Night fell, I heard, or seemed to hear,
Music that sorrow comes not near,
    A ritual hymn,   85
Chaunted in love that casts out fear
    By Seraphim.

THOUGHTS

SUGGESTED THE DAY FOLLOWING, ON THE BANKS OF NITH,
NEAR THE POET'S RESIDENCE.

Too frail to keep the lofty vow
That must have followed when his brow 5
Was wreathed—"The Vision" tells us how—
    With holly spray,
He faultered, drifted to and fro,
    And passed away.

Well might such thoughts, dear Sister, throng 10
Our minds when, lingering all too long,
Over the grave of Burns we hung
    In social grief—
Indulged as if it were a wrong
    To seek relief. 15

But, leaving each unquiet theme
Where gentlest judgments may misdeem,
And prompt to welcome every gleam
    Of good and fair,
Let us beside this limpid Stream 20
    Breathe hopeful air.

Enough of sorrow, wreck, and blight:
Think rather of those moments bright
When to the consciousness of right
    His course was true, 25
When wisdom prospered in his sight
    And virtue grew.

Yes, freely let our hearts expand,
Freely as in youth's season bland,
When side by side, his Book in hand,   30
        We wont to stray,
Our pleasure varying at command
        Of each sweet Lay.

How oft inspired must he have trode
These pathways, yon far-stretching road !   35
There lurks his home ; in that Abode,
        With mirth elate,
Or in his nobly-pensive mood,
        The Rustic sate.

Proud thoughts that Image overawes,   40
Before it humbly let us pause,
And ask of Nature, from what cause,
        And by what rules
She trained her Burns to win applause
        That shames the Schools.   45

Through busiest street and loneliest glen
Are felt the flashes of his pen :
He rules mid winter snows, and when
        Bees fill their hives :
Deep in the general heart of men   50
        His power survives.

What need of fields in some far clime
Where Heroes, Sages, Bards sublime,
And all that fetched the flowing rhyme
        From genuine springs,   55
Shall dwell together till old Time
        Folds up his wings !

Sweet Mercy! to the gates of Heaven
This Minstrel lead, his sins forgiven;
The rueful conflict, the heart riven   60
    With vain endeavour,
And memory of Earth's bitter leaven
    Effaced for ever.

But why to Him confine the prayer,
When kindred thoughts and yearnings bear   65
On the frail heart the purest share
    With all that live?—
The best of what we do and are,
    Just God, forgive!

TO THE CUCKOO.

O BLITHE New-comer! I have heard,
I hear thee and rejoice.
O Cuckoo! shall I call thee Bird,
Or but a wandering Voice?   5

While I am lying on the grass
Thy twofold shout I hear;
From hill to hill it seems to pass,
At once far off and near.

Though babbling only, to the Vale,   10
Of sunshine and of flowers,
Thou bringest unto me a tale
Of visionary hours.

Thrice welcome, darling of the Spring!
Even yet thou art to me   15
No Bird: but an invisible Thing,
A voice, a mystery;

The same whom in my School-boy days
I listened to ; that Cry
Which made me look a thousand ways   20
In bush, and tree, and sky.

To seek thee did I often rove
Through woods and on the green ;
And thou wert still a hope, a love ;
Still longed for, never seen.   25

And I can listen to thee yet ;
Can lie upon the plain
And listen, till I do beget
That golden time again.

O blessed Bird ! the earth we pace   30
Again appears to be
An unsubstantial, faery place ;
That is fit home for Thee !

YARROW VISITED,

SEPTEMBER, 1814.

AND is this—Yarrow ?—*This* the Stream
Of which my fancy cherished,
So faithfully, a waking dream ?   5
An image that hath perished !
O that some Minstrel's harp were near,
To utter notes of gladness,
And chase this silence from the air,
That fills my heart with sadness !   10

Yet why ?—a silvery current flows
With uncontrolled meanderings ;
Nor have these eyes by greener hills
Been soothed, in all my wanderings.
And, through her depths, Saint Mary's Lake   15
Is visibly delighted ;
For not a feature of those hills
Is in the mirror slighted.

A blue sky bends o'er Yarrow vale,
Save where that pearly whiteness   20
Is round the rising sun diffused,
A tender hazy brightness ;
Mild dawn of promise ! that excludes
All profitless dejection ;
Though not unwilling here to admit   25
A pensive recollection.

Where was it that the famous Flower
Of Yarrow Vale lay bleeding ?
His bed perchance was yon smooth mound
On which the herd is feeding :   30
And haply from this crystal pool,
Now peaceful as the morning,
The Water-wraith ascended thrice—
And gave his doleful warning.

Delicious is the Lay that sings   35
The haunts of happy Lovers,
The path that leads them to the grove,
The leafy grove that covers :
And Pity sanctifies the verse
That paints, by strength of sorrow,   40
The unconquerable strength of love ;
Bear witness, rueful Yarrow !

But thou, that didst appear so fair
To fond imagination,
Dost rival in the light of day   45
Her delicate creation :
Meek loveliness is round thee spread,
A softness still and holy ;
The grace of forest charms decayed,
And pastoral melancholy.   50

That Region left, the Vale unfolds
Rich groves of lofty stature,
With Yarrow winding through the pomp
Of cultivated nature ;
And, rising from those lofty groves,   55
Behold a Ruin hoary !
The shattered front of Newark's Towers,
Renowned in Border story.

Fair scenes for childhood's opening bloom,
For sportive youth to stray in ;   60
For manhood to enjoy his strength ;
And age to wear away in !
Yon Cottage seems a bower of bliss,
A covert for protection
Of tender thoughts that nestle there,   65
The brood of chaste affection.

How sweet, on this autumnal day,
The wild-wood fruits to gather,
And on my True-love's forehead plant
A crest of blooming heather !   70
And what if I enwreathed my own !
'Twere no offence to reason ;
The sober Hills thus deck their brows
To meet the wintry season.

I see—but not by sight alone,   75
Loved Yarrow, have I won thee;
A ray of Fancy still survives—
Her sunshine plays upon thee!
Thy ever-youthful waters keep
A course of lively pleasure;   80
And gladsome notes my lips can breathe,
Accordant to the measure.

The vapours linger around the Heights,
They melt—and soon must vanish;
One hour is theirs, nor-more is mine—   85
Sad thought, which I would banish,
But that I know, where'er I go,
Thy genuine image, Yarrow!
Will dwell with me—to heighten joy,
And cheer my mind in sorrow.   90

TO A SKY-LARK.

Up with me! up with me into the clouds!
    For thy song, Lark, is strong;
Up with me, up with me into the clouds!
    Singing, singing,   5
With clouds and sky about thee ringing,
    Lift me, guide me till I find
That spot which seems so to thy mind!

I have walked through wildernesses dreary,
And to-day my heart is weary;   10
Had I now the wings of a Faery,
Up to thee would I fly.

"To hear the lark begin his flight,
And, singing, startle the dull night,
From his watch-tower in the skies,
Till the dappled dawn doth rise."

         – L'Allegro.

There's madness about thee, and joy divine
In that song of thine ;
Lift me, guide me high and high   15
To thy banqueting-place in the sky.

    Joyous as morning,
Thou art laughing and scorning ;
Thou hast a nest for thy love and thy rest,
And, though little troubled with sloth,   20
Drunken Lark ! thou would'st be loth *lul. ur .*
To be such a traveller as I.
Happy, happy Liver,
With a soul as strong as a mountain River
Pouring out praise to the Almighty Giver,   25
    Joy and jollity be with us both !

Alas ! my journey, rugged and uneven,
Through prickly moors or dusty ways must wind
But hearing thee, or others of thy kind,
As full of gladness and as free of heaven,   30
I, with my fate contented, will plod on,
And hope for higher raptures, when Life's day is done.

TO A SKYLARK.

ETHEREAL Minstrel ! Pilgrim of the sky !
Dost thou despise the earth where cares abound ?
Or, while the wings aspire, are heart and eye
Both with thy nest upon the dewy ground ?   5
Thy nest which thou canst drop into at will,
Those quivering wings composed, that music still !

To the last point of vision, and beyond,
Mount, daring Warbler! that love-prompted strain,
('Twixt thee and thine a never-failing bond)   10
Thrills not the less the bosom of the plain:
Yet might'st thou seem, proud privilege! to sing
All independent of the leafy spring.

Leave to the Nightingale her shady wood;
A privacy of glorious light is thine;   15
Whence thou dost pour upon the world a flood
Of harmony, with instinct more divine;
Type of the wise who soar, but never roam;
True to the kindred points of Heaven and Home!

POEMS

AKIN TO THE ANTIQUE

AND

ODES.

—

"Then (last strain)
Of Duty, chosen laws, controlling choice,
Action and Joy!—An Orphic song indeed,
A song divine of high and passionate thoughts
To their own music chanted!"

—*Coler.dge.*

ODE TO DUTY.

Jam non consilio bonus, sed more eò perductus, ut non tantum rectè facere possim sed nisi rectè facere non possim."

STERN Daughter of the Voice of God !
O Duty ! if that name thou love
Who art a light to guide, a rod
To check the erring, and reprove;   5
Thou, who art victory and law
When empty terrors overawe ;
From vain temptations dost set free ;
And calm'st the weary strife of frail humanity !

There are who ask not if thine eye   10
Be on them; who, in love and truth,
Where no misgiving is, rely
Upon the genial sense of youth :
Glad Hearts ! without reproach or blot ;
Who do thy work, and know it not :   15
Long may the kindly impulse last !
But Thou, if they should totter, teach them to stand fast !

Serene will be our days and bright,
And happy will our nature be,
When love is an unerring light,   20
And joy its own security.
And they a blissful course may hold
Even now, who, not unwisely bold,
Live in the spirit of this creed ;
Yet seek thy firm support, according to their need.   25

I, loving freedom, and untried ; *unexps*
No sport of every random gust,
Yet being to myself a guide,
Too blindly have reposed my trust ;
And oft, when in my heart was heard 30
Thy timely mandate, I deferred
The task, in smoother walks to stray ;
But thee I now would serve more strictly, if I may.

Through no disturbance of my soul,
Or strong compunction in me wrought, 35
I supplicate for thy control ;
But in the quietness of thought :
Me this unchartered freedom tires ;
I feel the weight of chance-desires :
My hopes no more must change their name, 40
I long for a repose that ever is the same.

Stern Lawgiver ! yet thou dost wear
The Godhead's most benignant grace ;
Nor know we anything so fair
As is the smile upon thy face : 45
Flowers laugh before thee on their beds
And fragrance in thy footing treads ;
Thou dost preserve the Stars from wrong ;
And the most ancient Heavens, through Thee, are fresh and strong.

To humbler functions, awful Power ! 50
I call thee : I myself commend
Unto thy guidance from this hour ;
Oh, let my weakness have an end !
Give unto me, made lowly wise,
The spirit of self-sacrifice ; 55
The confidence of reason give ;
And in the light of truth thy bondman let me live !

ODE ON INTIMATIONS OF IMMORTALITY

FROM RECOLLECTIONS OF EARLY CHILDHOOD.

I.

THERE was a time when meadow, grove, and stream,
The earth, and every common sight,   5
    To me did seem
    Apparelled in celestial light,
The glory and the freshness of a dream.
It is not now as it hath been of yore ;—
    Turn wheresoe'er I may,   10
    By night or day,
The things which I have seen I now can see no more.

II.

    The Rainbow comes and goes,
    And lovely is the Rose ;   15
    The Moon doth with delight
Look round her when the heavens are bare ; .
    Waters on a starry night
    Are beautiful and fair ;
    The sunshine is a glorious birth ;   20
    But yet I know, where'er I go,
That there hath passed away a glory from the earth.

III.

Now, while the birds thus sing a joyous song,
    And while the young Lambs bound   25
    As to the tabor's sound,
To me alone there came a thought of grief :
A timely utterance gave that thought relief,
    And I again am strong :

The Cataracts blow their trumpets from the steep;   30
No more shall grief of mine the season wrong;
I hear the Echoes through the mountains throng,
The Winds come to me from the fields of sleep,
      And all the earth is gay;
          Land and sea   35
    Give themselves up to jollity,
        And with the heart of May
  Doth every beast keep holiday;—
      Thou child of joy,
Shout round me, let me hear thy shouts, thou happy Shepherd-
  boy!   40

IV.

Ye blessed Creatures, I have heard the call
    Ye to each other make; I see
The heavens laugh with you in your jubilee;
    My heart is at your festival,   45
      My head hath its coronal,
The fulness of your bliss, I feel—I feel it all.
      O evil day! if I were sullen
    While the Earth herself is adorning
      This sweet May-morning,   50
    And the children are pulling
      On every side,
      In a thousand valleys far and wide,
      Fresh flowers; while the sun shines warm,
And the babe leaps up on his mother's arm:—   55
      I hear, I hear, with joy I hear!
      —But there's a Tree, of many one,
A single Field which I have looked upon,
Both of them speak of something that is gone;
      The Pansy at my feet   60
      Doth the same tale repeat:

Whither is fled the visionary gleam?
Where is it now, the glory and the dream?

V.

Our birth is but a sleep and a forgetting :   65
The soul that rises with us, our life's Star,
  Hath had elsewhere its setting,
  And cometh from afar :
  Not in entire forgetfulness,
  And not in utter nakedness,   70
But trailing clouds of glory do we come
  From God, who is our home :
Heaven lies about us in our infancy !
Shades of the prison-house begin to close
  Upon the growing Boy,   75
But He beholds the light, and whence it flows
  He sees it in his joy ;
The Youth, who daily farther from the East
  Must travel, still is Nature's Priest,
  And by the vision splendid
  Is on his way attended ;   80
At length the Man perceives it die away,
And fade into the light of common day.

VI.

Earth fills her lap with pleasures of her own ;
Yearnings she hath in her own natural kind,   85
And even with something of a mother's mind,
  And no unworthy aim,
  The homely Nurse doth all she can
To make her foster-child, her inmate Man,
  Forget the glories he hath known,   90
And that imperial palace whence he came.

VII.

Behold the Child among his new-born blisses,
A six years' darling of a pigmy size !
See, where 'mid work of his own hand he lies,   95
Fretted by sallies of his Mother's kisses,
With light upon him from his Father's eyes !
See, at his feet, some little plan or chart,
Some fragment from his dream of human life,
Shaped by himself with newly-learnèd art ;   100
    A wedding or a festival,
    A mourning or a funeral,
      And this hath now his heart,
    And unto this he frames his song :
      Then will he fit his tongue   105
To dialogues of business, love, or strife ;
    But it will not be long
    Ere this be thrown aside,
    And with new joy and pride
The little Actor cons another part ;   110
Filling from time to time his " humorous stage "
With all the persons, down to palsied age,
That Life brings with her in her equipage ;
    As if his whole vocation
    Were endless imitation.   115

VIII.

Thou, whose exterior semblance doth belie
    Thy soul's immensity ;
Thou best Philosopher, who yet dost keep
Thy heritage, thou Eye among the blind,   120
That, deaf and silent, read'st the eternal deep,
Haunted for ever by the eternal mind,—
    Mighty Prophet ! Seer blest !

On whom those truths do rest,
Which we are toiling all our lives to find,   125
In darkness lost, the darkness of the grave ;
Thou, over whom thy immortality
Broods like the day, a master o'er a slave,
A presence which is not to be put by ;
Thou little Child, yet glorious in the might   130
Of heaven-born freedom on thy being's height,
Why with such earnest pains dost thou provoke
The years to bring the inevitable yoke,
Thus blindly with thy blessedness at strife ?
Full soon thy soul shall have her earthly freight,   135
And custom lie upon thee with a weight,
Heavy as frost, and deep almost as life !

IX.

O joy ! that in our embers
Is something that doth live,   140
That nature yet remembers
What was so fugitive !
The thought of our past years in me doth breed
Perpetual benediction : not indeed
For that which is most worthy to be blest ;   145
Delight and liberty, the simple creed
Of childhood, whether busy or at rest,
With new-fledged hope still fluttering in his breast :—
Not for these I raise
The song of thanks and praise ;   150
But for those obstinate questionings
Of sense and outward things,
Fallings from us, vanishings ;
Blank misgivings of a Creature
Moving about in worlds not realised,   155
High instincts before which our mortal Nature

Did tremble like a guilty thing surprised :
      But for those first affections,
      Those shadowy recollections,
        Which, be they what they may,   160
Are yet the fountain light of all our day,
Are yet a master light of all our seeing ;
      Uphold us, cherish, and have power to make
Our noisy years seem moments in the being
Of the eternal Silence : truths that wake,   165
        To perish never ;
Which neither listlessness, nor mad endeavour,
        Nor Man nor Boy,
Nor all that is at enmity with joy,
Can utterly abolish or destroy !   170
      Hence, in a season of calm weather,
        Though inland far we be,
Our souls have sight of that immortal sea
      Which brought us hither,
        Can in a moment travel thither,   175
And see the children sport upon the shore,
And hear the mighty waters rolling evermore.

               X.

      Then sing, ye Birds, sing, sing a joyous song !
        And let the young Lambs bound   180
        As to the tabor's sound !
    We in thought will join your throng,
        Ye that pipe and ye that play,
        Ye that through your hearts to-day
        Feel the gladness of the May !   185
What though the radiance which was once so bright
Be now for ever taken from my sight,
      Though nothing can bring back the hour
Of splendour in the grass, of glory in the flower ;

We will grieve not, rather find   190
Strength in what remains behind;
In the primal sympathy
Which having been must ever be,
In the soothing thoughts that spring
Out of human suffering,   195
In the faith that looks through death,
In years that bring the philosophic mind.

XI.

And O, ye Fountains, Meadows, Hills, and Groves,
Think not of any severing of our loves!   200
Yet in my heart of hearts I feel your might;
I only have relinquished one delight
To live beneath your more habitual sway.
I love the Brooks which down their channels fret,
Even more than when I tripped lightly as they;   205
The innocent brightness of a new-born Day
      Is lovely yet;
The Clouds that gather round the setting sun
Do take a sober colouring from an eye
That hath kept watch o'er man's mortality;   210
Another race hath been, and other palms are won.
Thanks to the human heart by which we live,
Thanks to its tenderness, its joys, and fears,
To me the meanest flower that blows can give
Thoughts that do often lie too deep for tears.   215

CHARACTER OF THE HAPPY WARRIOR.

Who is the happy Warrior?   Who is he
That every man in arms should wish to be?
——It is the generous Spirit, who, when brought

Among the tasks of real life, hath wrought   5
Upon the plan that pleased his childish thought:
Whose high endeavours are an inward light
That makes the path before him always bright :
Who, with a natural instinct to discern
What knowledge can perform, is diligent to learn ;   10
Abides by this resolve, and stops not there,
But makes his moral being his prime care ;
Who, doomed to go in company with Pain,
And Fear, and Bloodshed, miserable train !
Turns his necessity to glorious gain ;   15
In face of these doth exercise a power
Which is our human nature's highest dower ;
Controls them and subdues, transmutes, bereaves
Of their bad influence, and their good receives :
By objects, which might force the soul to abate   20
Her feeling, rendered more compassionate ;
Is placable—because occasions rise
So often that demand such sacrifice ;
More skilful in self-knowledge, even more pure
As tempted more ; more able to endure,   25
As more exposed to suffering and distress ;
Thence, also, more alive to tenderness.
—'Tis he whose law is reason ; who depends
Upon that law as on the best of friends ;
Whence, in a state where men are tempted still   30
To evil for a guard against worse ill,
And what in quality or act is best
Doth seldom on a right foundation rest,
He fixes good on good alone, and owes
To virtue every triumph that he knows :   40
—Who, if he rise to station of command,
Rises by open means, and there will stand
On honourable terms, or else retire,

And in himself possess his own desire ;
Who comprehends his trust, and to the same   40
Keeps faithful with a singleness of aim ;
And therefore does not stoop, nor lie in wait
For wealth, or honours, or for worldly state ;
Whom they must follow; on whose head must fall,
Like showers of manna, if they come at all :   45
Whose powers shed round him in the common strife,
Or mild concerns of ordinary life,
A constant influence, a peculiar grace ;
But who, if he be called upon to face
Some awful moment to which Heaven has joined   50
Great issues, good or bad for human kind,
Is happy as a lover ; and attired
With sudden brightness, like a man inspired ;
And through the heat of conflict, keeps the law
In calmness made, and sees what he foresaw ;   55
Or if an unexpected call succeed,
Come when it will, is equal to the need :
—He who though thus endued as with a sense
And faculty for storm and turbulence,
Is yet a Soul whose master-bias leans   60
To homefelt pleasures and to gentle scenes ;
Sweet images ! which, wheresoe'er he be,
Are at his heart ; and such fidelity
It is his darling passion to approve ;
More brave for this, that he hath much to love :—   65
'Tis, finally, the man, who, lifted high,
Conspicuous object in a Nation's eye,
Or left unthought-of in obscurity,—
Who, with a toward or untoward lot,
Prosperous or adverse, to his wish or not,   70
Plays, in the many games of life, that one
Where what he most doth value must be won :

Whom neither shape of danger can dismay,
Nor thought of tender happiness betray ;
Who, not content that former worth stand fast,   75
Looks forward, persevering to the last,
From well to better, daily self-surpast :
Who, whether praise of him must walk the earth
For ever, and to noble deeds give birth,
Or he must go to dust without his fame,   80
And leave a dead unprofitable name,
Finds comfort in himself and in his cause ;
And, while the mortal mist is gathering, draws
His breath in confidence of Heaven's applause :
This is the happy Warrior ; this is he   85
Whom every man in arms should wish to be.

REFLECTIVE AND ELEGIAC POEMS.

"Adieu! adieu! thy plaintive anthem fades."

—*Keats.*

TINTERN ABBEY.

LINES,

JULY 13, 1798.

Five years have past ; five summers, with the length,   5
Of five long winters ! and again I hear
These waters, rolling from their mountain-springs
With a sweet inland murmer.*——Once again
Do I behold these steep and lofty cliffs,
That on a wild secluded scene impress   10
Thoughts of more deep seclusion ; and connect
The landscape with the quiet of the sky.
The day is come when I again repose
Here, under this dark sycamore, and view
These plots of cottage-ground, these orchard-tufts,   15
Which at this season, with their unripe fruits,
Are clad in one green hue, and lose themselves
Among the woods and copses, nor disturb
The wild green landscape. · Once again I see
These hedgerows, hardly hedgerows, little lines   20
Of sportive wood run wild : these pastoral farms,
Green to the very door ; and wreaths of smoke
Sent up, in silence, from among the trees !
With some uncertain notice, as might seem
Of vagrant dwellers in the houseless woods,   25
Or of some Hermit's cave, where by his fire
The Hermit sits alone.
                    These beauteous Forms,
Through a long absence, have not been to me

---

* The river is not affected by the tides a few miles above Tintern.

As is a landscape to a blind man's eye :   30
But oft, in lonely rooms, and 'mid the din
Of towns and cities, I have owed to them,
In hours of weariness, sensations sweet,
Felt in the blood, and felt along the heart ;
And passing even into my purer mind,   35
With tranquil restoration :—feelings too
Of unremembered pleasure : such, perhaps,
As have no slight or trivial influence
On that best portion of a good man's life,
His little, nameless, unremembered acts   40
Of kindness and of love.   Nor less, I trust,
To them I may have owed another gift,
Of aspect more sublime ; that blessed mood,
In which the burthen of the mystery,
In which the heavy and the weary weight   45
Of all this unintelligible world,
Is lightened :—that serene and blessed mood
In which the affections gently lead us on,—
Until, the breath of this corporeal frame
And even the motion of our human blood   50
Almost suspended, we are laid asleep
In body, and become a living soul :
While with an eye made quiet by the power
Of harmony, and the deep power of joy,
We see into the life of things.   55
                        If this
Be but a vain belief, yet, oh ! how oft,
In darkness, and amid the many shapes
Of joyless daylight ; when the fretful stir
Unprofitable, and the fever of the world,   60
Have hung upon the beatings of my heart,
How oft, in spirit, have I turned to thee,
O sylvan Wye !   Thou wanderer thro' the woods,

How often has my spirit turned to thee !
  And now, with gleams of half-extinguished thought, 65
With many recognitions dim and faint,
And somewhat of a sad perplexity,
The picture of the mind revives again :
While here I stand, not only with the sense
Of present pleasure, but with pleasing thoughts   70
That in this moment there is life and food
For future years. And so I dare to hope,
Though changed, no doubt, from what I was when first
I came among these hills ; when like a roe
I bounded o'er the mountains, by the sides   75
Of the deep rivers, and the lonely streams,
Wherever nature led : more like a man
Flying from something that he dreads, than one
Who sought the thing he loved. For nature then
(The coarser pleasures of my boyish days,   80
And their glad animal movements all gone by)
To me was all in all.—I cannot paint
What then I was. The sounding cataract
Haunted me like a passion : the tall rock,
The mountain, and the deep and gloomy wood,   85
Their colours and their forms, were then to me
An appetite ; a feeling and a love,
That had no need of a remoter charm,
By thought supplied, or any interest
Unborrowed from the eye.—That time is past,   90
And all its aching joys are now no more,
And all its dizzy raptures. Not for this
Faint I, nor mourn nor murmur; other gifts
Have followed, for such loss, I would believe,
Abundant recompense. For I have learned   95
To look on nature, not as in the hour
Of thoughtless youth ; but hearing oftentimes

The still, sad music of humanity,
Nor harsh nor grating, though of ample power
To chasten and subdue.   And I have felt   100
A presence that disturbs me with the joy
Of elevated thoughts: a sense sublime
Of something far more deeply interfused,
Whose dwelling is the light of setting suns,
And the round ocean and the living air,   105
And the blue sky, and in the mind of man:
A motion and a spirit, that impels
All thinking things, all objects of all thought,
And rolls through all things.   Therefore am I still
A lover of the meadows and the woods,   110
And mountains; and of all that we behold
From this green earth; of all the mighty world
Of eye and ear, both what they half create,*
And what perceive; well pleased to recognise
In nature and the language of the sense,   115
The anchor of my purest thoughts, the nurse,
The guide, the guardian of my heart, and soul
Of all my moral being.
                         Nor perchance,
If I were not thus taught, should I the more   120
Suffer my genial spirits to decay:
For thou art with me, here, upon the banks
Of this fair river; thou, my dearest Friend,
My dear, dear Friend, and in thy voice I catch
The language of my former heart, and read   125
My former pleasures in the shooting lights
Of thy wild eyes.   Oh! yet a little while
May I behold in thee what I was once,
My dear, dear Sister! and this prayer I make,

---

* This line has a close resemblance to an admirable line of Young, the exact expression of which I do not recollect.

Knowing that Nature never did betray   130
The heart that loved her ; 'tis her privilege,
Through all the years of this our life, to lead
From joy to joy : for she can so inform   ⌐⌐∨०·
The mind that is within us, so impress
With quietness and beauty, and so feed   135
With lofty thoughts, that neither evil tongues,
Rash judgments, nor the sneers of selfish men,
Nor greetings where no kindness is, nor all
The dreary intercourse of daily life,
Shall e'er prevail against us, or disturb   140
Our cheerful faith, that all which we behold
Is full of blessings.   Therefore let the moon
Shine on thee in thy solitary walk ;
And let the misty mountain winds be free
To blow against thee : and in after years,   145
When these wild ecstasies shall be matured
Into a sober pleasure, when thy mind
Shall be a mansion for all lovely forms,
Thy memory be as a dwelling-place
For all sweet sounds and harmonies ; oh ! then,   150
If solitude, or fear, or pain, or grief,
Should be thy portion, with what healing thoughts
Of tender joy wilt thou remember me,
And these my exhortations !   Nor, perchance
If I should be where I no more can hear   155
Thy voice, nor catch from thy wild eyes these gleams
Of past existence, wilt thou then forget
That on the banks of this delightful stream
We stood together ; and that I, so long
A worshipper of Nature, hither came   160
Unwearied in that service : rather say
With warmer love, oh ! with far deeper zeal
Of holier love.   Nor wilt thou then forget,   ·

That after many wanderings, many years
Of absence, these steep woods and lofty cliffs,   165
And this green pastoral landscape, were to me
More dear, both for themselves and for thy sake!

THE FOUNTAIN.

A CONVERSATION.

WE talked with open heart, and tongue
Affectionate and true,
A pair of Friends, though I was young,   5
And Matthew seventy-two.

We lay beneath a spreading oak,
Beside a mossy seat;
And from the turf a fountain broke,
And gurgled at our feet.   10

"Now, Matthew!" said I, "let us match
This water's pleasant tune
With some old Border-song, or Catch,
That suits a summer's noon;

"Or of the Church-clock and the chimes   15
Sing here beneath the shade,
That half-mad thing of witty rhymes
Which you last April made!"

In silence Matthew lay, and eyed
The spring beneath the tree;   20
And thus the dear old man replied,
The grey-haired man of glee:

THE FAIRY GLEN.

" Down to the vale this water steers,
How merrily it goes !
'Twill murmur on a thousand years, 25
And flow as now it flows.

" And here, on this delightful day,
I cannot choose but think
How oft, a vigorous man, I lay
Beside this Fountain's brink. 30

" My eyes are dim with childish tears,
My heart is idly stirred,
For the same sound is in my ears
Which in those days I heard.

" Thus fares it still in our decay : ⌣ 35
And yet the wiser mind
Mourns less for what age takes away
Than what it leaves behind.

" The Blackbird in the summer trees,
The Lark upon the hill, 40
Let loose their carols when they please,
Are quiet when they will.

" With Nature never do *they* wage
A foolish strife ; they see
A happy youth, and their old age 45
Is beautiful and free :

" But we are pressed by heavy laws ;
And often, glad no more,
We wear a face of joy, because
We have been glad of yore. 50

" If there be one who need bemoan
His kindred laid in earth,
The household hearts that were his own,
It is the man of mirth.

" My days, my Friend, are almost gone,   55
My life has been approved,
And many love me ; but by none
Am I enough beloved."

" Now both himself and me he wrongs,
The man who thus complains !   60
I live and sing my idle songs
Upon these happy plains,

" And, Matthew, for thy children dead
I'll be a son to thee ! "
At this he grasped my hand, and said,   65
" Alas ! that cannot be."

We rose up from the fountain-side ;
And down the smooth descent
Of the green sheep-track did we glide ;
And through the wood we went ;   70

And, ere we came to Leonard's-rock,
He sang those witty rhymes
About the crazy old church-clock,
And the bewildered chimes.

PEELE CASTLE.

ELEGIAC STANZAS

SUGGESTED BY A PICTURE OF PEELE C   LE, IN, A STORM,
PAINTED BY SIR GEORGE   UMONT.

I was thy neighbour once, thou rugged Pile!
Four summer weeks I dwelt in sight of thee :   5
I saw thee every day ; and all the while
Thy Form was sleeping on a glassy sea.

So pure the sky, so quiet was the air !
So like, so very like, was day to day !
Whene'er I looked, thy Image still was there ;   10
It trembled, but it never passed away.

How perfect was the calm ! it seemed no sleep ;
No mood, which season takes away, or brings :
I could have fancied that the mighty Deep
Was even the gentlest of all gentle things.   15

Ah ! THEN, if mine had been the Painter's hand,
To express what then I saw ; and add the gleam,
The light that never was, on sea or land,
The consecration, and the Poet's dream ;

I would have planted thee, thou hoary Pile,   20
Amid a world how different from this !
Beside a sea that could not cease to smile ;
On tranquil land, beneath a sky of bliss.

A Picture had it been of lasting ease,
Elysian quiet, without toil or strife ;   25
No motion but the moving tide, a breeze,
Or merely silent Nature's breathing life.

Such, in the fond illusion of my heart,
Such Picture would I at that time have made :
And seen the soul of truth in every part,   30
A stedfast peace that might not be betrayed.

So once it would have been,—'tis so no more ;
I have submitted to a new control :
A power is gone, which nothing can restore ;
A deep distress hath humanised my Soul.   35

Not for a moment could I now behold
A smiling sea, and be what I have been :
The feeling of my loss will ne'er be old ;
This, which I know, I speak with mind serene.

Then, Beaumont, Friend! who would have been the Friend, 40
If he had lived, of Him whom I deplore,
This work of thine I blame not, but commend ;
This sea in anger, and that dismal shore.

O 'tis a passionate Work—yet wise and well,
Well chosen is the spirit that is here ;   45
That Hulk which labours in the deadly swell,
That rueful sky, this pageantry of fear !

And this huge Castle, standing here sublime,
I love to see the look with which it braves,
Cased in the unfeeling armour of old time,   50
The lightning, the fierce wind, and trampling waves.

Farewell, farewell the heart that lives alone,
Housed, in a dream, at distance from the Kind !
Such happiness, wherever it be known,
Is to be pitied ; for 'tis surely blind.   55

But welcome fortitude, and patient cheer,
And frequent sights of what is to be borne!
Such sights, or worse, as are before me here.—
Not without hope we suffer and we mourn.

FRENCH REVOLUTION.

AS IT APPEARED TO ENTHUSIASTS AT ITS COMMENCEMENT.

OH! pleasant exercise of hope and joy!
For mighty were the auxiliars, which then stood
Upon our side, we who were strong in love!
Bliss was it in that dawn to be alive,
But to be young was very heaven!—Oh! times,
In which the meagre, stale, forbidding ways
Of custom, law, and statute, took at once
The attraction of a country in Romance!   10
When Reason seemed the most to assert her rights
When most intent on making of herself   /
A prime enchantress—to assist the work,
Which then was going forward in her name!
Not favoured spots alone, but the whole earth,   15
The beauty wore of promise—that which sets
(As at some moment might not be unfelt
Among the bowers of paradise itself)
The budding rose above the rose full blown.
What temper at the prospect did not wake   20
To happiness unthought of? The inert
Were roused, and lively natures rapt away!
They who had fed their childhood upon dreams,
The playfellows of fancy, who had made
All powers of swiftness, subtilty and strength   25

9

Their ministers,—who in lordly wise had stirred
Among the grandest objects of the sense,
And dealt with whatsoever they found there
As if they had within some lurking right
To wield it; they, too, who, of gentle mood,   30
Had watched all gentle motions, and to these
Had fitted their own thoughts, schemers more mild,
And in the region of their peaceful selves;—
Now was it that *both* found, the Meek and Lofty
Did both find helpers to their heart's desire,   35
And stuff at hand, plastic as they could wish;
Were called upon to exercise their skill,
Not in Utopia, subterranean Fields,
Or some secreted Island, Heaven knows where!
But in the very world, which is the world   40
Of all of us,—the place where in the end
We find our happiness, or not at all!

A POET'S EPITAPH.

ART thou a Statesman, in the van
Of public business trained and bred?
—First learn to love one living man;
Then may'st thou think upon the dead.   5

A Lawyer art thou?—draw not nigh!
Go, carry to some fitter place
The keenness of that practised eye,
The hardness of that sallow face.

Art thou a Man of purple cheer?   10
A rosy Man, right plump to see?
Approach; yet, Doctor, not too near
This grave no cushion is for thee.

THE SKYLARK'S HOUR.

Or art thou one of gallant pride,
A Soldier, and no man of chaff?   15
Welcome!—but lay thy sword aside,
And lean upon a peasant's staff.

Physician art thou? One, all eyes,
Philosopher! a fingering slave,
One that would peep and botanize   20
Upon his mother's grave?

Wrapt closely in thy sensual fleece,
O turn aside,—and take, I pray,
That he below may rest in peace,
That abject thing, thy soul, away!   25

A Moralist perchance appears;
Led, Heaven knows how! to this poor sod:
And he has neither eyes nor ears;
Himself his world, and his own God;

One to whose smooth-rubbed soul can cling   30
Nor form, nor feeling, great or small;
A reasoning, self-sufficing thing,
An intellectual All-in-all!

Shut close the door; press down the latch;
Sleep in thy intellectual crust;   35
Nor lose ten tickings of thy watch
Near this unprofitable dust.

But who is He, with modest looks,
And clad in homely russet brown?
He murmurs near the running brooks   40
A music sweeter than their own.

He is retired as noontide dew,
Or fountain in a noon-day grove :
And you must love him, ere to you
He will seem worthy of your love.   45

The outward shows of sky and earth,
Of hill and valley, he has viewed ;
And impulses of deeper birth
Have come to him in solitude.

In common things that round us lie   50
Some random truths he can impart ;—
The harvest of a quiet eye
That broods and sleeps on his own heart.

But he is weak ; both Man and Boy,
Hath been an idler in the land ;   55
Contented if he might enjoy
The things which others understand.

—Come hither in thy hour of strength ;
Come, weak as is a breaking wave !
Here stretch thy body at full length ;   60
Or build thy house upon this grave !

SONNETS.

"*Scorn not the Sonnet; Critic you have frowned,
Mindless of its just honours; with this key
Shakespeare unlocked his heart;*"

SONNETS.

III.—ON THE EXTINCTION OF THE VENETIAN REPUBLIC.

ONCE did she hold the gorgeous East in fee ;
And was the safeguard of the West : the worth
Of Venice did not fall below her birth,   5
Venice, the eldest Child of Liberty.
She was a Maiden City, bright and free ;
No guile seduced, no force could violate ;
And, when She took unto herself a Mate,
She must espouse the everlasting Sea.   10
And what if she had seen those glories fade,
Those titles vanish, and that strength decay ;
Yet shall some tribute of regret be paid
When her long life hath reached its final day :
Men are we, and must grieve when even the Shade   15
Of that which once was great, is passed away.

VI.—THOUGHT OF A BRITON ON THE SUBJUGATION OF SWITZERLAND.

Two Voices are there ; one is of the Sea,
One of the Mountains ; each a mighty Voice :
In both from age to age Thou didst rejoice,   5
They were thy chosen Music, Liberty !
There came a Tyrant, and with holy glee
Thou fought'st against Him ; but hast vainly striven ;
Thou from the Alpine holds at length art driven,
Where not a torrent murmurs heard by thee.   10
Of one deep bliss thine ear hath been bereft :

Then cleave, O cleave to that which still is left;
For, high-souled Maid, what sorrow would it be
That Mountain Floods should thunder as before,
And Ocean bellow from his rocky shore,   . 15
And neither awful Voice be heard by thee !

XVII.—To Thomas Clarkson, on the Final Passing of the
Bill for the Abolition of the Slave Trade,
March 1807.

Clarkson ! it was an obstinate hill to climb :
How toilsome—nay, how dire it was, by Thee   5
Is known,—by none, perhaps, so feelingly ;
But Thou, who, starting in thy fervent prime,
Didst first lead forth this pilgrimage sublime,
Hast heard the constant Voice its charge repeat,
Which, out of thy young heart's oracular seat,   10
First roused thee. - O true yoke-fellow of Time,
Duty's intrepid liegeman, see, the palm
Is won, and by all Nations shall be worn !
The bloody Writing is for ever torn,
And Thou henceforth shall have a good man's calm,   15
A great man's happiness ; thy zeal shall find
Repose at length, firm Friend of human kind !

XIX.

Scorn not the Sonnet ; Critic, you have frowned,
Mindless of its just honours ; with this key
Shakespeare unlocked his heart ; the melody
Of this small lute gave ease to Petrarch's wound ;   5
A thousand times this pipe did Tasso sound ;
Camöens soothed with it an exile's grief ;

The Sonnet glittered a gay myrtle leaf
Amid the cypress with which Dante crowned
His visionary brow : a glow-worm lamp,   10
It cheered mild Spenser, called from Faery-land
To struggle through dark ways ; and, (when a damp
Fell round the path of Milton) in his hand
The Thing became a trumpet, whence he blew
Soul-animating strains—alas, too few !   15

XX.

NUNS fret not at their convent's narrow room,
And Hermits are contented with their cells,
And Students with their pensive citadels :
Maids at the Wheel, the Weaver at his loom,   5
Sit blithe and happy ; Bees that soar for bloom,
High as the highest Peak of Furness Fells,
Will murmur by the hour in foxglove bells:
In truth, the prison, unto which we doom
Ourselves, no prison is : and hence to me,   10
In sundry moods, 'twas pastime to be bound
Within the Sonnet's scanty plot of ground :
Pleased if some Souls (for such there needs must be)
Who have felt the weight of too much liberty,
Should find brief solace there, as I have found.   15

XXIII.—PERSONAL TALK.

I AM not One who much or oft delight
To season my fireside with personal talk,—
Of friends, who live within an easy walk,
Or neighbours, daily, weekly, in my sight :   5
And, for my chance-acquaintance, ladies bright,

Sons, mothers, maidens withering on the stalk,
These all wear out of me, like forms with chalk
Painted on rich men's floors for one feast-night.
Better than such discourse doth silence long,   15
Long, barren silence, square with my desire;
To sit without emotion, hope, or aim,
In the loved presence of my cottage-fire,
And listen to the flapping of the flame,
Or kettle whispering its faint undersong.   20

XXIV.—CONTINUED.

WINGS have we,—and as far as we can go
We may find pleasure: wilderness and wood,
Blank ocean and mere sky, support that mood
Which with the lofty sanctifies the low.   5
Dreams, books, are each a world; and books, we know,
Are a substantial world, both pure and good:
Round these, with tendrils strong as flesh and blood,
Our pastime and our happiness will grow.
There find I personal themes, a plenteous store,   10
Matter wherein right voluble I am,
To which I listen with a ready ear;
Two shall be named, pre-eminently dear,—
The gentle Lady married to the Moor;
And heavenly Una with her milk-white Lamb.   15

XXV.—CONCLUDED.

NOR can I not believe but that hereby
Great gains are mine; for thus I live remote
From evil-speaking; rancour, never sought,
Comes to me not; malignant truth, or lie.   5

Hence have I genial seasons, hence have I
Smooth passions, smooth discourse, and joyous thought:
And thus from day to day my little boat
Rocks in its harbour, lodging peaceably.
Blessings be with them—and eternal praise,   10
Who gave us nobler loves, and nobler cares—
The Poets, who on earth have made us heirs
Of truth and pure delight by heavenly lays !
Oh ! might my name be numbered among theirs,
Then gladly would I end my mortal days.   15

XXVL—To Sleep.

A FLOCK of sheep that leisurely pass by,
One after one ; the sound of rain, and bees
Murmuring ; the fall of rivers, winds and seas,
Smooth fields, white sheets of water, and pure sky,   5
By turns have all been thought of, yet I lie
Sleepless ; and soon the small birds' melodies
Must hear, first uttered from my orchard trees ;
And the first Cuckoo's melancholy cry.
Even thus last night, and two nights more, I lay,   10
And could not win thee, Sleep ! by any stealth :
So do not let me wear to-night away :
Without Thee what is all the morning's wealth ?
Come, blessed barrier between day and day,
Dear mother of fresh thoughts and joyous health !   15

XXIX.---Composed upon Westminster Bridge, Sept. 3, 1803.

EARTH has not anything to show more fair :
Dull would he be of soul who could pass by

A sight so touching in its majesty: 5
This City now doth like a garment wear
The beauty of the morning ; silent, bare,
Ships, towers, domes, theatres, and temples lie
Open unto the fields, and to the sky ;
All bright and glittering in the smokeless air. 10
Never did sun more beautifully steep
In his first splendour, valley, rock, or hill ;
Ne'er saw I, never felt, a calm so deep !
The river glideth at his own sweet will :
Dear God ! the very houses seem asleep, 15
And all that mighty heart is lying still !

DERWENTWATER AND SKIDDAW.

COMMENTARY.

" You might read all the books in the British Museum (if you could live long enough) and remain an utterly 'illiterate' uneducated person ; but if you read ten pages of a good book, letter by letter,—that is to say, with real accuracy,—you are forevermore in some measure an educated person. The entire difference between education and non-education (as regards the merely intellectual part of it) consists in this accuracy."

—*Ruskin.*

CHAPTER I.

MEMOIR OF WORDSWORTH.

Mark Antony.—His life was gentle; and the elements
So mixed in him, that Nature might stand up,
And say to all the world, "This was a man!"
                —Shakespeare's Julius Caesar.

WHERE WORDSWORTH WENT TO SCHOOL.

CHAPTER I.

Every great English poet has had a great lesson peculiarly his own to offer to his readers; however varied and voluminous his works, some dominant and central idea has given unity to them all and made them, as one may say, a single song of many notes. Milton's trumpet-voice proclaims the power and sublimity of the spirit world as conceived by the Puritan imagination; Pope asserts the superiority of reason as man's governing faculty; Byron stands for passion and liberty, even to excess; Shelley calls us to a revolt against conventionality and superstition; the inscrutable and god-like Shakespeare, while scorning any single truth, has taught us above all things to know the world rather than to judge it.

In fiction, also, this singleness of purpose has marked the efforts of our greatest novelists. Scott revived chivalry: he exerted his wonderful gift of historic imagination to show us " the storied past"; Dickens taught us the beauty and power of a warm and loving heart, the sweetness of cheerfulness and sentiment; Thackeray satirized all who make pretences, and exhibited the folly and meanness of sham and deceit; George Eliot was imbued with the importance of human life, and made us feel that it is as important in one class of society as in another.

Many gifted writers have failed to be great because they have failed to grasp any great central idea to give forth as a new and important truth for humanity. Many writers, on the other hand, have grasped truths of the highest value, and grasped them with wonderful power and originality, and yet, because of the want of artistic gifts, have failed to give us beautiful literary works. Carlyle with his lesson of hard work and sincere work might have been a sublime poet had he not lacked beauty of expression ; Emerson's great truth that the broadest view of a subject is the most truthful and enlightening, might have made him a great novelist had he possessed as much knowledge of story-telling as some of our weakest novelists.

The originality and importance to humanity of an author's great dominant idea, together with his gift of conveying that idea in a powerful form, go a long way toward making his rank and influence. Gray's idea that the villagers sleeping peacefully in their narrow cells under the twilight shadows of the churchyard at Stoke were worth writing beautifully about, has been considered so great an idea that Gray is a great poet though he wrote only a handful of verses.

Burns found that Gray's idea had not been exhausted ; he used the same great truth with so much love and warmth and life that he may be said to have made it his own. Perhaps this idea can never be exhausted until sorrow and poverty shall cease.

But, while a little work on such a truth has made such names as Gray and Burns, all the art of a Longfellow has failed to make an equal fame where no such powerful mission was felt, it is only when we find the great teacher and the great artist in the one man that we see a Spenser or a Tennyson.

It has never been claimed for Wordsworth that his art was equal to that of poets like Shelley and Swinburne ; when he first claimed attention for his verses he was sneered at as no gifted artist, however scanty his thought, is ever sneered at ; and yet he is reckoned among our first poets by a great majority of capable critics. Some rank him among the first three, some among the first five ; a few still sneer at his claims. Of his rank we shall speak again, but it must be certain that the great mission of this poet has appealed profoundly to the thoughtful classes; otherwise, with his small pretensions to skill as a versifier he could never hold the place he does.

If one were asked what subjects literature may deal with, one might conclude roughly that *humanity* and *nature* and the *unseen world* would cover the whole ground. Shakespeare has gone a long way toward covering all this ground, but he has certainly made human nature his own particular subject. Milton has told us of the invisible powers, and his name is in a sense identified with that division of the literary field. Now, it would seem that until Wordsworth came the other part of the field had never been appropriated, and he made it his own. Milton tells us to look within us and above for light and guidance; our path is that of *Christian*, we must keep our eye upon the end of the narrow way; Shakespeare tells us to look around us, to know our fellow-man, his actions and his motives; to learn how to live rather than how to die; our path is among men, our duty to our Creator is our duty to those among whom He has placed us. But Wordsworth tells us to look for the image of our Maker in the grass, the rocks, the starlit water; the daisy, the skylark, the innocent hart, are our examples because they draw their joy and peace from the source of it, and our wisdom is to see that the simple living of these is our guide to present and eternal happiness; our path is not among men so much as among the hills, the valleys, the meadows, along the streams, under the open sky of heaven. Milton was a man of books, Shakespeare was a man of the world, Wordsworth was neither. Milton was a man of strong ecclesiastical and scholastic opinions, Shakespeare has expressed no opinions, Wordsworth's opinions are the opinions of Nature herself.

When we say that Wordsworth is one of the three greatest poets, we mean that he has appropriated one of the three great divisions of the whole field of literary effort with so much power and success that no other poet has ever been thought of

as his rival. The substance of the views that people of a
scholastic and ecclesiastical turn of mind hold concerning the
unseen world may be found in the *Paradise Lost* and the
Paradise Regained. All that men think about each other (and
much more) may be found in Shakespeare's *Plays.* All our
tenderness for flowers, birds and natural objects generally is
voiced in Wordsworth, he tells us our ideal relation to nature,
we are to love nature and to learn from her. Nature teaches
us peace, happiness and duty. The stars in their orbits are
young and strong through obeying the law of their nature; if
we obey the law of our nature we shall be young and strong
always. If the stars could break the law ruin would result.
Duty, then, is our guide, but though our guide not our task-
master; we are to regard the law of duty as the law of perfect
liberty; liberty is the right to do right—to obey duty; the right
to do wrong is mere license. Liberty brings peace and happiness,
even a bright wholesome joy, but not pleasure. Pleasure is
something to be feared, it is unknown to the flower, and the
bird, and the star. Joy is the highest state of happiness that
brings no reaction, no misery or depression; pleasure is to be
shunned, it brings depression, remorse, decay.

It will be seen that the poet is not so much the poet who
glorifies nature as the poet who interprets man's relation to
nature. No more striking lesson could be had than to contrast
Shelley's verses about the skylark with Wordsworth's. Shelley's
song is indeed "harmonious madness," tremendous, wild and
passionate; Wordsworth's song is far more passionate than is
usual with him, indeed, it may be said to reach the highest
pitch of lyrical enthusiasm he permits himself, yet it ends thus:

> *"I, on the earth will go plodding on,
> By myself, cheerfully, till the day is done."

He does not wish to indulge in the wildness of joy though he

* Old reading.

envies the strong heart of this favourite of nature, a creature to whom the intoxication of joy is not an excess.

We have purposely said nothing of Wordsworth's life up to this point. It is not uncommon in memoirs to see such expressions as these: "an uneventful career," "a quiet and uninteresting life." Frankly then our poet never was a poacher, he never tramped through Europe supporting himself by playing a flute, he did not lead a band of disorderly Suliotes in the war of Greek Independence, nor was he drowned from a yacht at the age of thirty. No such amusing, exciting, or tragic tales are told of him. Nor had he any remarkable eccentricities to endear him to the reader; he did not quarrel with his wife, nor keep a pet bear, nor eat like a savage, nor drink tea excessively, nor ruin himself with opium; he did not commit suicide, nor die of a broken heart, nor at an early age. On the other hand he was a quiet, kindly, well-balanced man, of excellent habits and character; he lived in peace with all men, was a good neighbour and citizen, and through eighty long years kept plodding on cheerfully till his day was done. Not an eventful life in the common sense of the term; not an interesting life if one compare it with the life of a fiction-hero and on the same grounds of judgment. His own great dominant truth of book and life was that all morbid excitement, all passion, whether of pleasure or grief, is unmanly, undutiful and evil; he would have condemned no great tragic story if true and natural, but the morbid desire for all undue excitement was in his eyes the great evil of the world. He is the antithesis of Byron, he is the antithesis of Daudet and de Maupassant, he is the antithesis of cynicism and pessimism and of everything that destroys hope, and prevents effort, and paralyzes faith and love and health. No *blasé* heart will be stimulated into an hour's attention by his pen; no eye that cannot, with Carlyle see the fifth act of a tragedy in the death of every peasant, and weep over the field-mouse and the

uprooted daisy with Burns, will see what this poet has to
show.   But let no rash critic conclude that what he has no
eyes to see has no visible existence.   There are thousands of
" Wordsworthians" and tens of thousands who feel that life is
better worth living, and plodding less irksome, and simplicity
more charming, because Wordsworth lived uneventfully and
plodded cheerfully, and despised luxury.   Surely the best that
any poet can do is to make millions of people regard their
daily commonplace existence as being beautiful and worthy of
them and even ideal : and surely the worst any writer can do
is to make the people despise their poor surroundings, feel
wretched, envious, discontented, hopeless.

Had Wordsworth been of the latter class he might more
consistently have died a tragic early death after a tragic or
melodramatic life ; being of the former class preëminent, he
has left us only a simple record which the greatest of his readers
might wisely envy.

At Cockermouth, in April, when the buds break, in the year
1770, Wordsworth was born.   His father, an attorney, was
law-agent to the Earl of Lonsdale.   Both parents were of good
birth and education, both were wise, refined and capable.   The
mother died leaving her boy only eight years of age, very
young to be motherless, but not too young to have got a strong
impress of her love and wisdom.   He received his earliest
lessons at a dame-school in Penrith ; at nine he was sent to
Hawkeshead Grammar School in Lancashire ; at seventeen, to
St. John's College, Cambridge.   He was graduated Bachelor of
Arts in 1791, about a century ago.   The year before, he had
travelled in Europe with a College friend, Jones, and after his
graduation he went to France, where he remained about a year-
and-a-half, studying the French language, which he mastered
thoroughly, and the political situation of those stirring times.
At first he was an ardent Republican, but disgusted with the

WORDSWORTH'S HOME—RYDAL MOUNT.

excesses of the Revolutionists, he returned to England and rapidly became a staunch, not to say reactionary Conservative.

Though poor, he had relatives who made him an allowance on which he could live. His friends wished him to study for holy orders, but he felt a strong desire to live by writing, and soon published a small volume of verse. A friend, Raisley Calvert, for whom he felt a profound attachment, died after a lingering illness, in which Wordsworth had shown much devotion to him. Calvert having great faith in the young poet's genius left him £900, to enable him to follow literature without depending upon his relatives.

In 1797, Wordsworth met Coleridge, and the two ambitious young poets formed a strong friendship. They agreed to write a book of poems together, Coleridge to write about the supernatural, and Wordsworth to lend the charm of poetry to commonplace objects. This book appeared in '98 and contained "The Ancient Mariner," a ballad so powerful in presenting the strong reality of the invisible world that it carries more conviction of the existence of unseen and spiritual forces than even Milton's sublime works. The book (Lyrical Ballads, Vol. I.) was a flat failure however, and Wordsworth's part of it was much reviled by the critics.

After its publication the poets and Wordsworth's sister went to Germany to study. This visit to the continent had a striking influence upon Coleridge but Wordsworth returned without any strong marks of German culture. On his return to England in 1799, he settled down to live in seclusion as a poet-philosopher. He always lived near the English lakes, though in three or four different spots. In 1813, he went to Rydal Mount, the residence most famously associated with his name.

In 1802, the Wordsworth's got £8,500 in settlement of a lawsuit against the Earl of Lonsdale, and the poet's share was sufficient to warrant him in marrying; so at the age of thirty-two he was married to his own cousin, Mary Hutchinson, with whom as a child he had gone to school and played at Penrith. Their union was most happy. In his verses he often refers to her kindness and wisdom; there were five children, of whom the father was very fond, some of his sweetest verses describe his daughters. In 1813 he got a Government appointment as Distributor of Stamps for Cumberland and Westmoreland; this brought him about £500 a year, and the work was done by a deputy. In 1827 Sir George Beaumont, friend and patron of Wordsworth, died, leaving him £100 a year as a legacy.

Wordsworth worked steadily away with little encouragement except from a circle of cultivated friends such as Coleridge, Southey, De Quincey, and Arnold of Rugby, until about 1839, when he got more recognition. In 1840, he was pensioned by Sir Robert Peel, (the minister who never read poetry) receiving £300 yearly. In 1843 he was offered the honour of Poet Laureate upon the death of Southey; he declined the post because of his great age, but, being assured that no duties would be required of him, that the Queen heartily approved of his appointment, and that she could select for the place "no one whose claims for respect and honour on account of eminence as a poet" could be placed in competition with his, he withdrew his objections and honoured the English laurel by wearing it for his few remaining years.

When, a few years later, the present venerable Laureate inherited that decoration, he wrote with beautiful sincerity of his wreath as—

> "This laurel greener from the brows
> Of him that utter'd nothing base."

In 1850, once more in April, the star which had risen in 1770 was again upon the horizon. He had never known ill-

ness, but the weakness of fourscore left him unable to throw off
a cold, hence, on the 23rd of the month of buds, that beautiful
and perfect life returned unto God who gave it. In a moment
he returned from his journey far inland to that—

> "Immortal sea
> Which brought us hither."

He lies enshrined in a great temple. Its roof is fretted with
the clouds and stars, its carpet is the daisied grass, its pillars
are the ancient hills, its music the "murmuring Rotha" and
the restless wind. There, in the Grasmere churchyard he lies,
surrounded by his dear dalesmen, his wildflowers, and his birds.
What solemn pomp of stately edifice could equal the eternal
temple of nature. What noble company of the dead could be
so sweet to his ashes as that rustic fellowship. Were ever life,
death and burial-place more beautifully harmonious with a great
man's teaching than these? What dramatic touch, what
strange or eccentric story but would mar the steady consistent
life-record of this great, earnest, serious, humourless man.

A good citizen, good husband and father, good friend, good
neighbour, good poet—it is this that makes his life dull,
uneventful, undramatic ; it is this, that makes him worthy of
the highest praise—" This was a man."

> "The dew is on the Lotus ! Rise great Sun !
> And lift my leaf and mix me with the wave.
> Om Mani Padme Hum, the Sunrise comes !
> The dew-drop slips into the shining sea !"

CHAPTER II.

THE DEFINITION OF POETRY.

"In dreams we are true poets ; we create the persons of the drama ; we give them appropriate figures, faces, costume ; they are perfect in their organs, attitude, manners : moreover, they speak after their own characters, not ours ;—they speak to us, and we listen with surprise to what they say. Indeed I doubt if the best poet has yet written any five-act play that can compare in thoroughness of invention with the unwritten play in five acts, composed by the dullest snorer on the floor of the watch-house."

—Emerson

CHAPTER II.

When students begin to study Botany or Hydrostatics they naturally inquire for the definition of Botany or Hydrostatics so that they may grasp the meaning and aims of the new subject and its province of investigation; but every student begins the study of poetry with a more or less definite understanding of what a poem is, hence the formal definition of *poem* and *poetry* are usually passed over without direct notice. If, however, a more scientific mind should ask *What is poetry?* or *What are the characteristic marks of a poem?* it is probable that the question would meet with so great a variety of replies as to leave the questioner in a state of perplexity far deeper than he had at first experienced.

It is certain that many could say it is useless to seek for a rigid definition of a poem; nature tells her favoured few when they find the true metal and they do not care to divulge the secret nor to publish any tests by which less favoured readers may attempt the assay. But it is fairly certain that careful and even scientific scrutiny, with assaying tests and formulæ, do not lessen but increase our knowledge of poetry and our delight in it; it is also well known that many of our greatest poets, notably Wordsworth, have written learned essays upon the scientific aspects of their art and upon these grounds we may conclude that the hazy and indolent view which urges us not to attempt close observations for the sake of definition is merely a labour-saving caprice of those who would be critics without canons of criticism, and oracles without the authority of unquestioned knowledge. If then we err in attempting a scientific definition of poetry we err under the protection of such writers as Aristotle, Horace, Pope, Wordsworth, Goethe, Schiller, Ruskin, Poe, Swinburne, Matthew Arnold and a legion of others of almost equal fame.

All well-constructed definitions begin by placing the species to be defined in the genus or family to which it belongs. We have no difficulty in ascertaining that a poem is a work of art. Poems are one species of this genus, while pictures, musical pieces, pieces of statuary and of architecture are other species of the same large group. We know that a fine art is a method of appealing to the soul through the senses, as painting through the eye, and music through the ear; our inquiry then leads us to seek for the special mark or test which differentiates the art of poetry from the other fine-arts. We see at once that in the means used there is a decided difference between any two arts. Music uses combinations of sounds to arouse our thoughts and feelings; painting uses colours, lights and shadows; sculpture uses marble and differs from painting in using the white solid while painting uses the coloured surface.

Poetry is quite different from these, at first sight so different that we doubt whether we should call it an art; it uses *words* for its material and at first they seem to appeal to none of the senses. Of course we see printed words and they appeal, as bits of printing, to the eye, but unless the printing is very artistic they are not works of art merely considered as they appeal to the eye. Take for example the lines :—

> " Fair laughs the morn, and soft the zephyr blows,
>   While proudly riding o'er the azure realm
>   In gallant trim the gilded vessel goes,
>   Youth on the prow, and pleasure at the helm."

The mere fact that these irregular black characters on the white paper appeal to the eye does not make them a work of art; but, if these characters, on account of their conventional power as symbols of ideas, rouse in the *mind's eye* a picture of

the gilded vessel against the azure sea, of gay mariners and
reckless captain, the lines become as truly a work of art as if
the same picture were raised by colours skilfully spread on
canvas. After all it is not the eye which sees but the mind, and
though the pictures of words undoubtedly require more activity
of the sensuous imagination than the pictures of paint, they
are as truly (and probably in highly imaginative minds as
vividly) visible, as the most powerful painting. How powerfully is this claim of poetry to be ranked among the arts, set
forth by the actors when they represent the words of the poet
on the stage; what single other art can then vie with the
art of words in powerful and comprehensive mastery of the
human faculties; now every art is tributary, the hero is a
statue, a painting, the scene is a triumph of architecture, the
grand rhythm of the metre, if it be a masterpiece by our
greatest poet, is more thrilling and moving than the tones of
the sweetest and most powerful organ.

It would seem then that poetry is that means of appealing
to the soul of man which uses words as its medium of communication; but no sooner do we reach this conclusion than
we are confronted by the unquestionable fact that our natures
may be deeply stirred by prose and that the definition makes
nothing of a well-known distinction which differentiates prose
and poetry. Moreover we have used an expression "appealing
to the soul of man" which is so vague and uncertain as to
invalidate the definition from a scientific point of view.

Neglecting the second objection for the moment let us look
at the first. It cannot be doubted that prose is capable of
stirring our emotions deeply; think of the passage in the
"apology of Socrates" as translated by Jowett, where the great
ancient is described as speaking of the trials and sorrows of
life; think of Burke's defence of his pension where he speaks
of his personal misfortunes; or of the noble passage in which
he pays a chivalrous tribute to Marie Antoinette; read again

the ending of the second preface of *Sesame and Lilies* or the passage on "failure" in *The Mystery of Life*, read the punishment of Squeers in *Nicholas Nickleby*, or the quarrel between Adam Bede and Donnithorne, the concluding lines of Southey's *Life of Nelson* or Irving's sketch of *The Pride of the Village* ; above all perhaps, read the parts of Carlyle's writings which treat of death and sorrow and then say whether or not prose is a means of appealing to the soul of man.

What then is that mark which enables us to distinguish poetry from prose? In the high and intellectual sense there is none. But though prose at its very height may be said to be essentially one with poetry, there is a feeling, common to all peoples, that when an author's thoughts and feelings reach so lofty and elevating a pitch as to stir the feelings and thoughts of all other men to whom they may be communicated, they should be expressed in music; hence the most elevated productions of the mind have generally been expressed musically and when even the highest thoughts and emotions are expressed without this beautiful cadence men call the expression poetry only with a grudging feeling and usually they express a certain disapprobation by calling it merely prose. But, nevertheless they hold in high honour the writings of men who, lacking the gift of song, have done their best to express their noble thoughts adequately without it, and many have wished to call the most powerful prose by the name which is usually reserved for musical language. Now the ear of the reading public is not so cultivated as it might be, hence they have not called all musical writing of the best thoughts, poetry. Unless there is a music they can easily detect, a very regular cadence or falling of accents or stress, they do not call the writing musical; hence they mean by poetry, that means of appealing to the soul of man which uses words arranged in a regularly musical, or metrical way, as its means of communication. Some think

more of the sound than of the appeal to the soul of man, but
they are not of the best class perhaps.

But what is meant by "appealing to the soul"? Even the
most learned have various views as to the meaning of the word
"soul." Probably however the majority of thoughtful people
use it in the sense of "the immortal part of man." The soul
may include the stronger feelings of love and hate, joy and
sorrow, admiration and indignation, love of truth and hatred of
the false low and mean ; also the love of right for right's sake
and the hatred of wrong because it is not right ; and the joy
and pleasure in symmetry and harmony and activity and life,
and the grief and pain in the ugly malicious and stolid and
dead. When we say soul we may mean everything in us
except the material—the body ; but we usually mean the
reason, and the better, more refined and elevated emotions. A
soulless person is one who is lacking in these qualities ; a dull,
low, unjust, narrow person with no sense of beauty.

It will be seen that if poetry appeals to the soul and "the
soul" is so very uncertain a term, the term poetry must be
equally ambiguous and uncertain, and in fact such is the case.

Some of the accepted definitions are so framed as merely to
avoid the real issue ; some meet the difficulty in a bold but
one-sided manner ; few or none are so broad and tolerant as to
satisfy all who read and call the verses they like, poetry.

One enthusiastic reader loves Swinburne and thinks that
poetry, in the *true* sense of the word, always appeals to the
sensuous love of the beautiful. Another reads Charles Wesley
and is sure, equally, that *real* poetry is always employed in conveying ideas of worship, praise and supplication : each may
deride the other reader. A third admires Pope and feels convinced that any poetry that is merely an appeal to the senses or
to the moral fraction of a man is one-sided, to him reason is
first and the only real poetry is ratiocinative. "There is no
ratiocinative poetry" says Black the novelist, hence Pope is no

poet. " I would define in brief, the poetry of words as the
rhythmical creation of beauty ; its sole arbiter is taste; with
the intellect or with the conscience it has only collateral relations; unless incidentally, it has no concern whatever with
duty or truth," says Poe : hence verses in which duty and truth
are preëminent are not poetry, and Wesley, Havergal, and even
Browning are no poets.   These, in spite of great names are
but narrow views : the term *poetry* is but a word and those who
ardently desire to apply it to the works of their favourite .
authors should have that simple privilege: at best the definition
of it is but arbitrary.   If one were to define a natural species,
as *horse*, none would dispute the application of the term to individual examples hence the definition, if not easy, is possible ;
but, in defining poetry the right of a set of verses to be called
a poem is often disputed, hence the impossibility of a satisfactory definition of this artificial species.

The objection that the expression "appeals to the soul" is
vague and indefinite is unanswerable; its vagueness and in-
definiteness arise from infinite difference of opinion as to
the meaning of the word "soul" as concerned with poetry.
Some of the following definitions are popularly received because
they ignore the word entirely, "Poetry is the concrete expression of emotion," ("concrete" here, means appealing to
the sensuous imagination) ; "Poetry is the idealization of
the commonplace"; "Poetry is that one of the fine arts
which expresses its special powers and character by means of
language"; "Poetry is the art which has for its object the
creation of intellectual pleasures by means of imaginative and
passionate language, and language generally, though not necessarily formed in regular numbers"; or as Macaulay has it,
"By poetry we mean the art of employing words in such a
manner as to produce illusion upon the imagination—the art
of doing by words what the painter does by means of colours";
another has it "The language of imagination, or of the emotions,

rhythmically expressed, or language expressed in an elevated style of prose," or " Whatever embodies the products of the imagination and fancy, and appeals to those powers in others, as well as the finer emotions, the sense of ideal beauty."

Emerson's view is original and broad-minded but emphatic as one would expect from his character : "Poetry" says he "is the perpetual endeavour to express the *spirit* of the thing, to pass the brute body, and search the life and reason which caused it to exist." Again he says, " the poet discovers that what men value as substances have a higher value as symbols, that nature is the immense shadow of man." So ingenious, so important and so largely true are these pregnant sentences that it is profitable to pause and illustrate them. When, Tennyson says in *Ulysses* :—

> " The lights begin to twinkle from the rocks,
> The long day wanes."

he describes a merely natural appearance ; but few readers would fail to catch the echo of a deeper meaning ; the description has a high value as a picture of real tangible objects, but "a higher value " as a symbol of the closing of this our mortal life.

Sometimes the poet explains his symbolism as when Wordsworth says of the skylark that it is a

> " Type of the wise who soar, but never roam ;
> True to the kindred points of Heaven and Home."

In *The Cloud* Shelley gives no direct intimation of symbolism but study reveals a profound example of it in this wonderful poem. This piece of nature is no less than a symbol of life and all its vicissitudes, the fleeting moods and passions of the human heart.

But Emerson's symbolism has a very broad and deep meaning. Common sense is accepting the world about us at its apparent value and acting with a due regard for the importance of this material world; poetry is that uncommon sense which sees through the material envelope to the intelligent soul which made and animates it; but poetry does not reject the common sense view; the greatest poets Shakespeare, Homer, Burns, had the strongest common sense side by side with the strongest ideality—the mere absent-minded idealist is as pitiable as the most stolid Philistine, though not so gross.

But what are we to think of those definitions which insist upon beauty as the sum and end and height of poetry? Has poetry truly nothing to do with conscience and truth? Every man has a capacity for being pleased by beautiful things, objects that please him he calls beautiful but whether the beauty of an object is always something different from its utility or goodness it is difficult to say.

Few definitions of poetry have been more frequently quoted with approval than Poe's formula, "the rhythmical creation of beauty." Similar to this is the dictum of Theodore Watts, "absolute poetry is the concrete and artistic expression of the human mind in emotional and rhythmical language." These two critics are prominent exponents of a very large school; Swinburne, Rossetti, Keats and all poets whose chief appeal is to the sensuous imagination hold this belief firmly and some of them have asserted it strenuously. It is important to see clearly that there are two principal views of the question and it becomes necessary eventually to choose between them, though it never becomes necessary to declare the poets of either school to be distasteful or lacking in genius.

This first class of critics have their fixed and certain tests of true or absolute poetry:

(a) It must be musical.
(b) It must gratify the love of beauty.
(c) It must stir the emotions.
(d) It must be concrete in method.

These are their requirements, but of the "*beauty*" the "*music*" and the "*emotional power*" taste is the sole arbiter; unless incidentally poetry has no concern with *duty* or *truth*. All who declare that the aesthetic quality of poetry is its mark and brand hold these views more or less clearly. Good examples of work that satisfies these canons may be seen in·Rossetti's "*The Blessed Damozel*" Keats' "*Eve of St. Agnes*" and a great deal of Hugo's lyrical verse.

It seems incredible that English critics should ever have come to think and say that poetry should not be moral and didactic, as these critics have declared; it seems far more incredible that so un-English a dogma should have become popular with a nation

> "Who speak the tongue
> That Shakespeare spake, the faith and manners hold
> Which Milton held."

Indeed it would be quite entirely incredible were it not echoed to-day on every side so emphatically and so assiduously that one is apt to be ridiculed for rebelling against it and venturing to assert, however feebly, that whatever may be true of Italian art, or of French art, or of Japanese art, English art always was at its best and seems likely to be at its best most markedly and characteristically, and essentially, emphatically didactic and pointedly moral in tone and spirit: and by this is meant not that duty and truth have merely accidental relations to the beautiful and pleasing quality but that they are and constitute the pleasure of our greatest masterpieces according to the judgment of our greatest and wisest men in all ages; that with us truth and duty are so mingled, blended and unified with our conceptions of the highest beauty, that it is hardly a perversion of terms to use any one of the three indiscriminately to denote the highest attitude of the greatest poetry. It is true that Ouida has written cleverly to satirize the narrowness of the

English art, that Poe reviled the notion that poetry could have a well-defined didactic motive, that even Coleridge has warned us that ethical teaching should not narrow our love of beauty wherever we find it : it is no secret that the French literary critics sneer at our lack of freedom, as they are pleased to call our wholesome.decency, and that the amorous and military Italian is puzzled by our hopeless dullness. But while these taunts are frequent no English reader should doubt that our poetry both has been and is didactic and moral, nor should he say that it should be merely aesthetic, while considering that in so doing he would necessarily repudiate Shakespeare, Milton, Wordsworth, and Tennyson who have shown always by examples, and often by precept, that they think poetry at its best must do more than please and that the great poet must do more than charm, and charming in doing more. Who then need be ashamed, who at least of English speech and mind, to say boldly to all comers that, whatever may be true of European poetry or of poetry of the Swinburne and Oscar Wilde type, English poetry is and ought to be strongly intellectual, powerfully and actively stimulative of good, and pleasing only or chiefly because of these qualities.

What can be more shocking or unreasonable than to see an English school-boy praising English poetry for being melodious and sensuously beautiful, yet ashamed to say that it is powerfully thoughtful and morally sublime, while that very boy by reason of the strong English brain and virtuous English blood within him wants to give the higher praise because he deeply knows and feels it and doesn't care about the music and merely sensuous beauty, because they do not greatly appeal to his character and capacity.

Many may doubt whether this state of things exist. Let any one read to a class of young students the very best work of the so called aesthetic school, a picture of heavenly beauty appealing to eye, ear and imagination—such a passage as would have intoxicated Keats, for example his own ode, " *To the Nightingale*," which can hardly be surpassed surely in that way. Let him notice carefully the effect on the class : they will be pleased a little possibly, perhaps apathetic, at best they will' forget the impression in less than a week. Perhaps it may be argued that the piece is too difficult, but easier pieces will be equally ineffective. Next read them a poem full of thought, strong, didactic and like a lash to the will; let it be harsh in sound, clumsy in imagery, and obscure in meaning, for example George Meredith's "*England Before the Storm.*" Now note the effect ; nearly every pupil is deeply moved, the room is elec- tric with intense feeling, every muscle of the undemonstrative Canadian face is tense with a profound emotion that no other power on earth ever roused—that the very parents of these boys have never suspected in them. Some may conclude that they need more training in the emasculate, bloodless, brainless aestheticism of the Theodore Watts school; but, we conclude that boys who are so built that the dross of ugliness and coarseness of fibre must be purged out and refined by poetry with brains and morality in it would be wasting their time on merely aesthetic verses, and it seems to us that in this larger possession they have all the sensuous love of beauty that go well with strength and power. We do not want French or Japanese characters in this country, but English characters of the best and firmest type. It would be a long stride indeed if we could abolish at once and forever that wretched exotic caprice that "didactic poetry is no poetry, and that aesthetic poetry is the only poetry " and substitute for it the rule that poetry in which truth and duty do not mingle in equal pro- portions with pleasure and beauty is not the poetry that has made England first in the literature of the whole world ancient and modern.

It might now be wise to leave the reader to formulate his own definition of a poem. At best his definition must be in accordance with his own taste and as the Latin has it "*de gustibus non disputandum.*" Sitting before a few shelves of poetry one finds it difficult to take a narrow view. Shall one rule out Pope? Never, a single couplet would save him,—

> " Honour and shame from no condition rise
> Act well your part, there all the honour lies."

Is Scott a poet? who can read this symbol of the approach of the night when no man can labour without that indefinable charm called poetry?

> " The hills grow dark,
> On purple peaks a deeper shade descending ;
> In twilight copse the glow-worm lights her spark,
> The deer half-seen are to the covert wending."

But here is a volume by George Meredith, he surely is no poet: what do we read? He loves England and would warn her of blindness in neglecting her armaments:

> " The day that is the night of days
> With cannon fire for sun ablaze
> We spy from any billow's lift ;
> And England still this tidal drift!
> Would she to sainted forethought vow
> A space before the thunder's flood,
> That martyr of its hour might now
>   Spare her the tears of blood.
>   *   *   *   *   *
> They stand to be her sacrifice,
> The sons this mother plays like dice,
> To face the odds and brave the fates !
> As in those days of starry dates
> When cannon cannon's counterblast
> Awakened, muzzle muzzle bowled,
> And high in swathe of smoke the mast
> Its fighting rag outrolled."

What care we for bad grammar and outrageous diction, "fighting rag" alone repays us for all our trouble and we know that behind this Poet's forehead is a brain, kept alive by a heart.

And so it is from Chaucer to Kipling, from Milton to Havergal, from Shakespeare to Rossetti, we cannot spare one, we must stretch the definition to include every verse that ever roused or pleased anyone : we must conclude that poetry is the metrical expression of any thoughts or feelings that ever roused the soul of any reader whatever, even if the poet had but himself for audience.   No one has a right to limit this unless he adds to his definition " to me " and this is a case where it is less dogmatic to use the first personal pronoun than to omit it. If we limit poetry (in order to keep a high standard) to the work of the greatest men, we may very well accept Shelley's opinion that poetry is the best thoughts of the greatest men expressed in adequate language; but many would add "(to me) adequate language for the best thoughts must be metrical or highly musical."

If we might venture a new statement of the definition it would be :

Absolute poetry is an adequate (metrical) and fitting expression in language, of thoughts of a high didactic, moral, and aesthetic, value ; and the tests of such poetry would be,—

(*a*) It should be musical, but not necessarily sweet.

(*b*) Its language should be in keeping with its meaning.

(*c*) It should please the taste.

(*d*) It should interest the reason.

(*e*) It should arouse and instruct the conscience.

(*f*) It should stir the better feelings and strengthen and refine them.

(*g*) It should appeal to the mind through concrete symbols when possible, and through abstractions when necessary.

(*h*) It should leave a memory of wholesome pleasure and mental and emotional activity.

(*i*) It should not be morbid in tone, though melancholy and genius are perhaps inseparable.   .

But all these tests must be merely relative to the mind and tastes of each reader.

A poem has merit in proportion as it satisfies these tests. A few poems seem absolutely perfect.

CHAPTER III.

MINUTE CRITICISM OF POETRY.

"Poets are standing transporters, whose employment consists in speaking to the Father and to matter; in producing apparent imitation: of unapparent natures, and inscribing things unapparent in the apparent fabrication of the world." —*Zoroaster.*

"The poet's eye in a fine phrensy rolling
Glances from earth to heaven from heaven to earth;
And as imagination bodies forth
The forms of things unknown, the poet's pen
Turns them to shapes, and gives to airy nothing
A local habitation and a name." —*Shakespeare.*

CHAPTER III.

THE STUDY OF A POEM.

IT is always wise to keep the end of the journey conspicu ously before us; it strengthens the step and straightens the way. To what end do we study poems in our schools? All lessons in English have for their object the mastery of our mother tongue, and this mastery comprises two simple and definite elements, the power of *reading*, and the power of *writing* or composing English. Since grammar no longer deals with orthography, etymology and prosody, but only with syntax or sentence-building, it may be said to help us to write and speak English; any value the subject has beyond that of enabling us to appreciate sound syntax, arises from the fact that grammar is not altogether an English study, but to some extent—an increasingly large extent—a branch of science. It is not impossible that technical grammar may eventually fall to the lot of the science-master; if not, it will remain in the English division more on account of its subject matter, than on account of its objects and methods.

In literature we read that we may learn to read, that is to arrive at a full comprehension of masterpieces of our great English authors. In rhetoric we read not that we may learn to read, but that we may learn to write; that is, we contem- plate masterpieces that we may through reflection or unconscious imitation, catch some of the methods by which our great authors produced their successful works, and apply these methods to the feeble efforts at composition that our work or ambition may require us to make. Composition is a practical application of the principles of good writing, as we have learned them in grammar and rhetoric.

Now from this point of view the study of poetry has but little to do with writing; rhetoric will naturally use prose examples for its phenomena, inasmuch as prose is what the great majority would learn to compose. Though the study of poetry will tend to improve our thoughts and feelings, and to elevate our diction, it is best that it should be studied without much direct reference to composition, because it has an important purpose of its own, and because rhetoric is set apart for the purpose of improving our composing powers.

It may be concluded then that we study poetry exclusively for the purpose of learning to read the works of our great authors with appreciation and refined discernment. In the arguments that follow it will be taken for granted that improvement of the taste and understanding are the chief aim with beginners, and not immediate pleasure. Even should the poetry class prove duller than it should, the student would console himself with the fact that the drudgery of minute criticism brings its reward in after life, in the form of superior powers of grasping and appreciating new poems. Great care should be taken however, to see that no pupil should, in the discipline of minute reading, acquire a distaste for all poetry.

The ideal course for a young mind in this study would begin with such poems as children love without urging or much explanation, and would proceed by imperceptible steps upward, year by year, until the mind could enjoy such works as *The Grammarian's Funeral, In Memoriam,* and *Lear.* How practicable such a course is, and how blind are we who neglect the obvious blessings of it to study here and there from year to year without progress or systematic effort. Every boy of twelve with an average imagination can read Scott's poems with delight; but there are simpler rhymes for younger or weaker children. Suppose we begin with Nursery Rhymes and Andrew Lang's Poetry Book for Children, proceed to Scott and Campbell, and parts of Byron, thence to Longfellow and Tennyson's simpler poems, and through these and others on the same level to the light comedies of Shakespeare, is it not manifest that the young student may make a continuous study of poetry that will keep pace with the age, and promote his spiritual growth to the great and endless benefit of his character and habits of thought? Not only is this course ideal : it is perfectly feasible, and even easy. An anthology of a few hundred pages for use in the public schools, and another, or two or three others, properly graded for use in high schools, would accomplish the whole purpose. Who can fail to remember the ardent desire with which every piece in the Reader was searched for new thoughts and feelings in school days? Is not the wisest course to take advantage of this natural desire by putting in the Reader such a gradation of poems as will lead a pupil to the higher levels of taste? It would be a liberal education to many pupils to have even Mackay's " Thousand and One Gems of English Poetry " in their desks for use in " spare hours."

Having determined that we study poetry in order to make progress in the comprehension of the best poems, we meet another question which requires a definite answer : Are we to study each poem in order to make *it* our own ; that is, are we to regard the mastery of that particular poem as our object, or are we to study it in such a way that we may be able to read other poems more intelligently? The importance of this question will be seen immediately. Let us suppose that we read the beautiful *Ode to Immortality*, in the present volume, simply that we may master it for our own complete possession : if we do, it will be a noble piece of mental furniture for the remainder of life, and by its presence in the mind will do much to attract great thoughts, and to repel vulgar and commonplace views.

If the reading of it gave no reward but the possession of the piece itself, our time would still be well spent in studying it minutely. We may read it however, rather that we may study *poetry* than *the poems* ; that is we may approach it as a step

toward higher and more difficult work.   In the former case we
do well to throw all inductive and socratic methods aside, and
to get all the information we can about its meaning as rapidly
and easily as possible ; in the latter case we do well to do every
thing we can for ourselves, as in a mental gymnasium where
every feat we perform unaided makes us stronger to perform other and more difficult feats.   The second method
is slower, but while it gives more trouble, it gives greater
rewards.   When the former method is followed, care should
be taken to accept no opinions without careful consideration, and care should be taken that what is acquired so easily
is not forgotten with equal ease.   In the latter method the rule
is, "Let no one tell you anything that you can learn by your
own efforts."   The danger here is that time may be wasted in
work that is really not a study of poetry at all—for example,
in hunting up geographical and historical references which
ought to be given in a convenient form in the notes; also there
is the danger that your own efforts may never be sufficient to
put you in possession of the best qualities of the poem, and
that you will forget that this rule does not forbid you to learn
all that you can learn by any means from any one whatever,
after you have done your best for yourself.   Every good student
of arithmetic desires to know whether he has reached "the
right answer," and in order to know that, he turns to the
teacher or "the back of the book;" just so every good student
of a poem will desire to compare his own views with those of
his teacher or his editor; but *he should work out the problem
first, if he would improve his powers of reading with comprehension.*

    An old artist was once asked what he thought of the judg-
ment of the ordinary amateur with regard to pictures.   He
replied astutely, "An ordinary amateur doesn't know what to
look for in a picture."   Could any words express better the
relation of an ordinary reader to a poem?   An ordinary reader

does'nt know what to look for in a poem.   He is like a beggar
kicking precious gold ore aside with his tattered boots because he does not recognize its worth ; he may even go so. far
as to laugh at the miner who tells him of its value.

To tell a good poem from a poor one without assistance, even
the assistance of the author's name, is to be able to read poetry
with true critical acumen.   Of course critics differ, tastes differ,
but there are poems, as well as pictures and faces, of undisputed
beauty and worth, and the student is no longer an ordinary amateur critic who can discern such works unaided.   Perhaps then the best way to read poetry is to read some poems
chiefly for their own sakes—these would be acknowledged
masterpieces, concerning whose value and power all the world
agree ; and then also to read some poems chiefly for exercise of
the critical powers, avoiding the opinions of others until we
have reached a—not too dogmatic—opinion of our own.   In the
present voulme it would be well to master the *Ode to Duty*
and *The Ode to Immortality* in a reverent spirit of admiration.

These poems are so sublime and so generally command the awe
and wonder of the cultivated that it would not be amiss in a
young person to entertain an almost superstitious respect for
their genius, even before their merits are realized.   Respect for
the authority of universal cultivated opinion is not a mark of
weakness in a student.   With reference, however, to some of the
poems in this collection that are not so famous, greater freedom
of judgment may be exercised, and their rank may be assigned
with a due regard for their merits as discovered by diligent
search.   " Censure me in your wisdom," said Brutus, " but
awake your senses that ye may the better judge."

In order that the beginner may not be quite at a loss as to
how to proceed in studying a poem, a plan is appended below
which may be of some use to those who have not the guidance
of teachers.   Any such scheme of study must be used with

much judgment, and must be regarded not as rigid and dogmatic, but merely as tentative and suggestive.

No one can be said to understand a poem fully except its
author; we understand a poem in proportion as we approach
the author's intentions, mood and thoughts in the creation of
it. The poet proceeded from the thoughts and feelings to the
language, we must travel in the other direction. The more
closely we can imagine the author's mind in writing, the more
nearly we see the meaning of his language.

In the author's mind the first considerations are the choice
of subject and the main or central purpose or idea of his work;
second come the various thoughts and emotions that cluster
around this centre; finally comes the language in which these
are expressed to others. To the ordinary reader the language
as such is of small importance; even to the student the central
thought or subject of the poem and the various thoughts and
feelings which impress him are by far the most important part
—though it is impossible for the educated reader to ignore the
language of the poet. Hence, our plan should be to study the
poem under the following heads:

  (*a*) The choice of subject or central idea.

  (*b*) The various thoughts and emotions which enlarge upon
         the central idea.

  (*c*) The adaptation of language to the expression of the
         poet's mind.

When a poem is long and complex, it is often wise to consider the parts before considering the whole work very fully.
Still the first glance at a picture or group of statuary should
reveal its general purpose, and so, even a play three hours long
should reveal its general purpose at the first reading, however
indistinctly.

When the dominant central idea is found, the piece should
be analysed, or loosened up into stanzas or paragraphs (or acts
and scenes), and the central idea of each should be noted in

concise language. The synopsis thus made should be used to prove that the whole piece has unity as well as variety : *unity means singleness of purpose in a work of art.* Also the order in which the parts are introduced should be observed ; in narration the natural order is that of time : in argument we proceed from enunciation to illustration, proof, and conclusion, from cause to effect, from facts to inference and generalization ; in description we proceed from the outline to the details, preserving in the latter a certain climatic order. When a poet seems to violate the natural order of writing his reasons for so doing should be investigated ; it is in the departure from the regular and established way of writing that we perceive the individuality or style of the author.

Next test the unity of the paragraphs or stanzas ; those whose substance can be stated in a single clear sentence have unity ; those which seem to demand a second sentence on account of some secondary but important idea are likely to lack that quality.

It is well to memorize a great deal of poetry ; nothing has so refining an influence upon the taste and the language, as a memory stored with noble verses. In memorizing do not commit everything indiscriminately, but consider the value of the verses. Memorize

(a) Passages that have become the common property of all cultivated people.

(b) Passages that seem to you to be the perfect expression of some wise thought.

(c) Passages that seem to you to be very tender or beautiful.

(d) Passages very characteristic of the author, or of the motive or tone of the poem.

(e) Passages that you think you would often feel like repeating through life, to give a better expression to your own thoughts and feeling than you could give them in your own words.

(*f*) Passages that strikingly illustrate certain qualities of style and phases of emotion.

In some cases it is well to memorize the poem before studying it minutely ; generally perhaps it is better to defer the memorizing until after the poem has been thoroughly studied.

It is well to understand the classification of poems for this reason : an artist's success must be judged largely by his intentions ; if a poet designs a play for the stage, it is a failure if it does not please in the theatre ; but if he tells us that his play is meant to be read but not acted, he is judged by a different standard. It is not wise in a critic to say of a short story, "this is not a good novel," any more than it is to blame a schooner for not being a racing yacht. Hence, every student should know the kinds of poetry, and endeavour to learn the rules of structure that apply to each kind, so that he may praise or censure with due regard to the author's intentions ; the wild and lawless frenzy of Gray's *Bard* is not inappropriate in an *ode*, but the same license of language and passion would be shocking in an elegy. Matthew Arnold's defence of the illogical but natural and convenient Greek classification of poems into epic, lyric and dramatic, will commend itself to all who have compared it with more logical but less convenient divisions.

Although it is not well to consider the fame of the author when we read poems in a scientific spirit, it is certainly wise to learn all we can of his character, life, and motives, before considering that we have come into full possession of his works. This is the universally accepted view, and though it leads to serious abuses it also has many arguments to support it.

The danger of reading the life of an author is that the student will assume a spurious admiration for his works because he has accepted the opinions of the biographer without earning the right either to agree with him or to differ from him. Certain it is that weakminded readers are in danger of praising rapturously poems they have never read, and speaking of poets as their favourites whom they know only through the "books about books." And yet the spurious admiration is harmless ; it is the superstition of the worshipper who has faith because he cannot know, and being entirely *with* literature cannot be *against* it also. These same readers, if they had not this faith, would perhaps be Philistines of a deeper dye. Again is it not on the whole more conducive to sweetness and light that a large and wise authority such as the biographers possess should sway the ignorant than their own ugly and petty prejudices? It is the old question of authority against individual opinion. Our own opinion is that, after a fair effort at understanding the poet's work, the student should make a thorough study of the poet's life and times. Moreover, it seems likely that having experienced a reaction from the days when "Collier's Literature" took the place of the study of the masterpieces, and having on account of that reaction abandoned the study of the history of literature almost entirely, we have reached an extreme scarcely less detrimental to the best interests of the study of literature than the former condition had proved : "truth lies between" : a cultivated reader should have an intelligent knowledge of the schools of authors and of the biographies of authors, as well as a thorough acquaintance with their best productions. There *is* some use in lists of names of authors and books. Many a pupil is leaving our schools nowadays a positive ignoramus for lack of a few lessons in the history of literature.

Having thus finished the general consideration of the poem, we proceed to a detailed study of its words and sentences as shown in the table below.

After this it is sometimes helpful to write a critique of the poem, as if for publication in a review, dealing with the most striking and original qualities discerned in it.

Finally it is well to consider the poem as an exercise in elocution ; great care should be taken to read with feeling and thoughtfulness, and to avoid affectation of all kinds and mere declamation.

Sometimes it is a good means of getting at the style of a poet to compare what he says on a subject with the words of another writer on the same subject. Dozens of poems have been written on the sky-lark ; and it is very often possible for a well read person to find *parallel passages* from Shakespeare and Milton, and Coleridge and Shelley, for comparison with Wordsworth's poems.

The following table is offered not as exhaustive but merely as suggestive. Neither is the order in which the divisions are given meant to be followed nor is it intended that all these divisions should be applied to the study of every poem. It is hoped however, that it will, if kept before the student, prevent him from leaving the poem before he has considered the most important topics ; in reading a poem one may become so absorbed in one phase of it as to leave it without noticing other important matters. When this scheme is applied to a drama, it should be supplemented by other divisions, especially *(a)* Characterization, and *(b)* The *harmony* or *keeping* between the character and his words.

SOME OF THE POINTS TO CONSIDER IN THE STUDY OF A POEM.

I.—THE CENTRAL IDEA.

1. The choice of subject and its relation to the author's character and genius.

2. The name of the poem as compared with the central idea.

3. The synopsis by stanzas or sections.

4. The unity of the poem and of the sections.

5. The order of the sections.

6. The selection of material—what the author mentions, what he might have mentioned but omits.

7. The originality of the work : its relation to the period in which it was produced.

8. The harmony of the idea and the literary form selected : Is the form too insignificant for the thought, or the thought for the form ?

II.—THE MEMORIZING.

1. Memorize from motives suggested above.

2. Consider the grounds of popularity of all well-known or frequently-quoted parts.

III.—CLASSIFICATION.

1. Classify poem as epic, lyric, dramatic.

2. Classify poem as descriptive (perceptive), lyrical (feeling), reflective (thought), epic and dramatic (action).

3. Define great epic, historical epic, ballad epic, ballad, song, hymn, ode, elegy, dirge, sonnet, tragedy, comedy, and make a list o fsimilar technicalities.

4. Show clearly that one kind of poem may use devices that are not permissible in another.

IV.—THE AUTHOR.

1. Give some account of the life, works, style, rank and influence of the author.

2. To what extent do his works reveal his mind (subjective) ; to what extent do they deal purely with matters outside his own personality (objective) ?

3. Trace the rise and fall of English poetical power through its various stages since Chaucer's time.

4. Show the relation of the period in which Wordsworth wrote to the period preceding it, also to the Victorian period.

V.—DETAILED STUDY.

1. Consider peculiarities of spelling, use of capitals, marks of punctuation.

2. Consider the appearance of the book, and cultivate a taste in binding, printing, and similar matters.

3. Consider the vocabulary. Poetic words; prose words; precise synonyms; strong, metaphorical and picturesque words; archaic, long, technical, harsh, obscure, redundant words; words of interesting origin.

4. Consider diction; Arrangement of words and meaning of words and phrases are the most important. Diction may be verbose, full, foreign, English.

5. Consider the length and clearness of the sentences.

6. Consider the relation of the sentences to the lines.

7. Consider the devices of language which the poet uses to produce odd and beautiful effects.

It is probably wise to learn the names of these " figures of speech," not because hard names help us, but because a knowledge of the names leads us to observe the devices more frequently.

(The following list is given partly as an amusing curiosity of mediaeval pedantry. Paronomasia, metaphor, asyndeton, paraleipsis, proverb, simile, polysyndeton, allusion, repartee, personification, litotes, anacoenosis, sarcasm, allegory, epanerphosis, anagram, syllepsis, metonymy, epanorthosis, antonomasia, synecdoche, apostrophe, apologue, transferred epithet, vision, aposiopesis, alliteration, antithesis, hyperbole, enigma, assonance, oxymoron, climax, catachresis, ecphonesis, anaphora, erotesis, epizeuxis, epiphora, irony, epanalepsis, euphemism, anadiplosis, inuendo, hypotyposis, palilogia, zeugma, epanaphora, epigram, metalepsis, antistrophe, prolepsis, parable, aphaeresis, syncope, apocope, metathesis, onomatopoeia, imitative harmony, anacoluthon, tautology, redundancy, invocation, euphuism, anticipation, hendiadys, hypallage.)

Figures of comparison and contrast, figures of imitation of sound, and of repetition for emphasis, should be noticed most.

8. Consider the rhyme, metre, and rhythm of the poem, particularly the relation of the versification to the subject-matter.

9. Consider the emotions roused by the poem. Emotions range from the lofty and elevated sentiments of religion and sublimity through the middle octaves of every-day life to the dark passions of murder, revenge, hatred and jealousy. In which octaves of the emotional key-board does Wordsworth play?

VI.—THE CRITIQUE.

1. Write an essay on the poem—point out its beauties (and faults or defects) of language, thought, emotion and moral tone.

VII.—ELOCUTION.

1. Read the poem thoughtfully and with considerable feeling.

2. Write notes on the pauses, emphasis, inflections, rate, pitch, quality of voice, force, loudness, pronunciation, expression.

VIII.—STYLE.

1. State the respects in which your poet differs from other poets.

2. What adjectives would you use in describing his style of writing?

It is intended that the poem should be read twice for the meaning, once for the general, and once for the particular meaning. Of course the memorizing and the elocution may require several other readings.

It is the difficulty of carrying all the important considerations concerning the study of a poem in the mind at once that justifies one in keeping before the eye a table of this sort.

We trust that some readers may make this table a nucleus for their own notes and observations regarding the best plan for studying a poem.

CHAPTER IV.

CRITICAL ESTIMATES OF WORDSWORTH.

> *"I cannot tell how the truth may be;*
> *I say the tale as 'twas said to me."*
>
> —*Lay of the Last Minstrel.*

CHAPTER IV.

From James Russell Lowell—

The apostle of imagination.

From Hazlitt—

Nihil humani a me alienum puto is the motto of his works.

From Sir Walter Scott—

I do not know a man more to be venerated for uprightness of heart and loftiness of genius,

From Stopford A. Brooke—

The *greatest of the English poets of this century;* greatest not only as a poet, but as a philosopher.

From Professor Wilson—

Wordsworth's sonnets, were they all in one book, would be the statesman's, warrior's, priest's, sage's manual.

From Elizabeth Barrett [afterwards Mrs. Browning]—

Chaucer and Burns made the most of a daisy, but left it still a daisy ; Wordsworth leaves it transformed into his thoughts.

From Thomas Moore—

One of the very few original poets of this age (fertile as it is in rhymers *quales ego et Clavienus)* has had the glory of producing.

From Robert Southey—

Jeffrey, I hear, has written what his admirers call a *crushing* review of "The Excursion" He might as well seat himself upon Skiddaw and fancy that he crushed the mountain.

From Lord Jeffrey—

This will never do. . . . It ("The Excursion") is longer, weaker, and tamer than any of Mr. Wordsworth's other productions ; with less boldness of originality, and less even of that extreme simplicity and lowliness of tone which wavered so prettily in the "Lyrical Ballads" between silliness and pathos.

From Hazlitt—

Fools have laughed at, wise men scarcely understand them (Wordsworth's Ballads). He takes a subject or a story merely as pegs or loops to hang thought and feeling on ; the incidents are trifling in proportion to his contempt for imposing appearances ; the reflections are profound, according to the gravity and the aspiring pretensions of his mind.

WORDSWORTH'S MANNER OF USING BOOKS.

From Thomas De Quincey—

Wordsworth lived in the open air, Southey in his library, which Coleridge used to call his wife. Southey had particularly elegant habits (Wordsworth called them finical) in the use of books. Wordsworth, on the other hand, was so negligent and so self-indulgent in the same case that, as Southey, laughing, expressed it to me some years afterwards, when I was staying at Greta Hall on a visit, "To introduce Wordsworth into one's library is like letting a bear into a tulip garden."

WORDSWORTH'S GENIUS.

From S. T. Coleridge—

I think Wordsworth possessed more of the genius of a great philosophic poet than any man I ever knew, or, as I believe, has existed in England since Milton ; but it seems to me that he ought never to have abandoned the contemplative position which is peculiarly—perhaps I may say exclusively—fitted for him. His proper title is *Spectator ab extra*.

WORDSWORTH'S HEALTHFULNESS.

From Matthew Arnold—

Time may restore us, in his course,
Goethe's sage mind and Byron's force ;
But when will Europe's latter hour
Again find Wordsworth's healing power ?

Keep fresh the grass upon his grave,
O Rotha ! with thy living wave !
Sing him thy best, for few or none
Hear thy voice right, now he is gone.

WORDSWORTH'S UNIQUE DISTINCTION.

From Thomas Carlyle —

The incommunicable, the unmitigable might of Wordsworth,
when the god has indeed fallen on him, cannot but be felt by
all, and can but be felt by any ; none can partake and catch it
up. There are men much greater than he ; there are men
much greater ; but what he has of greatness is his only. His
concentration, his majesty, his pathos have no parallel ; none
have touched precisely the same point as he.

WORDSWORTH'S RANK.

From Robert Southey—

Wordsworth's residence and mine are fiften miles asunder—a
sufficient distance to preclude any frequent interchange of visits.
I have known him nearly twenty years, and for about half that
time intimately. The strength and the character of his mind you
see in "The Excursion;" and his *life does not belie his writings;*
for in *every relation of life* and *point of view* he is a truly
exemplary and admirable man. In conversation he is powerful
beyond any of his contemporaries ; and as a poet—I speak not
from the partiality of friendship, nor because we have been
absurdly held up as both writing upon one concerted system of
poetry, but with the most deliberate exercise **of** impartial

judgment whereof I am capable when I declare my full conviction that posterity will rank him with Milton.

EXCESSIVE SIMPLICITY.

From Elizabeth Barrett [afterwards Mrs. Browning].—

"Hero-worshippers," as we are, and sitting for all the critical
pretence—in right or wrong of which we speak at all—at the
feet of Mr. Wordsworth, recognizing him as we do a poet-hero
of a movement essential to the better being of poetry, as poet-
prophet of utterances greater than those who first listened
could comprehend, and of influences most vital and expensive,
we are yet honest to confess that certain things in the "Lyrical
Ballads," which most provoke the ignorant, innocent hootings
of the mob, do not seem to us all heroic. Love, like ambition,
may overvault itself, and Betty Foys of the Lake School (so
called) may be as subject to conventionalities as Pope's Lady
Betties. And perhaps our great poet might, through the very
vehemence and nobleness of his hero and prophet work for
nature, confound, for some blind moment, and by an association
easily traced and excused, nature with rusticity, the simple
with the bald, and even fall into a vulgar conventionality in
the act of spurning a graceful one.

A LAMPOON.

From Lord Byron—

We learn from Horace "Homer sometimes sleeps?"
    We feel without him, Wordsworth sometimes wakes—
To show with what complacency he creeps
    With his dear "Wagoners" around his lakes.
He wishes for a "boat" to sail the deeps—
    Of ocean? No, of air; and then he makes
Another outcry for a "little boat,"
    And drivels seas to set it well afloat.

If he must fain sweep o'er th' ethereal plain,
  And Pegasus runs restive in his "Wagon,"
Could he not beg the loan of Charles's Wain?
  Or pray Medea for a single dragon?
Or if, too classic for his vulgar brain,
  He fear'd his neck to venture such a nag on,
And he must needs mount nearer to the moon,
  Could not the blockhead ask for a balloon?

"Peddlers" and "Boats" and "Wagons!" Oh ye shades
  Of Pope and Dryden, has it come to this?
That trash of such sort not alone evades
  Contempt, but from the bathos' vast abyss
Floats scum-like uppermost, and these Jack Cades
  Of sense and song above your graves may hiss—
The "little boatman" and his "Peter Bell"
Can sneer at him who drew "Achitophel!"

From Whittier—

WORDSWORTH.

WRITTEN ON A BLANK LEAF OF HIS MEMOIRS.

Dear friends, who read the world aright,
  And in its common forms discern
A beauty and a harmony
  The many never learn!

Kindred in soul of him who found
  In simple flower and leaf and stone
The impulse of the sweetest lays
  Our Saxon tongue has known,—

Accept this record of a life
  As sweet and pure, as calm and good,
As a long day of blandest June
  In green field and in wood.

How welcome to our ears, long pained
  By strife of sect and party noise,
The brook-like murmur of his song
  Of nature's simple joys!

The violet by its mossy stone,
  The primrose by the river's brim,
And chance-sown daffodil, have found
  Immortal life through him.

The sunrise on his breezy lake,
  The rosy tints his sunset brought,
World-seen, are gladdening all the vales
  And mountain-peaks of thought.

Art builds on sand ; the works of pride
  And human passion change and fall ;
But that which shares the life of God
  With him surviveth all.

RUSKIN'S OPINION OF WORDSWORTH'S POWERS.

From Ruskin—

Wordsworth is simply a Westmoreland peasant, with considerably less shrewdness than most border Englishmen or Scotsmen inherit ; and sense of humor : but gifted (in this singularly) with vivid sense of natural beauty, and a pretty turn for reflections, not always acute, but, as far as they reach, medicinal to the fever of the restless and corrupted life around him. Water to parched lips may be better than Samian wine, but do not let us therefore confuse the qualities of wine and water. I much doubt there being many inglorious Miltons in our country churchyards ; but I am very sure there are many Wordsworths resting there, who were inferior to the renowned one only in caring less to hear themselves talk....

I am by no means sure that his influence on the stronger minds of his time was anywise hastened or extended by the spirit of tunefulness under whose guidance he discovered that Heaven rhymed to seven, and Foy to boy. Tuneful nevertheless at heart, and of the heavenly choir, I gladly and frankly acknowledge him ; and our English literature enriched with a new and singular virtue in the aerial purity and healthful rightness of his quiet song ; but *aerial* only—not ethereal; and lowly in its privacy of light.

A measured mind, and calm ; innocent, unrepentant ; helpful to sinless creatures and scatheless, such of the flock as do not stray. Hopeful at least, if not faithful ; content with intimations of immortality such as may be in skipping of lambs, and laughter of children—incurious to see in the hands the print of the nails. A gracious and constant mind ; as the herbage of its native hills, fragrant and pure ;—yet, to the sweep and the shadow, the stress and distress, of the greater souls of men, as the tufted thyme to the laurel wilderness of Tempê,—as the gleaming euphrasy to the dark branches of Dodona.

WORDSWORTH'S FAME.

From James Russell Lowell—

Of no other poet except Shakespeare have so many phrases become household words as of Wordsworth. If Pope has made current more epigrams of worldly wisdom, to Wordsworth belongs the nobler praise of having defined for us, and given us for a daily possession, those faint and vague suggestions of other-worldliness, · of whose gentle ministry with our baser nature the hurry and bustle of life scarcely ever allowed us to be conscious. He has won for himself a secure immortality by a depth of intuition which makes only the best minds at their best hours worthy, or, indeed, capable, of his companionship, and by a homely sincerity of human sympathy which reaches the humblest heart. Our language owes him gratitude for the habitual purity and abstinence of his style, and we who speak it for having emboldened us to take delight in simple things, and to trust ourselves to our own instincts. And he hath his reward. It needs not to bid

> " Renowned Chaucer lie a thought more nigh
>   To rare Beaumond, and learned Beaumond lie
>   A little nearer Spenser ; "

for there is no fear of crowding in that little society with
whom he is now enrolled as *fifth in the succession of the great
English poets.*

WORDSWORTH'S OFFICE.

From J. C. Shairp—

Perhaps I cannot better sum up the whole matter than by
adopting, if I may, the words of a correspondent.   He observes
(1) That while Wordsworth spiritualizes the outward world
more than any other poet has done, his feeling for it is essentially manly.   Nature he always insists, gives gladness to the
glad, comfort and support to the sorrowful.   (2) There is the
wondrous depth of his feeling for the domestic affections, and
more especially for the constancy of them.   (3) He must be
considered a leader in that greatest movement of modern
times—care for our humbler brethren ; his part being not to
help them in their sufferings, but to make as reverence them
for what they are, and what they have in common with us or
in greater measure than ourselves.   These are the tendencies
breathed from every line he wrote.   He took the commonest
sights of earth and the homeliest household affections, and
made you feel that these which men commonly take to be the
lowest things are indeed the highest.

If he seldom ventures within the inner sanctuary, he everywhere leads to its outer court, lifting our thoughts into a region
" neighbouring to heaven, and that no foreign hand."   If he
was not universal in the sense in which Shakespeare was and
Goethe aimed to be, it was because he was smitten with too
deep an enthusiasm for these truths by which he was possessed.
His eye was too intense, too prophetic to admit of his looking

at life dramatically. In fact, no poet of modern times has had in him so much of the prophet. In the world of nature, to be a revealer of things hidden, the sanctifier of things common, the interpreter of new and unsuspected relations, the opener of another sense in men ; in the moral world, to be the teacher of truths hitherto neglected or unobserved, the awakener of men's hearts to the solemnities that encompass them, deepening our reverence for the essential soul, apart from accident and circumstance, making us feel more truly, more tenderly, more profoundly, lifting the thoughts upward through the shows of time to which is permanent and eternal, and bringing down on the transitory things of eye and ear some shadow of time to that which is permanent and eternal, till we

> " Feel through all this fleshly dress
> Bright shoots of everlastingness."

This is the office which he will not cease to fulfil as long as the English language lasts.

THE LOST LEADER.*

From Robert Browning—

I.

Just for a handful of silver he left us,
　Just for a ribbon to stick in his coat—
Found the one gift of which fortune bereft us.
　Lost all the others, she lets us devote ;
They, with the gold to give, doled him out silver,
　So much was theirs who so little allowed :
How all our copper had gone for his service !
　Rags --were they purple, his heart had been proud ! ·

---

* This poem is always taken as referring to Wordsworth. Wordsworth in youth was a revolutionist, in age a strong conservative. Browning, writing of this poem admits that he thought of Wordsworth's change of views, but says the work was rather a work of art with him than an attack upon that poet ; rather ideal than individual.

We that had loved him so, followed him, honored him,
   Lived in his mild and magnificent eye,
Learned his great language, caught his clear accents,
   Made him our pattern to live and to die !
Shakespeare was of us, Milton was for us,
   Burns, Shelley, were with us,—they watch from their graves !
He alone breaks from the van and the free man,
   He alone sinks to the rear and the slaves !

II.

We shall march prospering,—not through his presence ;
   Songs may inspirit us,—not from his lyre ;
Deeds will be done,—while he boasts his quiescence,
   Still bidding crouch whom the rest bade aspire ;
Blot out his name, then, record one lost soul more,
   One task more declined, one more footpath untrod,
One more devil's-triumph and sorrow for angels,
   One wrong more to man, one more insult to God !
Life's night begins : let him never come back to us !
   There would be doubt, hesitation, and pain,
Forced praise on our part—the glimmer of twilight,
   Never glad confident morning again !
Best fight on well,—for we taught him—strike gallantly,
   Menace our heart ere we master his own ;
Then let him receive the new knowledge and wait us,
   Pardoned in heaven, the first by the throne !

A FRENCH ESTIMATE.

From H. A. Taine—

Wordsworth's moulds are of bad, common clay, cracked,
unable to hold the noble metal which they ought to contain.
But the metal is really noble, and besides several very beautiful
sonnets, there is now and then a work—among others his
largest, "The Excursion"—in which we forget the poverty of
the getting up to admire the purity and elevation of the
thought. In truth, the author hardly puts himself to the

trouble of imagining ; he walks along, and converses with a pious Scotch peddler—this is the whole of the story. The poets of this school always walk, look at nature, and think of human destiny—it is their permanent attitude. He converses, then, with the peddler—a meditative character who has been educated by a long experience of men and things, who speaks very well (too well!) of the soul and of God, and relates to him the history of a good woman who died of grief in her cottage ; then he meets a solitary, a sort of sceptical Hamlet—morose, made gloomy by the death of his family and the disappointments suffered during his long journeyings ; then a clergyman, who took them to a village church-yard and described to them the life of several interesting people who are buried there. Observe that just in proportion as reflections and moral discussions arise, and as scenery and moral descriptions spread before us in hundreds, so also dissertations entwine their long thorny hedge-rows, and metaphysical thistles multiply in every corner. In short, the poem is as grave and dull as a sermon. And yet in spite of this ecclesiastical air, and the tirades against Voltaire and his age, we feel ourselves impressed as by a discourse of Théodore Jouffroy. After all, Wordsworth is convinced. He has spent his life meditating on these kinds of ideas—they are the poetry of his religion, race, climate ; he is imbued with them ; his pictures, stories, interpretations of visible nature and human life tend only to put the mind in a grave disposition which is proper to the inner man. I enter here as in the valley of Port Royal : a solitary nook, stagnant waters, gloomy woods, ruins, grave-stones, and above all the idea of responsible man and the obscure beyond, to which we involuntarily move. I forget the careless French fashions, the customs of not disturbing the even tenor of life. There is an imposing seriousness, an austere beauty in this sincere reflection ; we begin to feel respect, we stop, and are moved. This book is like a Protestant temple—august, though bare and monotonous.

. . . . The verses sustain these serious thoughts by their grave harmony, as a motet accompanies meditation or prayer. They resemble the grand and monotonous music of the organ, which in the eventide, at the close of the service, rolls slowly in the twilight of the arches and pillars.

WORDSWORTH IN CONVERSATION.

From Sir Charles Gavan Duffy—

On our first day's journey the casual mention of Edmund Burke induced me to ask Carlyle who was the best talker he had met among notable people in London. He said that when he met Wordsworth first he had been assured that he talked better than any man in England. It was his habit to talk whatever was in his mind at the time, with total indifference to the impression it produced on his hearers ; on this occasion he kept discoursing on how far you could get carried out of London on this side and on that for sixpence. One was disappointed perhaps, but, after all, this was the only healthy way of talking to say what is actually in your mind, and let sane creatures who listen make what they can of it. Whether they understood it or not, Wordsworth maintained a stern composure, and went his way, content that the world went quite another road. When he knew him better, he found that no man gave you so faithful and vivid a picture of any person or thing which he had seen with his own eyes

I inquired if Wordsworth came up to this description he had heard of him as the best talker in England.

Well, he replied it was true you would get more meaning out of what Wordsworth had to say to you than from anybody else, Leigh Hunt would emit more pretty, pleasant ingenious flashes in an hour than Wordsworth in a day. But in the end you would find, if well considered, that you had been drinking perfumed water in one case, and in the other you got the sense of a deep, earnest man, who had thought silently and painfully on many things. There was one exception to your satisfaction with the man. When he spoke of poetry he harangued about meters, cadences, rhythms, and so forth, and one could not be at the pains of listening to him. But on all other subjects he had more sense in him of a sound and instructive sort than any other literary man in England.

I suggested that Wordsworth might naturally like to speak of the instrumental part of his art, and consider what he had to say as very instructive, as by modifying the instrument he had wrought a revolution in English poetry. He taught it to speak in unsophisticated language, and of the humbler and more familiar interests of life.

Carlyle said no, not so; all he had got to say in that way was like a few driblets from the great ocean of German speculation on kindred subjects by Goethe and others. Coleridge, who had been in Germany, brought it over with him, and they translated Teutonic thought into a poor, disjointed, whitey-brown, sort of English, and that was nearly all. But Wordsworth, after all, was a man of most practical mind of any of the persons connected with literature whom he had encountered though his pastoral pipings were far from being of the importance his admirers imagined. He was essentially a cold, hard, silent, practical man, who, if he had not fallen into poetry, would have done effectual work of some sort in the world. This was the impression one got of him as he looked out of his stern blue eyes, superior to men and circumstances.

I said I had expected to hear of a man of softer mood, more sympathetic and less taciturn.

Carlyle said no, not at all; he was a man quite other than that; a man of an immense head and great jaws like a crocodile's cast in a mould designed for prodigious work.

DE QUINCEY'S PEN-PORTRAIT OF WORDSWORTH.

From Literary Reminiscences—

Wordsworth was, upon the whole, not a well-made man. His legs were pointedly condemned by all the female connoisseurs in legs that ever I heard lecture upon that topic; not that they were bad in any way which *would* force itself upon your notice—there was no absolute deformity about them, and undoubtedly they had been serviceable legs beyond the average standard of human requisition; for I calculate, upon good data, that with these identical legs Wordsworth must have traversed a distance of one hundred and seventy-five to one hundred and eighty thousand English miles—a mode of exertion which to him, stood in the stead of wine, spirits, and all other stimulants whatsoever to the animal spirits; to which he has been indebted for a life of unclouded happiness, and we for much of what is most excellent in his writings. But useful as they have proved themselves the Wordsworthian legs were certainly not ornamental; and it was really a pity, as I agreed with a lady in thinking, that he had not another pair for evening-dress parties, when no boots lend their friendly aid to mask our imperfections from the eyes of female rigorists—the *elegantes formarum spectatrices*. A sculptor would certainly have disapproved of their contour. But the worst part of Wordsworth's person was the bust; there was a narrowness and a droop about the shoulders which became striking, and had an effect of meanness when brought into close juxtaposition with a figure of a most statuesque order.... But the total effect of Wordsworth's person was always worst in a state of motion; for according to the remark I have heard from many country people, "he walked like a cade"—a cade being some sort of insect which advances by an oblique motion. Meantime his face—that was one which would have made amends for greater defects of figure; it was certainly the noblest for intellectual effects that, in actual life, I have seen, or at least have consciously been led to notice. Many such, or even finer, I have seen among the portraits of Titian, and, in a later period, among those of Vandyck, from the great era of Charles I., as also from the court of Elizabeth and of Charles II.; but none which has so much impressed me in my own time. It was a face of the long order, often falsely classed as oval. The forehead was not remarkably lofty, but it *is* perhaps remarkable for its breadth and expansive development. Neither are the eyes of Wordsworth "large," as is erroneously stated somewhere in "Peter's Letters;" on the contrary they are (I think) rather small; but that does not interfere with their effect, which at times is fine and suitable to his intellectual character.....I have seen Wordsworth's eyes oftentimes affected powerfully in this respect; his eyes are not, under any circumstances, bright, lustrous, or piercing; but, after a long day's toil in walking, I have seen them assume an appearance the most solemn and spiritual that it is possible for the human eye to wear. The light which resides in them is at no time a superficial light, but under favorable accidents it is a light which seems to come from depths below all depths; in fact, it is more truly entitled to be held "The light that never was on land or sea"—a light radiating from some far spiritual world than any the most idealizing light that ever yet a painter's hand created. The nose, a little arched and large, which, by the way (according to a natural phrenology existing centuries ago among some of the lowest among the human species), has always been accounted an unequivocal expression of animal appetites organically strong. And that was in fact the basis of Wordsworth's intellectual power; his intellectual passions were fervent and strong, because they rested upon a basis of animal sensibility superior to that of most men, diffused through *all* the animal passions (or appe tites); and something of that will be found to hold of all poets who have been great by original force and power, not (as Virgil) by means of fine management and exquisite artifice of com-

14

position applied to their conceptions. The mouth, and the region of the mouth—the whole circumjacencies of the mouth— were about the strongest feature in Wordsworth's face.

THE FIVE CHARACTERISTIC DEFECTS OF
WORDSWORTH'S POEMS.

From Coleridge's Biographia Literaria.

The first characteristic, though only occasional defect, which I appear to myself to find in these poems is the inconstancy of the style. Under this name I refer to the sudden and unprepared transitions from lines or sentences of peculiar felicity (at all events striking and original) to a style, not only unimpassioned but undistinguished. He sinks too often and too abruptly to that style which I should place in the second division of language, dividing it into the three species: first, that which is peculiar to poetry; second, that which is only proper in prose; and third, the neutral or common to both. There have been works, such as Cowley's Essay on Cromwell, in which prose and verse are intermixed (not as in the Consolation of Boetius, or the Argenis of Barclay, by the insertion of poems supposed to have been spoken or composed on occasions previously related in prose, but) the poet passing from one to the other as the nature of the thoughts or his own feelings dictated. Yet this mode of composition does not satisfy a cultivated taste. There is something unpleasant in the being thus obliged to alternate states of feeling so dissimilar, and this too in a species of writing, the pleasure from which is in part derived from the preparation and previous expectation of the reader. A portion of that awkwardness is felt which hangs upon the introduction of songs in our modern comic operas; and to prevent which the judicious Metastasio (as to whose exquisite taste there can be no hesitation, whatever doubts may be entertained as to his poetic genius) uniformly placed the *aria* at the end of the scene, at the same time that he almost always raises and impassions the style of the recitative immediately preceding. . . . .

The second defect I could generalize with tolerable accuracy, if the reader will pardon an uncouth and new-coined word. There is, I should say, not seldom a matter-of-factness in certain poems. This may be divided into, first, a laborious minuteness and fidelity in the representation of objects, and their positions, as they appeared to the poet himself; secondly, the insertion of accidental circumstances, in order to the full explanation of his living characters, their dispositions and actions : which circumstances might be necessary to establish the probability of a statement in real life, where nothing is taken for granted by the hearer, but appear superfluous in poetry, where the reader is willing to believe for his own sake. . . . . . .

Third ; an undue predilection for the dramatic form in certain poems, from which one or other of two evils result. Either the thoughts and diction are different from that of the poet, and then there arises an incongruity of style ; or they are the same and indistinguishable, and then it presents a species of ventriloquism where two are represented as talking, while in truth one man only speaks. . . . . . .

The fourth class of defects is closely connected with the former; but yet are such as arise likewise from an intensity of feeling disproportionate to such knowledge and value of the objects described, as can be fairly anticipated of men in general, even of the most cultivated classes ; and with which therefore few only, and those few particularly circumstanced, can be supposed to sympathize : in this class I comprise occasional prolixity, repetition, and an eddying instead of progression of thought. As instances, see page 27, 28, of the Poems, vol. i.,* and the first eighty lines of the Sixth Book of The Excursion. . . . .

Fifth and last; thoughts and images too great for the subject.

---

* The Anecdote for Fathers.

This is an approximation to what might be called mental bombast, as distinguished from verbal; for as in the latter there is a disproportion of the expressions to the thoughts, so in this there is a disproportion of thought to the circumstance and occasion.   This, by-the-by, is a fault of which none but a man of genius is capable.   It is the awkwardness and strength of Hercules with the distaff of Omphale. . . . . . .

SONNET TO WORDSWORTH.*

From Shelley—

 Poet of Nature, thou hast wept to know
  That things depart which never may return :
 Childhood and youth, friendship, and love's first glow,
  Have fled like sweet dreams, leaving thee to mourn,
 These common woes I feel.   One lost is mine,
  Which thou too feel'st, yet I alone deplore.
 Thou wert as a lone star whose light did shine
  On some frail bark in winter's midnight roar :
 Thou hast like to a rock-built refuge stood
  Above the blind and battling multitude :
 In honored poverty thy voice did weave
  Songs consecrate to truth and liberty.
 Deserting these thou leavest me to grieve,
  Thus, having been, that thou shouldst cease to be.

COLERIDGE'S ODE TO WORDSWORTH.

 Friend of the wise ! and teacher of the good !
 Into my heart have I received that lay
 More than historic, that prophetic lay
 Wherein (high theme by thee first sung aright)
 Of the foundations and the building up
 Of a Human Spirit thou hast dared to tell*

-----

* This sonnet alludes to Wordsworth's conversion to conservative views.

What may be told to the understanding mind
Revealable ; and what within the mind
By vital breathings secret as the soul
Of vernal growth, oft quickens in the heart
Thoughts all too deep for words !—

       Theme hard as high
Of smiles spontaneous, and mysterious fears,
(The first-born they of Reason and twin-birth)
Of tides obedient to external force,
And currents self-determined, as might seem,
Or, by some inner power ; of moments awful,
Now in thy inner life, and now abroad,
When power streamed from thee, and thy soul received
The light reflected, as a light bestowed—
Of fancies fair, and milder hours of youth,
Hyblean murmurs of poetic thought
Industrious in its joy, in vales and glens
Native or outland, lakes and famous hills !
Or on the lonely high-road, when the stars
Were rising ; or by secret mountain streams,
The guides and the companions of thy way !

 Of more than Fancy, of the Social Sense
Distending wide, and man, beloved as man,
Where France in all her towns lay vibrating
Like some becalmed bark beneath the burst
Of Heaven's immediate thunder, when no cloud
Is visible, or shadow on the main.
For thou wert there, thine own blows garlanded
Amid the tremor of a realm aglow,
Amid a mighty nation jubilant,
When from the general heart of human kind
Hope sprang forth like a full-born Deity !
——Of that dear Hope afflicted and struck down,
So summoned homeward, thenceforth calm and sure
From the dread watch-tower of man's absolute self.
With light unwaning on her eyes to look
Far on—herself a glory to behold,

The Angel of the vision !   Then (last strain)
Of duty, chosen laws controlling choice,
Action and joy !—An orphic song indeed,
A song divine of high and passionate thoughts
To their own music chanted !

                                    O great Bard !
Ere yet that last strain dying awed the air,
With steadfast eye I viewed thee in the choir
Of ever-enduring men.   The truly great
Have all one age, and from one visible space
Shed influence !   They, both in power and act,
Are permanent, and Time is not with them,
Save as it worketh for them, they in it.
Not less a sacred roll, than those of old,
And to be placed, as they, with gradual fame
Among the archives of mankind, thy work
Makes audible a linked lay of Truth,
Of Truth profound a sweet continuous lay,
Not learnt, but native, her own natural notes!
Ah: as I listened with a heart forlorn,
The pulse of my being beat anew ;
And even as life returns upon the drowned.
Life's joy rekindling roused a throng of pains—
Keen pangs of Love, awakening as a babe
Turbulent, with an outcry in the heart ;
And fears self-willed, that shun the eye of hope ;
And hope that scarce would know itself from fear ;
Sense of past youth, and manhood come in vain,
And genius given, and knowledge won in vain ;
And all which I had culled in wood-walks wild,
And all which patient toil had reared, and all,
Commune with thee had opened out—but flowers
Strewed on my course, and borne upon my bier,
In the same coffin, for the self same grave !

   That way no more ! and ill beseems it me,
Who came a welcomer in herald's guise,
Singing of glory, and futurity,

To wander back on such unhealthful road,
Plucking the poisons of self-harm !   And ill
Such intertwine beseems triumphal wreaths
Strewed before thy advancing !

                    Nor do thou,
Sage Bard ! impair the memory of that hour
Of thy communion with my nobler mind
By pity or grief, already felt too long !
Nor let my words import more blame than needs.
The tumult rose and ceased : for peace is nigh
Where wisdom's voice has found a listening heart.
Amid the howl of more than wintry storms,
The halcyon hears the voice of vernal hours
Already on the wing.

                  Eve following eve,
Dear tranquil time, when the sweet sense of Home
In sweetest ! moments for their own sake hailed
And more desired, more precious for thy song,
In silence listening, like a devoted child,
My soul lay passive, by the various strain
Driven as in surges now beneath the stars,
With momentary stars of my own birth,
Fair constellated foam,* still darting off
Into the darkness ; now a tranquil sea,
Outspread and bright, yet swelling to the moon.

    And when—O Friend ! my comforter and guide !
Strong in thyself, and powerful to give strength !—
Thy long sustained Song finally closed,
And thy deep voice had ceased—yet thou thyself
Wert still before my eyes, and round us both
That happy vision of beloved faces—

---

* "A beautiful white cloud of foam at momentary intervals coursed by the side of
the vessel with a roar, and little stars of the flame danced and sparkled and went out in
it ; and every now and then light detachments of this white cloud-like foam darted off
from the vessel's side, each with its own small constellation, over the sea, and soared
out of sight like a Tartar troop over a wilderness."—*The Friend* p. 220.

Scarce conscious, and yet conscious of its close
I sate, my being blended in one thought
(Thought was it? or aspiration? or resolve?)
Absorbed, yet hanging still upon the sound—
And when I rose, I found myself in prayer.

CHAPTER V.

SELECTED POEMS FOR SIGHT-WORK.

"There is sweet music here that softer fall
Than petals from blown roses on the grass,
Or night dews on still waters between walls
Of shadowy granite, in a gleaming pass;
Music that gentlier on the spirit lies,
Than tired eyelids upon tired eyes;
Music that brings sweet sleep down from the blissful skies."

·—The Lotos-Eaters.

CHAPTER V.

SELECTED POEMS FOR SIGHT-WORK.

BREAK, BREAK, BREAK.*

Break, break, break,
    On thy cold gray stones, O Sea !
And I would that my tongue could utter
    The thoughts that arise in me.

O well for the fisherman's boy,
    That he shouts with his sister at play !
O well for the sailor lad,
    That he sings in his boat on the bay !

And the stately ships go on
    To their haven under the hill ;
But O for the touch of a vanish'd hand,
    And the sound of a voice that is still !

Break, break, break,
    At the foot of thy crags, O Sea !
But the tender grace of a day that is dead
    Will never come back to me.

1. State and account for the author's mood in this poem. What is the subject of the poem ?

2. Describe the scene before the poet's mind, accounting for the order in which he notices the different objects.

3. Explain how ll. 3-4, 11-12, and 15-16 are respectively connected in sense with the preceeding context.

4. Show how the poet has harmonized his language and versification with his thoughts and feelings. When qualities of style are exemplified in the poem ?

5. Write brief elocutionary notes on the poem,

---

* These questions are from a paper set by Mr. Seath, in 1887. To answer them is to show a knowledge of the essential meaning of the poem. Nothing helps good teaching more than such questioning at examinations.

SPEECH BY ULYSSES.

Time hath, my lord, a wallet at his back,
Wherein he puts alms for oblivion,
A great-sized monster of ingratitudes :
Those scraps are good deeds past ; which are devour'd,
As fast as they are made, forgot as soon
As done : perseverance, dear my lord,
Keeps honour bright : to have done is to hang
Quite out of fashion, like a rusty mail
In monumental mockery.   Take the instant way ;
For honour travels in a strait so narrow,
Where one but goes abreast : keep then the path ;
For emulation hath a thousand sons
That one by one pursue : if you give way,
Or hedge aside from the direct forthright,
Like to an enter'd tide, they all rush by
And leave you hindmost ;
Or, like a gallant horse fall'n in first rank,
Lie there for pavement to the abject rear,
O'er-run and trampled on ; then what they do in present,
Though less than yours in past, must o'ertop yours ;
For *time* is like a fashionable host
That slightly shakes his parting guest by the hand,
And with his arms outstretch'd, as he would fly,
Grasps in the comer : welcome ever smiles,
And farewell goes out sighing.   O, let not virtue seek
Remuneration for the thing it was ;
For beauty, wit,
High birth, vigour of bone, desert in service,
Love, friendship, charity, are subjects all
To envious and calumniating *time*.
One touch of nature makes the whole world kin.

—Troilus and Cressida.

(*a*) In a prose paragraph of half a dozen lines, express the outline of thought in this extract.

(*b*) Criticize the principal similitudes on the following canons of criticism :

1. There should be a marked difference between the *original* and the *comparison*.

2. There should be a marked resemblance in the relevant point of comparison.

3. The comparison should be more effective with the reader than the original.

4. The comparison should not be too obvious.

5. The comparison should not be trite or worn out.

6. The comparison should not be degrading to the original.

7. The comparison should not be so elevated as to render the original absurd.

8. The emotion of the comparison should be in line with that of the original.

9. The comparison should lend the charm of novelty, remoteness, ingenuity.

10. There should not be a mixture of similitudes in the one figure.

ENGLAND BEFORE THE STORM.

THE day that is the night of days,
With cannon-fire for sun ablaze,
We spy from any billow's lift ;
And England still this tidal drift !
Would she to sainted forethought vow
A space before the thunders flood,
That martyr of its hour might now
    Spare her the tears of blood ?

Asleep upon her ancient deeds,
She hugs the vision plethora breeds,
And counts her manifold increase
Of treasure in the fruits of peace.
What curse on earth's improvident,
When the dread trumpet shatters rest,
Is wreaked, she knows, yet smiles content
    As cradle rocked from breast.

She, impious to the Lord of Hosts,
The valour of her offspring boasts,
Mindless that now on land and main
His heeded prayer is active brain.
No more great heart may guard the home,
Save eyed and armed and skilled to cleave
You swallower wave with shroud of foam,
     We see not distant heave.

They stand to be her sacrifice,
The sons this mother flings like dice,
To face the odds and brave the Fates;
As in those days of starry dates,
When cannon cannon's counterblast
Awakened, muzzle muzzle bowled,
And high in swathe of smoke the mast
     Its fighting rag outrolled.
         —*George Meredith, in the Athenæum.*

(a) State in a sentence the substance of this poem.

(b) State the substance of each stanza concisely.

(c) Simplify the expressions you find obscure.

EARTH'S PREFERENCE.

EARTH loves her young : a preference manifest :
She prompts them to her fruits and flower-beds ;
Their beauty with her choicest interthreads,
And makes her revel of their merry zest.

As in our East much were it in our West,
If men had risen to do the work of heads.
Her gabbling grey she eyes askant, nor treads
The ways they walk ; by what they speak oppressed.

How wrought they in their zenith ? 'Tis not writ ;
Not all ; yet she by one sure sign can read :
Have they but held her laws and nature dear,

They mouth no sentence of inverted wit,
More prizes she her beasts than this high breed
Wry in the shape she wastes her milk to rear.

—*George Meredith.*

(*a*) Express the central thought of this sonnet.
(*b*) Paraphrase it into simple prose.

THE SEA-LIMITS.

CONSIDER the sea's listless chime :
    Time's self it is, made audible,—
    The murmur of the earth's own shell.
Secret continuance sublime
    Is the sea's end : our sight may pass
    No furlong further.   Since time was,
This sound hath told the lapse of time.

No quiet, which is death's,—it hath
    The mournfulness of ancient life,
    Enduring always at dull strife.
As the world's heart of rest and wrath,
    Its painful pulse is in the sands.
    Last utterly, the whole sky stands,
Gray and not known, along its path.

Listen along beside the sea,
    Listen along among the woods ;
    Those voices of twin solitudes
Shall have one sound alike to thee :
    Hark where the murmurs of thronged men
    Surge and sink back and surge again.—
Still the one voice of wave and tree.

Gather a shell from the strewn beach,
    And listen at its lips : they sigh
    The same desire and mystery,
The echo of the whole sea's speech.

And all mankind is thus at heart
Not anything but what thou art :
And Earth, Sea, Man, are all in each.

—*Dante Gabriel Rosetti.*

(*a*) Develop the metaphor "*shell*" in line 3.

(*b*) Explain "*Secret continuance sublime.*"

(*c*) Explain "*Our sight may pass no furlong further.*"

(*d*) Explain "*No quiet, which is death's.*"

(*e*) Explain line 4 and 5, stanza II.

(*f*) Write notes on the motive, tone, harmony, and melody, of the poem.

NIGHT AND DEATH.

MYSTERIOUS Night ! when our first parent knew
  Thee from report divine, and heard thy name,
  Did he not tremble for this lovely frame,
This glorious canopy of light and blue ?
Yet 'neath a curtain of translucent dew
  Bathed in the rays of the great setting flame,
  Hesperus with the host of heaven came,
And lo ! creation widened in man's view.

Who could have thought such darkness lay concealed
  Within thy rays, O Sun, or who could find,
Whilst fly and leaf and insect stood revealed,
  That to such countless orbs thou mad'st us blind ?
Why do we then shun death with anxious strife,
If Light can thus deceive, wherefore not life ?

—*Joseph Blanco White.*

(*a*) Express briefly the central thought of this sonnet.

(*b*) Explain the allusion in "*our first parent knew thee from report divine*" and in "*Hesperus.*"

(*c*) How do you reconcile the expressions "our first parent" and "in man's view"?

(*d*) Explain "such darkness lay concealed within thy beams."

(*e*) Develop fully the comparison of Night and Death showing all points of similarity.

Whither, 'midst falling dew,
While glow the heavens with the last steps of day,
Far through their rosy depths dost thou pursue
    Thy solitary way ?

Vainly the fowler's eye
Might mark thy distant flight to do thee wrong,
As darkly limned on the crimson sky,
    Thy figure floats along.

Seek'st thou the plashy brink
Of weedy lake, or marge of river wide,
Or where the rocking billows rise and sink
    On the chafed ocean side ?

There is a power whose care
Teaches thy way along that pathless coast,—
The desert and illimitable air,—
    Lone wandering, but not lost.

All day thy wings have fanned,
At that far height, the cold, thin atmosphere ;
Yet stoop not, weary, to the welcome land,
    Though the dark night is near.

And soon that toil shall end ;
Soon shalt thou find a summer home, and rest,
And scream among thy fellows ; reeds shall bend
    Soon o'er thy shelter'd nest.

Thou'rt gone ; the abyss of heaven
Hath swallow'd up thy form ; yet on my heart
Deeply hath sunk the lesson thou hast given,
    And shall not soon depart.

He who, from zone to zone,
Guides through the boundless sky thy certain flight,
In the long way that I must tread alone,
    Will lead my steps aright.

15

1. State fully the circumstances under which the different parts of this poem have professedly been written.

2. Give a fully descriptive title; and state, connectedly and without the poet's amplification, the leading thoughts.

3. State the poetic (or symbolic) meaning you attach to the long high flight of the bird and develop its significance in the details.

4. Would the deeper meaning not be obvious without the last stanza? Is it artistic to enlarge upon obvious abstractions in poetry? Underline parts in which the poet fails to use the concrete method. Justify the last stanza.

5. Poetic imagination consists largely in finding analogies between the world of mind and the external world; in seeing deep truths in material objects: illustrate this from the poem above and from other poems.

Ich weiss nicht was soll es bedeuten.

I CANNA tell what has come ower me
  That I am sae eerie and wae;
An auld-warld tale comes before me,
  It haunts me by nicht and by day.

From the cool lift the gloamin' draps dimmer,
  And the Rhine slips saftly by;
The taps of the mountains shimmer
  I' the lowe o' the sunset sky.

Up there, in a glamour entrancin',
  Sits a maiden wondrous fair;
Her gowden adornments are glancin',
  She is kaimin' her gowden hair.

As she kaims it the gowd kaim glistens,
  The while she is singin' a song
That hauds the rapt soul that listens,
  With its melody sweet and strong.

The boy, floating by in vague wonder,
  Is seized with a wild weird love;

He sees na the black rocks under,—
He sees but the vision above.

The waters their waves are flingin'
Ower boatie and boatman anon ;
And this, with her airtful singin',
The Waterwitch Lurley hath done.

ALEXANDER MACMILLAN.

a. Give any reason why this dialect is suitable for translating Heine's ballad into English.

b. State the substance of the poem in your own words: suggest a title for the poem.

c. What may be taken as the allegorical or symbolic meaning of this simple song?

THE CASTAWAY.*

OBSCUREST night involved the sky,
  The Atlantic billows roar'd,
When such a destined wretch as I,
  Wash'd headlong from on board,
Of friends, of hope, of all bereft,
His floating home for ever left.

No braver chief could Albion boast
  Than he with whom he went,
Nor ever ship left Albion's coast
  With warmer wishes sent.
He loved them both, but both in vain ;
Nor him beheld, nor her again.

Not long beneath the whelming brine
  Expert to swim, he lay ;
Nor soon he felt his strength decline,
  Or courage die away ;
But waged with death a lasting strife,
Supported by despair of life.

---

* This was Cowper's last poem. It is founded on an anecdote in *Anson's Voyages.* (March 20th, 1799.)

He shouted ; nor his friends had fail'd
   To check the vessel's course,
But so the furious blast prevail'd,
   That pitiless perforce
They left their outcast mate behind,
And scudded still before the wind.

Some succour yet they could afford ;
   And, such as storms allow,
The cask, the coop, the floated cord,
   Delay'd not to bestow :
But he, they knew, nor ship nor shore,
Whate'er they gave, should visit more.

Nor, cruel as it seem'd, could he
   Their haste himself condemn,
Aware that flight, in such a sea,
   Alone could rescue them ;
Yet bitter felt it still to die
Deserted, and his friends so nigh.

He long survives, who lives an hour
   In ocean, self-upheld :
And so long he, with unspent power,
   His destiny repell'd ;
And ever, as the minutes flew,
Entreated help, or cried—"Adieu !"

At length, his transient respite past,
   His comrades, who before
Had heard his voice in every blast,
   Could catch the sound no more :
For then, by toil subdued, he drank
The stifling wave, and then he sank.

No poet wept him ; but the page
   Of narrative sincere,
That tells his name, his worth, his age,
   Is wet with Anson's tear :
And tears by bards or heroes shed
Alike immortalise the dead.

I therefore purpose not, or dream,
  Descanting on his fate,
To give the melancholy theme
  A more enduring date :
But misery still delights to trace
Its semblance in another's case.

No voice divine the storm allay'd,
  No light propitious shone,
When, snatch'd from all effectual aid,
  We perish'd, each alone :
But I beneath' a rougher sea,
And whelm'd in deeper gulfs than he.

1. State in two or three sentences the line of thought in this poem.

2. Explain the expression " Such a destined wretch as I."

3. Explain the pronouns of the second stanza.

4. Paraphrase the third stanza into simple prose: what is Litotes ? (How is the word pronounced ?)

5. What is the charm of the line " That pitiless perforce" ? (IV. 4.)

6. Compare "respite" (VIII. 1.) with *reprieve*, considering *sense* not *sound*.

7. Why is "descanting" (X. 2.) a well chosen word ?

8. How many lines in the eleven stanzas refer to himself directly ? What is gained by the abruptness of the conclusion ? (XI. 4, 5, 6.)

9. Why is a knowledge of the author's life more important when the author is a lyric poet than when he is a dramatic poet ?

10. Pick out short quotable passages sufficiently general and proverbial to rank as aphorisms.

11. Point out expressions in the description of the castaway and his fate that might apply to Cowper almost without change.

12. Shew how the pathos of loneliness is used to intensify the emotions of sorrow and despair.

ODE TO A NIGHTINGALE.

My heart aches, and a drowsy numbness pains
  My sense, as though of hemlock I had drunk,
Or emptied some dull opiate to the drains
  One minute past, and Lethe-wards had sunk :
'Tis not through envy of thy happy lot,
  But being too happy in thy happiness,—
    That thou, light-winged Dryad of the trees,
      In some melodious plot
  Of beechen green, and shadows numberless,
    Singest of summer in full-throated ease.

O for a draught of vintage, that hath been
  Cool'd a long age in the deep-delved earth,
Tasting of Flora and the country-green,
  Dance, and Provençal song, and sun-burnt mirth !
O for a beaker full of the warm South,
  Full of the true, the blushful Hippocrene,
    With beaded bubbles winking at the brim,
      And purple-stained mouth :
  That I might drink, and leave the world unseen,
    And with thee fade away into the forest dim :

Fade far away, dissolve, and quite forget
  What thou among the leaves hast never known,
The weariness, the fever, and the fret
  Here, where men sit and hear each other groan ;
Where palsy shakes a few, sad, last grey hairs,
  Where youth grows pale, and spectre-thin, and dies ;
    Where but to think is to be full of sorrow
      And leaden-eyed despairs ;
  Where Beauty cannot keep her lustrous eyes,
    Or new Love pine at them beyond to-morrow.

Away ! away ! for I will fly to thee,
  Not charioted by Bacchus and his pards.
But on the viewless wings of Poesy,
  Though the dull brain perplexes and retards ;
Already with thee ! tender is the night,

And haply the Queen-Moon is on her throne,
  Cluster'd around by all her starry Fays ;
    But here there is no light,
Save what from heaven is with the breezes blown
  Through verdurous glooms and winding mossy ways.

I cannot see what flowers are at my feet,
  Nor what soft incense hangs upon the boughs,
But, in embalmed darkness, guess each sweet
  Wherewith the seasonable month endows
The grass, the thicket, the fruit tree wild ;
  White hawthorn, and the pastoral eglantine ;
    Fast-fading violets cover'd up in leaves ;
      And mid-May's eldest child,
The coming musk-rose, full of dewy wine,
  The murmurous haunt of the flies on summer eves.

Darkling I listen ; and, for many a time
  I have been half in love with easeful Death,
Call'd him soft names in many a mused rhyme,
  To take into the air my quiet breath ;
Now more than ever seems it rich to die,
  To cease upon the midnight with no pain,
    While thou art pouring forth thy soul abroad
      In such an ecstacy !
Still wouldst thou sing, and I have ears in vain—
  To thy high requiem become a sod.

Thou wast not born for death, immortal Bird !
  No hungry generations tread thee down :
The voice I hear this passing night was heard
  In ancient days by emperor and clown :
Perhaps the self-same song that found a path
  Through the sad heart of Ruth, when, sick for home,
    She stood in tears amid the alien corn ;
      The same that oft-times hath
Charm'd magic casements, opening on the foam
  Of perilous seas, in faëry lands forlorn.

Forlorn ! the very word is like a bell
  To toll me back from thee to my sole self !
Adieu ! the fancy cannot cheat so well
  As she is famed to do, deceiving elf.
Adieu ! adieu ! thy plaintive anthem fades
  Past the near meadows, over the still stream,
    Up the hill-side ; and now 'tis buried deep
      In the next valley-glades :
Was it a vision, or a waking dream ?
  Fled is that music :—Do I wake or sleep ?

1. "An ode is a lofty utterance of intense feeling and remarkable for its elaborate versification." How does this poem answer the description quoted ?

2. "Generally speaking, modern odes are distinguished from other poems by their form—the character of the feet, the length of the verses, and the construction of the divisions or stanzas being varied in accordance with the changes in the flow of the feeling." How does the quotation apply to this ode ?

3. Point out passages in which the music of the verse seems to fit the subject-matter closely.

4. The line of thought in this ode is somewhat as follows : (1) The poet is intoxicated with the happy melody of the bird : (2) He desires a magic drink that will enable him to join the bird in its retreat : (3) He would leave this poor world of men and dwell with the bird among the leaves : (4) Without magic wine, but aided by fancy he joins the bird : (5) He is delighted with the fragrance of his dark retreat : (6) He could now die contented, but dead he would be deaf to the bird's song : (7) The bird is immortal : (8) The spell is broken by the bird's departure. What is the central idea of all this ? Has it any significance beneath the surface ?

5. Explain the relation of "That thou" (I. 7.)

6. Explain "drains" (I. 3.)

7. Explain the compound words.

8. Comment on the use of epithets.

9. Explain the last three lines of the seventh stanza.

10. Does "mused" (VI. 3.) mean *fanciful*, or *muse-inspired*, or *thought, but not given utterance* ?

CHAPTER VI.

QUESTIONS ON THE SELECTIONS.

"All hope abandon ye who enter here.
. . . . We are come
Where I have told thee we shall see the souls
To misery doomed, who intellectual good
Have lost." —*Divine Comedy.*

CHAPTER VI.

QUESTIONS.

I.—PEELE CASTLE.

S. J. Radcliffe, Esq., B.A., English Master, London, O. I.

1. Describe the pictures of Peele Castle presented to the poet and the painter.

2. What two views of human life correspond to these two pictures?

3. Show that the first picture, and the first view of life are mistaken.

4. What caused this change of opinion? Quote any passages to illustrate your answer.

5. Show that the tone and diction of the poem are characteristic of Wordsworth.

6. What impressions has the study of the poem left on you (1) as to mood (2) as to beauty.

II.—THE POET'S EPITAPH.

A. E. Lang, Esq., B.A., Eng. Master, Napanee O. I.

1. Outline briefly the argument of this poem.

2. Describe in your own words the "types" of stanzas 1-9, (Statesman, Lawyer, etc.) and show how these in some degree anticipate the character of stanzas 10-15.

3. Compare Wordsworth's conception of the Poet, with Tennyson's (in "the Poet" and "the Poet's mind.")

4. Show how stanzas 12 and 13, are particularly applicable to Wordsworth himself.

5. Point out the force of the following words :—" Sallow," l. 8, "fingering," l. 18, "smooth-rubbed," l. 29, "random," l. 50, "breaking," l. 58.

6. Explain fully what is meant by :—

" Lean upon a peasant's staff."

" Would peep and botanize upon his mother's grave."

" An intellectual all in all."

" Impulses of deeper birth have come to him in solitude."

" The harvest of a quiet eye."

"Contented if he might enjoy the things which others understand."

7. Criticise the structure, form and metre of this Poem, and show the suitability of the metre to a theme of this kind."

III.—THE SOLITARY REAPER.*

Cephas Guillet, Esq., B.A., Mod. Lang. Master, Ottawa C. I.

1. Show the plan of the poem.

2. Show fully the harmony between the thought and the rhythm and melody in the first stanza. Mention what you consider the best example of effective change of rhythm in rest of poem.

(Compare with Lamartine's " O Père qu' adore mon père " &c in the new *High School French Reader !* It really would be interesting to you, to compare that sample of Lamartine's harmonious verse with a poem by Fréchette on the opposite page. They form a striking contrast in point of melody.)

3. What aspect of the picture is chiefly emphasized in the first stanza? State effect of this emphasis. (Of course I refer

---

*The parentheses in this paper were not intended for publication, but they are too interesting to be omitted.—ED.

to repetition of idea of solitude in "single" "solitary," "by her-self," "alone" all in harmony with the "melancholy strain.")

4. Explain the effect of the comparisons in stanza II. (He has chosen favorite birds of the poets. His own poem on the Cuckoo might well be read here to enhance the beauty of the comparison in the pupil's mind. And what more fitting than the mention of the nightingale in trying to impress us with the plaintive beauty of the maiden's song.

> " Sweet bird that shunn'st the noise of folly,
> Most musical, most melancholy !
> Thee, chantress, oft the wood among
> I woo, to hear thy even-song.")

5. Note the felicity with which the poet has clothed the thought in stanza III ; and mention what you consider the best example of the union of thought and diction in the rest of the poem. (Of course I am thinking of the simplicity and terse suggestiveness eminently Wordsworthian of " old unhappy, far-off things . . . ago" "Some natural sorrow," to end of stanza. The last two lines of stanza I. were also in my mind ; fine use of *profound* and *overflowing*. In second part of second question I was thinking of the line " Breaking the silence of the seas "—but of course the main point is to give good reason for one's choice whatever it be. They might mention use of feminine rhymes in last stanza.)

6. What is the tone and effect of the poem ? (Or what is the thought, or feeling to which the poet is giving expression ?) Compare it in this respect with *The Highland Girl*.

(It is a sweet and melancholy strain thrilling in its very simplicity and plaintiveness. It fills the heart with calm, soothing images and attunes it to a lasting sympathy. We seem indeed to be listening to the " still sad music of humanity."

IV.—HART-LEAP WELL.

L. M. Levan, Esq., B.A., Principal, Owen Sound Coll. Inst.

1. Describe the metrical structure of this poem.

2. Show clearly the meaning and the poetical value of all the similes and metaphors.

3. Show the force of all the epithets in the poem.

4. In every case where the prose order of words is not observed, show why it has been departed from.

5. What thought is the poem meant to illustrate? Where is it expressed?

6. Why is this poem divided into two parts. Show the bearing of each part on the central thought.

7. Where has Coleridge treated the same theme? What are the main differences between his mode of treatment and Wordsworth's?

8. From what characteristics would you judge this poem, if you had never seen it before, to be Wordsworth's?

V.—SONNET XIX.

W. H. Schofield, Esq., B.A., Mod. Lang. Master, Hamilton C. I.

1. Discuss the appropriateness and force of the metaphors in this sonnet.

2. Explain the allusions in "Petrarch's wound"; "an exile's grief"; "mild Spenser"; "when a damp fell round the path of Milton"; also the meaning of "The Sonnet glittered . . . brow."

3. What places do Shakspeare, Petrarch, Tasso, Camöens, Dante, Spenser, and Milton occupy as sonneteers? When and where did they live? Very briefly state the work of each.

4. What key have we to the strength and suggestiveness of

Wordsworth's style in the use of such expressions as "mindless of its just honours"; "a glow-worm lamp"; "soul-animating strains"?

5. Discuss the one-sentence structure, the impressiveness of the ending, and the general effect.

6. What characteristics of Wordsworth as *man* do we see here revealed?

7. What are the chief features of Wordsworth's poems as regards (*a*) theme (*b*) style (*c*) influence.

VI.—AT THE GRAVE OF BURNS.

A. W. Burt, Esq., B.A., Principal, Brookville O. I.

1. Describe this poem under the heads, subject, matter and style.

2. What other poems of Wordsworth does it most closely resemble? Indicate the points of similarity.

3. Compare it with "*A Poet's Epitaph*."

4. How far does it conform with the canons of poetry laid down by Wordsworth?

5. What features of its author's character and genius does it illustrate?

6. To what circumstances in the life, character and work of Burns does it call attention?

7. Describe the metrical structure of the poem and discuss its suitability to the theme.

8. Show the force of the figures of speech in I, 3-4. IV, 3-6. VI, 5-6.

9. Explain the meaning of the following expressions: "fierce and bold," I, 1; "struggling" V, 2 ; "with the obscurest" V, 5; "current," VII, 1 ; " when the main fibres are entwined closely

still" VIII, 3-6. "this dread moment," IX, 3. "a ritual hymn," XIV, 4.

VII.—CHARACTER OF THE HAPPY WARRIOR.

John Jeffries, Esq., B.A., Eng. Master, Peterborough C. I.

1. With what great field of thought does the poet in this poem deal?

2. What is his special theme?

3. To what extent is it an important theme?

4. What feelings were associated with the thoughts of this theme.

5. Do the ideas and feelings expressed in this poem appear to you to be due to some immediate external excitement, or to be the result of the poet's reflection and constitution of mind?

6. Does thought or expression appear to have received chief attention here?

7. Wordsworth has said that a large portion of the language of every good poem can in no respect differ from that of prose. Refer to the use of prosaic language in this poem.

8. Discuss the extent and degree of elevation possessed by the language.

9. Matthew Arnold has said that Wordsworth's greatness lies in his energetic and profound application of ideas to life— to the question: How to live. Apply the criticism to this poem.

10. Describe the versification.

11. To what category of poetry does the poem belong?

12. Outline its contents.

VIII.—ODE ON INTIMATIONS OF IMMORTALITY FROM RECOLLECTIONS OF EARLY CHILDHOOD.

Miss Nellie Spence, B.A., English Specialist, Parkdale C. I.

1. Explain clearly the philosophical teaching of this ode. From what school of philosophy did Wordsworth borrow his ideas on this subject? Did he *only* borrow? Or do his ideas differ in any way from those of the original expounders? By what argument does he support his view?

2. Discuss the *aesthetic* as distinguished from the *logical* value of the theory and arguments here given.

3. What modern school of philosophic thought (now attracting a good deal of attention) teaches doctrines not unlike, in one respect at least, those here stated? What living poet has made similar doctrines the theme of his most famous work?

4. What are the most important theories that have been held at one time or another regarding the origin and destiny of the human soul? Compare Wordsworth's with these, in so far as the poetic beauty of the different conceptions is concerned.

5. Make a logical analysis of this ode by stating as concisely as possible the theme of each stanza, and showing the development of the main thought from stanza to stanza. In which stanza is the philosophic theory most clearly stated.

6. Is the general tone of the ode characteristic of Wordsworth? If so, show the resemblance, if not, the contrast, between it and some other of his poems. In the details of the ode, point out, in diction, sentence-structure, or thought, any Wordsworthian tendencies.

Make a comparison between :

> (a) " Trailing clouds of glory do we come
> From God, who is our home ;
> Heaven lies about us in our infancy."—

16

and

> " I have not so far left the coasts of life
> To travel inland, that I cannot hear
> That murmur of the outer Infinite
> Which unweaned babies smile at in their sleep'
> When wondered at for smiling."—*Mrs. Browning.*

and also between the foregoing lines of Mrs. Browning and

> " Hence in a season of calm weather.
> Though inland far we be
> Our souls have sight of that immortal sea
> That brought us hither
> Can in a moment travel thither,
> And see the children sport upon the shore,
> And hear the mighty waters rolling evermore."

(*b*) " Though nothing can bring back the hour
>   Of sunshine in the grass, of splendor in the flower."

and

" Our delight in the sunshine on the deep-bladed grass to-day
might be no more than the faint perception of wearied souls, if it
were not for the sunshine and the grass in the far-off years, which
still live in us and transform our preception into love."

—*George Eliot.*

(*c*) " To me the meanest flower that blows can give
>   Thoughts that do often lie too deep for tears."

and

> " Thee neither know I nor thy peers ;
> And yet my eyes are filled with tears."
>   —*To a Highland Girl.*

(*d*) " There hath pass'd away a glory from the earth."

and

> " The world is too much with us ; late and soon,
> Getting and spending, we lay waste our powers ;
> Little we see in nature that is ours :
> We have given our hearts away, a sordid boon !
> The sea that bares her bosom to the moon,

The winds that will be howling at all hours,
And are up-gathered now like sleeping flowers ;
For this, for everything we are out of tune,
It moves us not."

8. Wordsworth is always a nature-worshipper. Illustrate from this ode. Compare the descriptions of nature here with those given by him elsewhere, *e.g.*, in *The Excursion*.

9. To what extent does Wordsworth observe his own rules of diction in this ode?

10. "Did I not know for a.certainty that this ode was written by Wordsworth, I should be much more inclined to think it came from Shelley's pen." Examine this statement.

11. What use is made of the principle of contrast in this ode? By what other means is force received?

12. Point out and critically examine any examples of per-sonification, metaphor, simile, apostrophe, climax, and other figures of speech which you observe.

13. One of the tests of the poet lies in the figures of speech by which he beautifies his thought. Applying this test to Wordsworth and judging from this ode, what status would you assign to him? Compare his figures in boldness, origin-ality, power, and beauty, with those of Tennyson, Longfellow, Coleridge,·Shelley, Keats, or any other poets with whom you are familiar.

14. The saying "Beauty unadorned is adorned the most" applies as well to literary as to physical beauty. In what sense is this statement true? Is it, in that sense, applicable to Wordsworth generally? Is it applicable in this particular poem?

15. What qualities of style are exemplified in this ode? Point out one marked example of each.

16. By careful analysis, reveal, if possible, the secret of the wonderful charm of this ode.

17. What is an ode?   Name some celebrated odes in the English language.   What rank does this one hold?

18. Show, if possible, from this ode, how Wordsworth represents the *natural* as opposed to the *artificial* school of English poetry.   Of English poets name the one whom you consider most emphatically opposed to Wordsworth.

19. Wordsworth is the poet of the few, Tennyson of the many.   From this ode, show how this is (if it be) the case.

20. Examine the appropriateness of the introductory stanza? How far does it suggest the main theme?   Show how the two concluding stanzas summarize and apply what has been developed in the preceding part of the poem?   Are the rhetorical laws with regard to the beginning and the end of a composition well observed.

21. Write what you consider the two finest parts of the ode. Why do you so consider them?

22. Make explanatory remarks on the following :—

" Celestial light," " of yore," " the fields of sleep," " the heart of May," "jubilee," "I hear, I hear, with joy I hear." (Why the repetition?), "something that is gone," "the visionary gleam," " the soul———our life's star," " trailing clouds of glory do we come from God," " shades of the prison-house," (quote similar metaphors), "nature's priest," the light of common day," "the homely nurse," "her foster-child," " the inevitable yoke," " in our embers," " those obstinate questionings———high instincts———shadowy recollections," " the fountain light of all our day," "that immortal sea," "my heart of hearts," " thoughts———too deep for tears."

23. Describe the metrical structure of this ode.   Examine its appropriateness.   What advantage has the iambic over the trochaic metre which would make the latter unsuitable for a composition such as this?

IX.—MICHAEL.

W. H. Libby, Esq., B.A., Eng. Master, Ottawa C. I.

1. Wherein does the poem "Michael" differ from prose in its language, thought and feeling?

2. Coleridge analyzing Wordsworth's style, assigns it five characteristic defects, and six characteristic merits, as follows:

Defects—1. Inconstancy of style: sometimes flat and prosy.

  2. Frequent "matter-of-factness."

  3. Weak use of dramatic form. (When characters speak for themselves they seem unreal—mere echoes of Wordsworth.)

  4. Prolixity and repetition, resulting from an uncommon interest in things not usually considered worthy of emphasis.

  5. Disproportion between subject in hand and comparisons used to illustrate it: not a defect of strength but a fault of excess.

Merits—1. Austere use of language—grammatically and logically.

  2. Truth and sanity of thought and sentiments—absence of exaggeration of feeling and undue prominence to half-truths.

  3. Felicity in single lines and paragraphs.

  4. Faithful description of nature.

  5. Meditative pathos—union of deep thoughtfulness with sensibility: sympathy with man as man.

  6. Imagination in the highest and strictest sense of the word—the power to "add the gleam, the light that never was on sea or land, the consecration and the poet's dream" to any subject even, indeed, especially, to the most commonplace.

Matthew Arnold says: " If I had to pick out poems of a kind most perfectly to show Wordsworth's unique power, I should rather choose poems such as *Michael, The Fountain, The Highland Reaper.*   •

Illustrate these characteristic defects and merits of Words-worth's style, by references to this characteristic poem.   Dis-cuss the statement that he who likes the poem " *Michael,*" is " a Wordsworthian."

3.   " It was the first,
          Of these domestic tales that spake to me
          Of Shepherds, dwellers in the valleys, men
          Whom I already loved ; not verily
          For their own sakes, but for the fields and hills
          Where was their occupation and abode.
          And hence this tale, while I was yet a boy
          Careless of books, yet having felt the power
          Of Nature, by the gentle agency
          Of natural objects led me on to feel
          For passions that were not my own, and think
          (At random and imperfectly indeed)
          On man, the heart of man, and human life."

What do we learn from these lines of the awakening and development of the "social sense" of "man beloved as man" in Wordsworth, and of the relation of nature and man to his poetry.

4. In what respects may *Michael* be called a dramatic poem, (suited in any way or degree to stage representation) and in what respects is it strikingly non-dramatic?

What qualities distinguish Michael, Isabel and Luke from ordinary peasants?   Is it as types or as individuals that Words-worth selects them for description?   Compare them in this respect with the characters of Chaucer's *Prologue* and of Shakespeare's Plays.

5. What were Wordsworth's views concerning poetic diction?
(Read preface to second edition of *Lyrical Ballads*, chapters
xvii., xviii., xix., Coleridge's *Biographia Literaria* and Minto's
Wordsworth in the Encyc. Brit.) Does his own diction conform
to his theory? What are the "vulgar errors" with regard to
his views of poetic diction? Is his theory broad enough to
cover the great variety of diction shown in *Lucy Gray*, *Michael*,
and the *Ode on Intimations of Immortality*? Or is some of his
work written in defiance of his reasoned views? If you found
him inconsistent would you consider his theory or his practice
the more authoritative in fixing a canon of diction?

6. Compare Shelley with Wordsworth in the matter of the
selection of subject-matter and treatment. Contrast *The Cloud*
with *Michael* in these respects.

7. In your own words, and concisely, tell the story of *Michael*
with the purpose of setting forth its value as poetical material.

8. "He assailed the public taste as 'depraved,' first and
mainly in so far as it was adverse to simple incidents simply
treated, being accustomed to 'gross and violent stimulants,'
'craving after extraordinary incident,' possessed with a 'degrading thirst after outrageous stimulation,' 'frantic novels, sickly
and stupid German tragedies, and deluges of idle and extrava-
gant stories in verse.'"—*Minto*.

Mention with comments works of his period that come within
the meaning of his strictures. How would Shakespeare's
tragedies bear the charge of depraving the public taste by
"sensationalism"? What are the negative (as distinguished
from the actual) merits of the story of Michael as told by
Wordsworth?

X.—ODE TO DUTY.

1. Is this subject suited to the character and genius of the poet? Compare it with some of his other subjects in this respect.

2. Write if you can a name for the poem more fully significant of its central idea, yet artistic and concise.

3. State the principal idea of the poem in one clear sentence.

4. Set forth the line of thought of the poem more fully: state the substance of each stanza in a clear sentence.

5. Show that the thought of each stanza has a duty in working out the thought of the whole work, and show the effect of deleting any stanza.

6. State with reasons whether any of the stanzas might in your opinion be placed in a different order from that in which you find them.

7. In selecting material for an Ode to Duty the poet might have chosen to speak of religious, civic, intellectual, moral, physical, social and domestic duties; he might have indicated what our duties are in regard to many virtues and vices; none of this material is directly touched upon; how do you account for his selection and rejection of material in a subject where material is so plentiful?

8. Is there anything original in this poem? Is there anything in the classical literature of Greece and Rome that has the same spirit as this ode? Can you mention any other great poet who might have written this ode? Would the poem if appearing now for the first time be likely to command as great admiration as it has in fact commanded?

9. Is the ode the best form for the material of this poem? Why should it not have been a sermon or a hymn? Is the ode a dignified form of verse? Name other great odes and compare them with this in form and substance.

10. State what reasons account, in your opinion, for the statement that "all lovers of Wordsworth have, or ought to have by heart," the *Ode to Duty.*

11. Is this ode purely lyrical, or has it dramatic or epic qualities? Compare it in this respect with Gray's "*The Bard.*"

12. Is it a poem of *Perception, Feeling, Thought,* or *Action ?*

13. Is the poem intended to impress us chiefly as a work of artistic beauty, of elevating morality, or of profound truth?

14. How does a sonnet differ from an ode? Can you give any reason why the substance of this ode might not have been as well embodied in a sonnet ?

15. The central idea of this poem might have been worked out concretely in a tale similar to *Michael.* What is the advantage of this comparatively abstract method ! What relieves this poem from the charge of being an abstract moral essay in verse ?

16. To what extent is this poem subjective ?

17. Is the poem a result to any degree of the historical and social circumstances of Wordsworth's day, or does it rest upon less fleeting foundations ?

18. Is there anything remarkable about the use of capitals or the punctuation of the poem? If so do these peculiarities seem to you to be in keeping with the substance ?

19. Are there any words or forms of words used in the ode that would not be used in (*a*) *prose* (of the grade of Macaulay's Essays) ; (*b*) *conversation ?*

20. Are there any words used that Pope, Gray or Tennyson would reject as unpoetical or prosy ?

21. Are there any words that seem to be chosen less from the fact that they say precisely what the poet means than because they suit the exigencies of rhyme, metre, rhythm, euphony, or poetic diction ?

22. There sometimes appears a curious felicity of expression in Wordsworth's poems, beautiful junctures of words not in themselves remarkable for beauty : can you point out such here ?

23. Indicate any epithets or other words that strike you as strong or picturesque.

24. What proportion of words here are of foreign origin ! How do the percentages of English and borrowed words in this work compare with the average percentages of literary works ?

25. In the *order* of words and phrases are there many departures from the English prose order ? What is Spencer's *principle of economic order* ? Do the inversions here seem to be for economy of effort in understanding or from exigencies of verse ?

26. Explain clearly what Wordsworth means by the following expressions ; simplify for the understanding of a child if possible :

    (a) " *Daughter of the Voice of God.*"
    (b)   " *Who art victory and law*
           When empty terrors overawe."
    (c) " *Who do thy work ; and know it not.*"
    (d) " *The kindly impulse.*"
    (e) " *When love is an unerring light.*"
    (f) " *No Sport if every random gust.*"
    (g) " *Unchartered freedom.*"
    (h) " *The weight of chance desires.*"
    (i) " *My hopes no more must change their name.*"
    (j) " *Thou dost preserve the stars from wrong.*"
    (k) " *The confidence of reason.*"

27. Are the sentences used long or short, loose or periodic ?

28. Does the length of the sentences fit well with the length of the line, judging by the number of unstopt and of end-stopt lines ?

2. Point out and name every figure or device of language used by the poet in this ode, and indicate the effect of each. Develop the comparisons by indicating the resemblances and the differences between the things compared.

30. If English were to you an unknown tongue, and if this ode were read to you with good voice, feeling, and general expression, do you think it would impress you as a pleasant tune? Would it stand on its merits as music? Would the "tunes of speech" running through it convey to you any inkling of its tenor, feeling, thought?

31. Justify or criticize the following rhymes: *God—rod; love—reprove; free—humanity; be—security; wise—sacrifice.* A famous critic, Palgrave, says, "we should require finish in proportion to brevity;" how might Wordsworth have defended his ode with reference to this canon?

32. What is the artistic justification of the monotonous iambic tetrameters ending in a dragging hexameter?

33. Are all the feet iambic? Illustrate the truth that emphasis may be given by using an irregular foot. In *Sir Galahad* Tennyson changes the whole movement of the sense by this simple device:

"They réel, they róll in clánging lísts,
And whén the tíde of cómbat stánds,
Pérfume and flówers fáll in shówers,
That lightly ráin from ládies hánds."

34. Define satisfactorily the term *rhythm.* Is metre rhythm? Is rhythm a matter of *duration, intervals, loudness, pitch,* or *tone-colour?* Is it concerned with *syllables, words, phrases, lines* or *stanzas?* Illustrate from this ode.

35. In what respects do you fancy you discern *harmony* or *keeping* between the subject-matter and the versification of this ode?

36. Even the most thoughtful poetry is usually imbued with emotion : our emotions may be roughly classified as *sublime*, (pertaining to powerful and elevated objects), *common*, (pertaining to our likes and dislikes for nature and human nature in the ordinary relations of life), and *passionate*, (pertaining to the animal instincts and to the darker phases of the human heart). Of which order are the emotions af this ode? In this respect is this ode a representative work of the author? Give names to the main emotions evoked by the ode, and account for their order.

37. What constitutes the poetic charm peculiar to this poem?

38. Would the moral tone of this poem be universally regarded as sound and right?

39. Make an elocutionary analysis of the poem on the following table:

Rate	Pitch.	ODE TO DUTY.	Voice.	Force.	Expression.
		Stern Daughter of the Voice of God!			
		O Duty! if that name thou love			
		Who art a light to guide, a rod			
		To check the erring, and reprove ;			
		Thou, who art victory and law			
		When empty terrors overawe;			
		From vain temptations dost set free ;			
		And calm'st the weary strife of frail			
		humanity!			
		There are who ask not if thine eye			
		Be on them ; who, in love and truth,			
		Where no misgiving is, rely			
		Upon the genial sense of youth :			
		Glad Hearts! without reproach or blot ;			
		Who do thy work, and know it not :			
		Long may the kindly impulse last !			
		But Thou, if they should totter, teach			
		them to stand fast !			
		Serene will be our days and bright,			
		And happy will our nature be,			
		When love is an unerring light,			
		And joy its own security.			

Rate.	Pitch.	(Continued).	Voice.	Force.	Expression.

And they a blissful course may hold
Even now, who, not unwisely bold,
Live in the spirit of this creed ;
Yet seek thy firm support, according to
  their need.

I, loving freedom, and untried ;
No sport of every random gust,
Yet being to myself a guide,
Too blindly have reposed my trust ;
And oft, when in my heart was heard
Thy timely mandate, I deferred
The task, in smoother walks to stray :
But thee I now would serve more strictly,
  if I may.

Through no disturbance of my soul,
Or strong compunction in me wrought,
I supplicate for thy control ;
But in the quietness of thought :
Me this unchartered freedom tires :
I feel the weight of chance-desires :
My hopes no more must change their name,
I long for a repose that ever is the same.

Stern Lawgiver! yet thou dost wear
The Godhead's most benignant grace ;
Nor know we anything so fair
As is the smile upon thy face :
Flowers laugh before thee on their beds
And fragrance in thy footing treads ;
Thou dost preserve the Stars from wrong,
And the most ancient Heavens, through
  Thee, are fresh and strong.

To humbler functions, awful Power!
I call thee: I myself commend
Unto thy guidance from this hour ;
Oh, let my weakness have an end !
Give unto me, made lowly wise,
The spirit of self-sacrifice ;
The confidence of reason give ;
And in the light of truth thy bondman let
  me live !

NOTE.—In the columns at the sides indicate the directions for reading by such terms as *fast, moderate, slow ; high, middle, low ; pure, orotund ; loud, medium, low ; solemn, fervent, sublime.*

In the text itself underline the emphatic **words**; mark rhetorical pauses by vertical lines; and indicate inflections by accents (` and ').

Add any necessary warnings concerning pronunciation and articulation.

40. State any features of this poem that seem to you to be distinctively Wordsworthian: could you in fact tell whether or not the poem deserves to be classed as a great work? Could you believe it to be the work of a poet of little genius? Give reasons. Write a list of adjectives that may qualify the word *style*, when *style* means characteristic literary expression of an author. From your list choose such terms as describe Wordsworth's style in this poem.

CHAPTER VII.

NOTES.

"I wish either to be considered as a teacher or as nothing."
—*Wordsworth.*

LANGDALE.

CHAPTER VII.

THE REVERIE OF POOR SUSAN.--Page 33.

Of this poem Wordsworth says, "The feeling therein developed gives importance to the action and situation, and not the action and situation to the feeling." He adds that his purpose is to excite the interest of the reader without the use of "gross and violent stimulants."

"*Poor Susan*" not only excites our compassion for the unfortunate, but lends dignity to the lower class by showing that they may have tender and even poetic sensibilities such as the touching recollections and the vivid imagination of this poor outcast.

Wordsworth's biographer in the *English Men of Letters Series*, says: "He became, as one may say, the poet not of London considered as London, but of London considered as a part of the country. Like his own *Farmer of Tilsbury Vale*—

> In the throng of the Town like a stranger is he,
> Like one whose own Country's far over the sea ;
> And Nature, while through the great city he hies,
> Full ten times a day takes his heart by surprise.

Among the poems describing these sudden shocks of vision and memory, none is more exquisite than the *Reverie of Poor Susan*. The picture is one of those which come home to many a country heart with one of those sudden revulsions into the natural which philosophers assert to be the essence of human joy."

The poem exhibits his regard for the common people and his preference for nature.

"**Reverie**."—The French *rêver* means to *dream*. A *reverie* is a waking dream. When *dream* is used in a metaphorical sense it differs from *reverie* in the respect that *reverie* points to inconsecutiveness of thought, *dream* to unreality. Absent-minded persons fall into *reveries*, ambitious and ardent persons have *dreams*.

2. "**Wood Street**."—A street in London running north from Cheapside.

"**when daylight appears.**"—Suggests the wretched condition of Susan.

3. "**a Thrush.**"—"The song of the Thrush (or Throstle) is peculiarly rich, mellow and sustained, and is remarkable for the full purity of its intonation, and the variety of its notes."

"**three years.**"—This caged Thrush seems like a symbolical shadow of Poor Susan, there is something in common between them. Poets often use the numbers *three* and *seven*. Shakespeare says, "They say there's a divinity in odd numbers."

5. "**silence of morning.**"—The only silence known in parts of London. A good background for the Thrush's song.

6. "**a note of enchantment.**"—*Enchant*, as it happens, comes from *cano*, I sing; what is the association between *singing* and *enchantment?*

"**what ails her?**"—What causes this question?

8 "**volumes of vapour.**"—What actual phenomena may suggest *vapour* and *river* to Susan's enchanted fancy? What would "volumes of vapour" have meant in Susan's childhood home?

"**Lothbury.**"—A street behind the Bank of England.

9. "**Cheapside.**"—From M. E. *cheap* meaning *trade.*

12. "**like a dove's.**"—In what respects?

14. "**in heaven.**"—What is meant?

15. "**mist,**" "**river,**" "**hill**" and "**shade,**" are in distributive apposition with "they:" note the expressions in stanza 2 to which these allude.

16. "**will not.**"—Suggests the reluctance with which Susan relinquishes her reverie: the roar of London has drowned the enchanter's song.

Show the reason of each stanza in the development of the poem.

Tell the story of Susan as suggested to your imagination by this poem.

Would the poem be improved by adding the following stanza as its conclusion?—

> "Poor Outcast! Return—to receive thee once more
> The house of thy father will open its door.
> And then once again, in thy plain russet gown,
> May'st hear the Thrush sing from a tree of its own."

It occurs in the first edition; what has been gained by its suppression?

WE ARE SEVEN.—(1798)—Page 33.

2. In the first edition of the *Lyrical Ballads* the first line of this poem is—

A simple child, dear brother Jim :

The following note is by Wordsworth :

" To return to '*We are Seven*,' the piece that called forth this note, I composed it while walking in the grove at Alfoxden. My friends will not deem it too trifling to relate that while walking to and fro I composed the last stanza first, having begun with the last line. When it was all but finished, I came in and recited it to Mr. Coleridge and my sister, and said, 'A prefatory stanza must be added, and I should sit down to our little tea-meal with greater pleasure if my task were finished.' I mentioned in substance what I wished to be expressed, and Coleridge immediately threw off the stanza thus :

' A little child, dear brother Jem,' etc.

I objected to the rhyme, 'dear brother Jem,' as being ludicrous, but we all enjoyed the joke of hitching in our friend, James T——'s name, who was familiarly called Jem."

20. " Conway."—Town in North Wales.

24. " churchyard cottage."—State condition of family from evidence in poem.

38, 40. Middle rhyme, a device of emphasis.

52. " released."—Does this harmonize with the language of this simple child of eight? What preposition usually follows *release* in such constructions ?

53. " when the grass was dry."—What is this meant to suggest ?

60. " forced."—Notice the pathos of this simple view expressed in the passive voice.

66. " dead."—No syllable rhymes with *dead*. Account for irregularities of rhyme in first and last stanzas.

LUCY GRAY.—Page 36.

This ballad occurs in the second volume of the *Lyrical Ballads ;* the second title, *Solitude,* is not found in the first editions.

The Modern English ballad had its origin in the ancient ballads of the Northumbrian dialect. This form of verse has flourished in the southern

Scotch and in the northern English dialects for ages.   Bishop Percy,
Burns and Scott, gave the ballad a wonderful vogue in the reign of
George III., and many more recent writers have given us excellent work
fashioned more or less directly upon the old border songs.   The answer
to the question why Coleridge and other modern writers use the
archaisms of the northern ballad-writers in their own ballads, is that
the ballad had flourished so famously in the northern tongue that
modern writers judged it wise to preserve the forms in which it had
seen great days.

No description of these poems can do so much for the student as even
a careless study of Percy's *Reliques*, where he will find such poems as
*Sir Patrick Spence, King Cophetua and The Beggar Maid, Gernutus the
Jew of Venice,* and many more famous for beauty and literary interest.

The ballad was usually a song of love or war.   Its versification is
often, indeed usually, that of *Lucy Gray*—a quatrain of two tetrameters
and two trimeters arranged alternately,   Usually only the second and
fourth lines rhyme.   The weakness of the versification of Lucy Gray
arises largely from the fact that in more than a dozen instances the
accent falls upon a weak word, such as *a, the, to, there, in, from, by ;* one
line reads—

"Into the middle of the plank,"

and unless care is taken to shift the stress away from the syllables *to* and
of, the effect is absurd.   In the last stanza those who feel the beauty of
the poem will be careful to read it so as to avoid making it sound
ridiculous : (indeed this is true of nearly every stanza :) *to* in the first
line of it, *is* in the second, and *you* in the third will not bear the stress
their position implies.

By common consent a ballad must be simple and direct : they usually
open abruptly ; they are fond of the numbers *three* and *seven.*   Coleridge's *Ancient Mariner* is the greatest ballad in English.   Heine's Ballads are perhaps the sweetest and tenderest in the world : there is a
beautiful translation in the Canterbury Series, but the German is very
easy.

2. What attitude does the poet take towards the story, judging from
the first stanza ?

8. Notice all the expressions that impress the feelings of solitude.

12, 13. Account for the apparent irrelevance.

34. "**But never reached the town.**" Is this abrupt or euphem-
istic ?

43. The old reading is interesting,—

> " And now they homeward turned, and cried,"

The next stanza began with—

> " Then downward from the steep hill's edge,"

Compare these readings with those in the text, and endeavour to put yourself in the place of the poet as he makes the changes.

MICHAEL.—Page 41.

Much has been said of the slurs and ridicule heaped upon Wordsworth because of his simple style and homely characters. In the *English Bards and Scotch Reviewers*, Byron indulges in a coarse and rather witty sketch of the poet, with a pointed allusion to the *Idiot Boy*, ending thus :

> " So close on each pathetic part he dwells,
> And each adventure so sublimely tells,
> That all who view the 'idiot in his glory,'
> Conceive the bard the hero of the story."

Wordsworth despised rank, (at least in his earlier days) and his defence is well expressed by Coleridge when he says, " I honour a wise and virtuous man without reference to the presence or absence of artificial advantages.' In Michael and in poems of similar motive, Wordsworth owes much to Burns. whom he greatly loved and heartily admired : he had the power, preëminent in Burns of touching the hearts of the refined classes with a powerful sense of their common humanity, he " astounded bosoms habitually enveloped in the thrice-piled folds of social reserve, by compelling them to tremble—nay, to tremble visibly— beneath the fearless touch of natural pathos." " Is there not the fifth act of a tragedy in every death-bed, though it were a peasant's, and a bed of heath ?" exclaims Carlyle. Wordsworth had the eye of sympathy which makes the Story of Michael as great and significant as the story of Macbeth, and while we may trust that Shakespeare had the larger sounder judgment in attaching more importance to the prominent and powerful, yet we must revere the grand democratic spirit of Wordsworth, Burns, Coleridge, and Carlyle.

A Pastoral poem is a narrative of simple rustic life, containing descriptions of nature, and of the manners and morals of peasants.

4. **"Green-head Ghyll."**—Ghyll or gill, a ravine.

7. "pastoral."—In its radical sense.

13. "kites."—A fierce bird of prey.

32. "led."—Ta'e....led.

38. "a few natural hearts."—Those who cannot like Wordsworth for his positive merits, should remember his negative merits : the meanness, the sensationalism, the nasty sentiment, the bad taste, the unnatural forced literary or bookish point of view are all absent.

45. "bodily frame."—Contrasted with *mind* in line 46.

47. "frugal."—Not self-indulgent, requiring little pleasure.

53. "subterraneous."—In the valley.

58-62. These lines are a harmonious symbol of his inner life ; " the traveller " is a less heroic type.

71. "hardship, skill or courage, joy or fear."—His own acts.

76. "Those fields, those hills."—See eight lines above.

94. "The one."—One of them.

101. "cleanly."—They were habitually clean.

115. "duly."—As regularly as the darkness required it.

117. "utensil."—L. *utensilis*=fit for use.

120. "uncounted."—The lamp by long association had become a friend, a character.

123. "with objects."—The worst misery is total lack of interest in things : but this never comes to these self-respecting people.

125. "by the light of this old lamp."—The lamp may be fancied to stand as a symbol of constant virtue, old-fashioned and far from gay, but trustworthy : it was a benign influence in the neighbourhood.

130. Worthy of Swinburne in imitative power.

131. "Easedale, Dunmail-Raise."—Ten miles south of Keswick.

142-159. What is the terror of old age from which Luke saved Michael?

160-177. To say that this passage is not poetical is to beg the whole question of Wordsworth's claims : Wordsworth himself was a man of great intellectual power, and as regards academic culture and literary associations "in the foremost files ;" yet he renounced the unquestioned fame of works like the *Ode to Duty* and *Laodamia,* to glory in works like *Michael.*

180. Criticize.

181. "coppice."—A thicket of brushwood.

217. "**but.**"—Only a.

225. "**patrimonial.**"—The continuity of the family adds greatly to the effect when the succession is disturbed.

229-242. This struggle with doubts, murmurs and uncharitableness, makes Michael human : but his triumph makes him noble. The refined morality of line 242 is a greater dignity than wealth or rank, Wordsworth means to tell us.

260. "**Parish-boy.**"—Depending on charity.

269. "**monies.**"—Expresses Isabel's feelings accurately.

283. "**the Boy should go to-night.**"—Why ?

326. "**melancholy.**"—Transferred epithet.

355. "**in us.**"—In our case.

364. Michael has as deep a sense of family continuity as an earl.

380. "**It looks as if.**"—The land was so identified with its owner that his imagination could grapple with no other condition.

389. "**Nay, Boy.**"—Dramatic touch : what does it suggest ?

393. This most pathetic line owes much to the context.

412. How is innocence a cause of energy in good deeds ?

415. What were the parts of this covenant ?

417. "**I shall love thee to the last.**"—He was eighty-four.

449-451. Coleridge admired Wordsworth for the number and beauty of his aphorisms.

455. Cf. line 45.

460. "**inheritance.**"—Appositive.

467. "**never lifted up a single stone.**"—What does this tell indirectly ?

469. "**that.**"—Cf. line 94, where the clumsy expression "*the one*" to which this clumsy demonstrative refers, is used.

476. "**a stranger's hand.**"—Michael's worst fears in regard to his boy and his estate are realized.

HEART-LEAP WELL.—(1800)—Page 56.

Of the origin of this story Wordsworth says : "My sister and I had passed the place a few weeks before in our wild winter journey from Lockburn on the banks of the Tees, to Grasmere. A peasant whom we met near the spot told us the story so far as concerned the name of the well and the hart, and pointed out the stones. Both the stones and the well are objects that can easily be missed ; the tradition by this time may be extinct in the neighbourhood : the man who related it to us was very old." Scott's " *Lady of the Lake* " appeared ten years later, and the first canto of it gives a description of the chase quite different from Wordsworth's. But Cowper in *The Task*, (Book III.) had spoken bitterly against the—

> " Detested sport,
> That owes its pleasures to another's pain."

Burns had wept over a field-mouse or a wounded hare : and many writers of sensibility, notably Bishop Butler, had spoken of the kindness men owe the lower animals. Butler and Agassiz both speak of a possible immortality for animals. While many poets warn us not to be unkind to helpless creatures, Coleridge takes a more positive strain in the story of the murdered albatross, and in a noble and popular passage says,

> " He prayeth well, who loveth well
> Both man and bird and beast.
> He prayeth best who loveth best
> All things both great and small."

And it is this universal love that makes men like Burns seem the best of men.

12. " **falcon.**"—The bird is also a hunter.

14. " **rout.**"—Band of hunters.

14. " **this morning.**"—Vivid use of adjective *this*.

18. " **veering.**"—Changing direction ; cf. *vibrate*.

22. " **chid.**"—Chide sometimes means *to cause to come or go*.

23. " **With suppliant gestures.**"—Not suitable diction.

28. " **not like an earthly Chase.**"—Why !

32. " **what death he died.**"—How.

51. " **rods**," also written *roods* : five yards and a half.

74. Does this stanza exaggerate ?

97. " **And I to this would add another tale.**—The unconscious humour of this appendage suggests the " happy happy liver " of the *Sky-Lark*.

100. " **To freeze the blood I have no ready arts.**"—" I could a tale unfold whose lightest word, would harrow up thy soul, freeze thy young blood."

120. The verbosity of this part throws doubt upon the opinion that there was. "matter for a second rhyme."

130. "**finest palace**," etc.—Is this stated as a fact?

140. "**And blood cries out for blood**."—Is this a generalization by the shepherd?

146. "**has been**."—Cf. *was*.

148. "**my simple mind**."—Is this the language a shepherd would use of himself? What different meanings has *simple?*

The last five stanzas of the shepherd's speech are imbued with tender imagination; is Wordsworth false to nature in this? Compare the characters of Adam and Corin, (Shakespeare's *As You Like It*, Act II, Sc. 3, and Act III, Sc. 2), with the characters of Wordsworth's peasants.

167-170. Are these lines intentionally or carelessly vague and periphrastic?

177. "**the milder day**."—"The larger heart, the kindlier hand."

180. "**what she shows, and what conceals**."—What nature in an angry mood makes clear as well as what she charitably covers over.

FIDELITY.—Page 62.

If the poet had chosen to call this poem by a less didactic title, it might be more popular. There is something natural and pleasing about the order in which the details of the first stanza are told. The description in stanzas three and four is so picturesque, simple and withal artistic, that one wishes the poet had given himself over to sensuous verse, and left moralizing to others. However, the lofty sentiment of the last stanza of the poem seems to justify Wordsworth's method. The general regard for the dog as a faithful companion of man, calls for poetical expression, and most people who are not "too clever by half," will like this simple poem on account of the sincere admiration it expresses for the hero.

Coleridge says of *Fidelity*: "The poem is for the greater part written in language as unraised and naked as any perhaps in the two volumes." He calls attention to the superior style of stanza four, and of the last half of the last stanza. Comparing these parts with the rest of the work, he exclaims: "Can any candid and intelligent mind hesitate in determining which of these best represents the tendency and native

character of the poet's genius?" He concludes that Wordsworth is sadly
cramped by his theories.

27. " cheer."—Sign of life.

29. " symphony."—Echoing harshly.

51. " whose."—Cf. "a triangle *whose sides.*"
Criticize the versification.

THE LEECH-GATHERER.—Page 65.

Of this poem Mr. R. H. Hutton says it treats of Wordsworth's
favourite theme—'· the strength which the human heart has, or ought to
have, to contain itself in adverse circumstances." Again he says, " *The
Leech-Gatherer* has much less of buoyancy than the earlier poems, and
sometimes here and there the stateliness of the later style." Coleridge
finds in this work all the characteristic defects and merits of its author.
Wordsworth in a characteristic note says: "I describe myself as having
been exalted to the highest pitch of delight by the joyousness and
beauty of Nature ; and then as depressed, even in the midst of those
beautiful objects, to the lowest dejection and despair. A young poet in
the midst of the happiness of Nature is described as overwhelmed by
the thoughts of the miserable reverses which have befallen the happiest
of all men, namely, poets. I think of this till I am so deeply impressed
with it that I consider the manner in which I am rescued from my dejection and despair almost as an interposition of Providence. A person
reading the poem with feelings like mine will have been awed and con-
trolled, expecting something spiritual or supernatural. What is brought
forward? A lonely place, 'a pond, by which an old man *was,* far from
all house or home:' not *stood,* nor *sat,* but *was*—the figure presented in
the most naked simplicity possible. The feeling of spirituality or
supernaturalness is again referred to as being strong in my mind in this
passage. How came he here? thought I, or what can he be doing? I
then describe him, whether ill or well is not for me to judge with perfect
confidence ; but this I *can* confidently affirm, that though I believe God
has given me a strong imagination, I cannot conceive a figure more impressive than that of an old man like this, the survivor of a wife and ten
children, travelling alone among the mountains and all lonely places,
carrying with him his own fortitude, and the necessities which an unjust
state of society has laid upon him. You speak of his speech as tedious.
Everything is tedious when one does not read with the feelings of the

author. . . . It is in the character of the old man to tell his story, which an impatient reader must feel tedious But, good heavens! such a figure, in such a place; a pious, self-respecting, miserably infirm and pleased old man, telling such a tale!"

8. "Stock-dove."—A wild-pigeon.

9. "Jay."—A handsomely coloured bird with a crest.

9. "Magpie."—Allied to the Jays.

25. "from the might," etc—The excess brings reäction.

46. "Chatterton."—Thomas Chatterton died by his own hand in 1770, aged seventeen. He pretended to have discovered in a muniment room at Bristol, the *Death of Sir Charles Bawdin*, and other poems, by a monk, Thomas Rowley: these raised a controversy.

49. "Following his plow."—Read Carlyle's *Essay on Burns*.

50. "By our own spirits are we deified."—The power is from within, not from circumstances.

52. "despondency and madness."—Is this view Wordsworth's belief, or a dramatic expression of a mood?

56. "untoward."—Vexatious.

59. "that ever wore grey hairs."—What characteristic defect?

60. "As a huge Stone."—How is this comparison justified and rendered credible?

62. "the same."—What peculiarity of diction?

65. "Sea-beast."—Why this simile within a simile?

78. "as a Cloud."—Note all the points of likeness.

137. "blended,"—Observe the change of movement and of emotion effected by the double rhyme.

What is the effect of ending a stanza of pentameters with a hexameter? Be careful not to speak too positively of the intellectual value of sounds.

Indicate the stanzas that seem to you least poetical and most poetical.

TO THE DAISY.—Page 73.

Wither, a poet ridiculed by Pope in the *Dunciad*, is the author of the following verses, which Wordsworth prefixed as a keynote to this song to the Daisy:

By a daisy whose leaves spread
Shut when Titan goes to bed,
Or a shady bush or tree,
She could more infuse in me
Than all Nature's beauties can
In some other wiser man.

Her divine skill taught me this,
That from everything I saw
I could some instruction draw,
And raise pleasure to the height
Through the meanest object's sight.
By the murmur of a spring,
Or the least bough's rustling.

It will be observed that the lines are very much in the spirit of our author, and suggest the conclusion of his great *Ode*.

This poem offers an example of the general truth concerning Wordsworth's relation to nature—he was less the poet who describes than the interpreter : the daisy is not merely a sweet little flower, but it is a local habitation and a name, a symbol for those airy nothings that lived in his own spirit.

8. " **Nature's love partake of thee.**"—Love nature through this flower.

18. " **morrice train.**"—(Sp. morisco=moorish.) A grotesque holiday dance.

26. " **mews.**"—A confined place.

27. " **wanton Zephyrs.**"—The amorous west-wind.

31. " **thy fame.**"—Chaucer's verses to the daisy are beautiful.

38. " **fare**".—To fare at length=to be stretched on the grass. Cf. Gray's *Elegy*.

45. " **apprehension.**"—Not a happy choice of word.

62. " **by dews opprest.**"—" Dew-drops are the gems of morning, but the tears of mournful eve."

75. " **lover of the sun.**"—*Daisy = Day's eye.*

77. " **leveret.**"—A young hare.

TO THE SAME.—Page 75.

This is not the second but the third song of this series. Matthew Arnold omits the second from his selections : it is interesting to compare it with the other two, in order to judge whether the critic rejected it on account of inferiority :

TO THE SAME FLOWER.

WITH little here to do or see
Of things that in the great world be,
Daisy, again I talk to thee,
  For thou art worthy,
Thou unassuming common-place
Of nature, with that homely face,
And yet with something of a grace
  Which Love makes for thee !

Oft on the dappled turf at ease
I sit and play with similes.
Loose types of things through all degrees,
  Thoughts of thy raising ;
And many a fond and idle name
I give to thee for praise or blame,
As in the humour of the game,
  While I am gazing.

A nun demure of lowly port ;
Or sprightly maiden of Love's court,
In thy simplicity the sport
  Of all temptations ;
A queen in crown of rubies drest ;
A starveling in a scanty vest ;
Are all, as seems to suit thee best,
  Thy appellations.

A little Cyclops, with one eye
Staring to threaten and defy,
That thought comes next—and instantly
  The freak is over,
The shape will vanish—and behold
A silver shield with boss of gold,
That spreads itself, some faery bold
  In fight to cover !

I see thee glittering from afar,
And then thou art a pretty star ;
Not quite so fair as many are
    In heaven above thee,
Yet like a star with glittering crest,
Self-poised in air thou seem'st to rest ;—
May peace come never to his nest
    Who shall reprove thee !

Bright *flower !* for by that name at last,
When all my reveries are past,
I call thee, and to that cleave fast !
    Sweet silent creature,
That breath'st with me in sun and air,
Do thou, as thou art wont, repair
My heart with gladness and a share
    Of thy meek nature !

TO A HIGHLAND GIRL.—Page 76.

The author is full of enthusiasm for the beauty of a Highland lass whom he saw in a northerly excursion. One might fancy the motive of the piece to be merely an artistic portrait of the child, but there is too much of

> " The homely sympathy that heeds
> The common life our nature breeds,"

to admit of this opinion. While he takes perhaps a little too superior and scientific a relation to the girl to strike our sympathies deeply, there are proofs that he felt that touch of nature which makes the whole world kin.

5. "**consenting.**"—In radical sense: in harmony with her well-being.

11. "**a quiet road.**"—In Sonnet XXV. Wordsworth says, "My little boat rocks in its harbour, lodging peaceably." *Road* has the stem-notion of *riding;* one meaning is a place where boats may ride at anchor. Sketch a picture (however rudely) indicating the position of each detail of this picture.

13. "**together do ye seem.**"—The girl and her surroundings.

15-16. Notice the light, fanciful, and tender use of a sober imagination.

36. "**seemliness complete.**"—The pleasing grace of a good heart

unsullied by any evil, and having the absence of restraint that Raphael admired in infants.

37. "**about thee**."—As if the charm were an illusion, a glamour, not assignable to her material being : this is the language of one enchanted.

38. "**such as springs**."—The passage has for its general notion : the girl could not speak English freely, but the very effort showed her beauty in a more interesting light.

50-51. "**thee**"—"**your**."—Which pronoun prevails in the poem ?

69. "**her**."—Memory. At seventy-three the poet writes that his prophecy that memory would preserve this picture for his pleasure had "through God's goodness been realized." Cf. line 70 *Tintern Abbey*.

STEPPING WESTWARD.—Page 78.

The beautiful interpretation of the greeting illustrates the poetic method :

"In common things that round us lie
 Some random truths he can impart."

2. "**westward**."—Compare George Meredith's *Earth's Preference*, (page 108, line 4) ; also the *Ode on Immortality*, (page 99, line 78). The *east*, in his poetic vocabulary signifies *heaven from which we come*, *westward* signifies *toward our destiny*.

3. "**wildish**."—Rather ill-directed.

11. "**all**."—Adverb.

14. "**A sound of something without place or bound**."—Suggesting a large abstract meaning.

THE SOLITARY REAPER.—Page 79.

The date of this work is 1803. When Keats was seven years old this poem was written, and when Keats was eleven *The Solitary Reaper* was published. The similarity in tone, spirit and details between Keats' *Ode to a Nightingale* and this work is so obvious as to render their dates interesting. (See Chapter V.)

17. "**Hebrides**."—That is, lonely western isles.

AT THE GRAVE OF BURNS.—Page 81.

This touching tribute to the memory of Burns is written in metre most strikingly reminding us of that poet : it is the metre of *The Mountain Daisy* itself, as well as of many of his other songs.   There is something paradoxical in Wordsworth's love of Burns, when we consider the vulgar estimate of the character of the latter which prevailed in the early part of this century.   It is much to the credit of Wordsworth's insight that he was one of the first to recognize the greatness of soul of the plowman-poet.   The noble essay on Burns by Carlyle, (written before the prose of the great moralist had become irregular and eccentric) is at once a charming piece of English and wonderful piece of critical sympathy : the following passage gives some idea of the view held in common by Carlyle and our author :

" We had something to say on the public moral character of Burns ; but this also we must forbear.   We are far from regarding him as guilty before the world, as guiltier than the average ; nay from doubting that he is less guilty than one of ten thousand.   Tried at a tribunal far more rigid than that where the *Plebiscita* of common civic reputations are pronounced, he has seemed to us even there less worthy of blame than of pity and wonder.   But the world is habitually unjust in its judgments of such men ; unjust on many grounds, of which this one may be stated as the substance : it decides, like a court of law, by dead statutes ; and not positively but negatively, less on what is done right, than on what is or is not done wrong.   Not the few inches of deflection from the mathematical orbit, which are so easily measured: but the *ratio* of these to the whole diameter, constitutes the real aberration.   This orbit may be a planet's, its diameter the breadth of the solar system ; or it may be a city hippodrome ; nay the circle of a ginhorse, its diameter a score of feet or paces.   But the inches of deflection only are measured : and it is assumed that the diameter of the ginhorse, and that of the planet, will yield the same ratio when compared with them !   Here lies the root of many a blind, cruel condemnation of Burnses, Swifts, Rousseaus, which one never listens to with approval.   Granted, the ship comes into harbor with shrouds and tackle damaged ; the pilot is blameworthy ; he has not been all-wise and all-powerful : but to know *how* blameworthy, tell us first whether his voyage has been round the Globe, or only to Ramsgate and the Isle of Dogs.

" With our readers in general, with men of right feeling anywhere, we are not required to plead for Burns.   In pitying admiration he lies enshrined in all our hearts, in a far nobler mausoleum than that one of marble ; neither will his Works, even as they are, pass away from the memory of men.   While the Shakespeares and Miltons roll on like mighty rivers through the country of Thought, bearing fleets of traffickers and assiduous pearl-fishers on their waves ; this little Valclusa Fountain will also arrest our eye : for this also is of Nature's own and most cunning workmanship, bursts from the depths of the earth, with a full gushing current, into the light of day ; and often will the traveller turn aside to drink of its clear waters, and muse among its rocks and pines ! "

23. **" glinted."**—Read Burns' *The Daisy*.

29. **" be."**—Old indicative form.

30. **" soon."**—See last stanza of *The Daisy*, by Burns.

31. **" The prompt, the brave."**—Quick and violent champion of freedom.

40. **" the current."**—Of life.

42. **" Criffel."**—Near Skiddaw.

43. **" Skiddaw."**—Hill four miles north of Keswick.

46. **" diversely."**—Divers (some times spelled diverse) took accent on first.

48. **" the main fibres."**—The essential respects.

53. **" poor Inhabitant below."**—The quotation touchingly applied to its author.   (See *The Bard's Epitaph*).

55. **" sate."**—Săt ; rarely säte.

56. **" gowans."**—Gaelic for flower ; especially the daisy.

59. **"of knowledge graced by fancy what a rich repast."**— Delightful conversation.

77. **" devious."**—From L. *de* and *via*.

85. **" ritual."**—Music of a noble ceremony.

87. **" Seraphim."**--Cherubs are infant angels.

Read Campbell's beautiful *Ode to the Memory of Burns*: one stanza reads :

> " O deem not, 'midst this worldly strife,
> An idle art the poet brings :
> Let high Philosophy control,
> And sages calm, the stream of life,
> 'Tis he refines its fountain-springs,
> The nobler passions of the soul."

18

THOUGHTS.—Page 84.

The refined humility, the grace and sympathy of judgment shown in Wordsworth's estimate of the character of Burns, go far to prove that Ruskin's opinion of him as helpful only to the sinless, was shallow and ill-considered.

The poem is a climax in the radical sense of the word, a veritable ladder from the humble dwelling of Burns "to the gates of Heaven," and the broad clear atmosphere of the last stanzas is reminiscent of Burns at his best.

6. "**The Vision.**"—Read the poem by Burns.

17. "**Where gentlest judgments may misdeem.**"—Where the utmost charity may be too harsh a judge.

40. "**Image.**"—His picture of Burns.

45. "**shames the Schools.**"—Conventional poetry.

TO THE CUCKOO.—Page 86.

The pleasing power of the simplest natural phenomena to arouse those recollections of early childhood which to him were intimations of another world, is set forth fully and grandly in his great *Ode* ; this little poem bears some such relation to the *Ode on Intimations of Immortality*, as *Break, Break, Break*, bears to the *In Memoriam*. The main outlines of the *Ode* are here in miniature, and the elevation of the last stanza shows that mingling of the child-philosopher and the student-philosopher which makes the ending of the *Ode* so obscurely impressive. In Arnold's Selections the following stanzas are added under the heading, *The Cuckoo Again:*

> Yes, it was the mountain Echo,
> Solitary, clear, profound,
> Answering to the shouting Cuckoo,
> Giving to her sound for sound !
>
> Unsolicited reply
> To a babbling wanderer sent ;
> Like her ordinary cry,
> Like——but oh, how different!
>
> Hears not also mortal life ?
> Hear not we, unthinking creatures !
> Slaves of folly, love, or strife—
> Voices of two different natures ?

Have not *we* too?—yes, we have
Answers, and we know not whence ;
Echoes from beyond the grave,
Recognized intelligence !

Often as thy inward ear
Catches such rebounds, beware !—
Listen, ponder, hold them dear ;
For of God,—of God they are.

Wordsworth wrote a sonnet to the same bird, and a poem entitled *The Cuckoo at Laverna :* both are interesting for comparison with the verses above.

2. "**New-comer.**"—The lark, the cuckoo, and the swallow are the birds of early spring.

29. "**golden time.**"—Cf. *visionary hours* in line 13.

YARROW VISITED.—Page 87.

The famous ballad by Hamilton entitled *The Braes of Yarrow*, may be found in Percy's *Reliques*, Second Series, Book III, Number 24. It was itself an imitation of "an old Scottish ballad on a similar subject, with the same burden to each stanza." The three poems on Yarrow by Wordsworth, were written respectively in the years 1803, 1814, and 1831 : they are the direct offspring of Hamilton's ballad, as will be seen by the allusions to it in the first of them. In the Mother country they are regarded with great favour, and indeed there is a repose, a strong unquestionable sense of beauty, a sober right-minded joy in *Yarrow Visited*, that makes one think of pictures of English landscapes.

For comparison, and on account of their literary interest, the three poems shoud be read as a series.

YARROW UNVISITED.

(See the various Poems the Scene of which is laid upon the Banks of the Yarrow; in particular the exquisite Ballad of Hamilton, beginning

"Busk ye, busk ye, my bonny, bonny bride
Busk ye, busk ye, my winsome Marrow !"—)

FROM Stirling Castle we had seen
The mazy Forth unravelled ;
Had trod the banks of Clyde, and Tay,
And with the Tweed had travelled ;

And when we came to Clovenford,
Then said my " *winsome Marrow,*"
" What'er betide, we'll turn aside,
And see the Braes of Yarrow."

" Let Yarrow Folk, *frae* Selkirk Town,
Who have been buying, selling,
Go back to Yarrow, 'tis their own ;
Each Maiden to her Dwelling !
On Yarrow's banks let herons feed,
Hares couch, and rabbits burrow !
But we will downward with the Tweed,
Nor turn aside to Yarrow.

" There's Galla Water, Leader Haughs,
Both lying right before us ;
And Dryborough, where with chiming Tweed
The Lintwhites sing in chorus ;
There's pleasant Tiviot-dale, a land
Made blithe with plow and harrow :
Why throw away a needful day
To go in search of Yarrow ?

" What's Yarrow but a River bare,
That glides the dark hills under ?
There are a thousand such elsewhere
As worthy of your wonder."
—Strange words they seemed of slight and scorn;
My True-love sighed for sorrow ;
And looked me in the face, to think
I thus could speak of Yarrow !

" Oh ! green," said I, " are Yarrow's Holms,
And sweet is Yarrow's flowing !
Fair hangs the apple frae the rock,
But we will leave it growing.
O'er hilly path, and open Strath,
We'll wander Scotland thorough ;
But, though so near, we will not turn
Into the Dale of Yarrow.

"Let beeves and home-bred kine partake
The sweets of Burn-mill meadow ;
The swan on still St. Mary's Lake
Float double, swan and shadow !
We will not see them ; will not go,
To-day, nor yet to-morrow ;
Enough if in our hearts we know
There's such a place as Yarrow.

"Be Yarrow Stream unseen, unknown !
It must, or we shall rue it :
We have a vision of our own ;
Ah ! why should we undo it ?
The treasured dreams of times long past,
We'll keep them, winsome Marrow !
For when we're there, although 'tis fair,
'Twill be another Yarrow.

"If Care with freezing years should come,
And wandering seem but folly,—
Should we be loth to stir from home,
And yet be melancholy ;
Should life be dull, and spirits low.
'Twill soothe us in our sorrow,
That earth has something yet to show,
The bonny Holms of Yarrow !"

YARROW REVISITED.

[The following Stanzas are a memorial of a day passed with Sir Walter Scott, and other Friends visiting the Banks of the Yarrow under his guidance, immediately before his departure from Abbotsford for Naples.]

THE gallant Youth, who may have gained,
Or seeks, a "winsome Marrow,"
Was but an infant in the lap
When first I looked on Yarrow ;
Once more, by Newark's Castle-gate
Long left without a warder,
I stood, looked, listened, and with Thee,
Great Minstrel of the Border !

Grave thoughts ruled wide on that sweet day,
   Their dignity installing
In gentle bosoms, while sere leaves
   Were on the bough, or falling ;
But breezes played, and sunshine gleamed—
   The forest to embolden ;
Reddened the fiery hues, and shot
   Transparence through the golden.

For busy thoughts the Stream flowed on
   In foaming agitation ;
And slept in many a crystal pool
   For quiet contemplation :
No public and no private care
   The freeborn mind enthralling,
We made a day of happy hours,
   Our happy days recalling.

Brisk Youth appeared, the Morn of youth,
   With freaks of graceful folly—
Life's temperate Noon, her sober Eve,
   Her Night not melancholy ;
Past, present, future, all appeared
   In harmony united,
Like guests that meet, and some from far,
   By cordial love invited.

And if, as Yarrow, through the woods
   And down the meadow ranging,
Did meet us with unaltered face,
   Though we were changed and changing ;
If, *then*, some natural shadows spread
   Our inward prospect over,
The soul's deep valley was not slow
   Its brightness to recover.

Eternal blessings on the Muse,
   And her divine employment !
The blameless Muse, who trains her Sons
   For hope and calm enjoyment ;

Albeit sickness, lingering yet,
  Has o'er their pillow brooded ;
And Care waylays their steps—a Sprite
  Not easily eluded.

For thee, O SCOTT ! compelled to change
  Green Eildon-hill and Cheviot
For warm Vesuvio's vine-clad slopes,
  And leave thy Tweed and Teviot
For mild Sorrento's breezy waves ;
  May classic Fancy, linking
With native Fancy her fresh aid, ·
  Preserve thy heart from sinking !

O ! while they minister to thee,
  Each vying with the other,
May Health return to mellow Age
  With Strength her venturous brother ;
And Tiber, and each brook and rill
  Renowned in song and story,
With unimagined beauty shine,
  Nor lose one ray of glory !

For Thou, upon a hundred streams,
  By tales of love and sorrow,
Of faithful love, undaunted truth,
  Hast shed the power of Yarrow ;
And streams unknown, hills yet unseen,
  Wherever they invite Thee,
At parent Nature's grateful call,
  With gladness must requite Thee.

A gracious welcome shall be thine,
  Such looks of love and honour
As thy own Yarrow gave to me
  When first I gazed upon her ;
Beheld what I had feared to see,
  Unwilling to surrender
Dreams treasured up from early days,
  The holy and the tender.

And what, for this frail world, were all
    That mortals do or suffer,
Did no responsive harp, no pen,
    Memorial tribute offer ?
Yea, what were mighty Nature's self ?
    Her features, could they win us,
Unhelped by the poetic voice
    That hourly speaks within us ?

Nor deem that localized Romance
    Plays false with our affections ;
Unsanctifies our tears—made sport
    For fanciful dejections :
Oh, no ! the visions of the past
    Sustain the heart in feeling
Life as she is—our changeful Life,
    With friends and kindred dealing.

Bear witness, Ye, whose thoughts that day
    In Yarrow's groves were centred ;
Who through the silent portal arch
    Of mouldering Newark enter'd ;
And clomb the winding stair that once
    Too timidly was mounted
By the "last Minstrel," (not the last !)
    Ere he his Tale recounted.

Flow on for ever, Yarrow Stream !
    Fulfil thy pensive duty,
Well pleased that future Bards should chant
    For simple hearts thy beauty ;
To dream-light dear while yet unseen,
    Dear to the common sunshine,
And dearer still, as now I feel,
    To memory's shadowy moonshine !

Hutton says : "Mr. Arnold places all the really first-rate work of
Wordsworth in the decade between 1798 and 1808. I think he is right
here. But I should put Wordsworth's highest perfection of style much
nearer the later date than the earlier." In a contrast of the earliest
with the latest *Yarrow*, Hutton shows us with much skill the changes

that had come over Wordsworth's style in twenty-eight years. The first poem is self-contained, swift, bare and rapid, the third is slow and sweet, rich, free and mellow, and gives no such impression of powerful repression as the first. The criticism may be extended to apply to a great deal of the poet's earlier and later work.

In the *Yarrow Unvisited*, the poet and his sister decide not to visit the famous stream for fear their lovely picture of it got from what they had read and imagined should be injured by the scene itself. The poet first visited Yarrow in the company of the Ettrick shepherd, Hogg, author of that sweetest of ballads, *Kilmeny* : the second poem records the impressions of this occasion. The third poem is "a memorial of the very last visit Scott (in company with Wordsworth) ever paid, not to Yarrow only, but to any scene in that land which he had so loved and glorified."

Just as the first is strong and almost humourous, the second strong and sweet, so the third is sweet and sad, and the three have a unity which suggests that Wordsworth's life gave vital unity to all his work.

6. **"An image that hath perished !"** The imaginary Yarrow of his first poem.

15. **"Saint Mary's Lake."**—In *Yarrow Unvisited*, he says :

> "The swan on still Saint Mary's Lake
> Float double, swan and shadow !"

This is the couplet that Scott misquoted by pluralizing *swan*. Wordsworth corrects him, and adds that the swan with no companion but its own reflection is a symbol of the utter loneliness of the scene : but Scott was misled by taking *float* for an assertive word in the plural, whereas it depends on *let*.

Wordsworth's note concludes with this sentence: "I have hardly ever known any one except myself who had a true eye for nature—one that thoroughly understood her meanings and her teachings."

27. **"the famous Flower of Yarrow Vale."**—The poet is showing interest in the legends of the place ; that they were not so familiar to him as to Scott is shown by using an expression to denote the youth who was killed, which was regularly applied not to the youth but to the lady.

33. **"The Water-wraith."**—Mr. Rolfe quotes from an old Yarrow ballad :

"Scarce was he gone, I saw his ghost ;
It vanished with a shriek of sorrow ;
Thrice did the water-wraith ascend
And gave a doleful groan through Yarrow."

57. Newark's Towers."—A castle on the banks of the Yarrow near
Selkirk, made famous by Scott's *Lay of the Last Minstrel.*
Wordsworth uses some pet thoughts again and again. Lines 75-78
make one think of "the light that never was ;" and the last three lines
of the poem remind one of the conclusion of *The Highland Girl.*

TO A SKYLARK.—Page 90.

In the sympathy bred by his love of nature, the poet contrasts the
happy elevation of the bird with his own lowly lot, and aspires to
heavenly joys and triumphs ; but reflection comes to his aid, and instead
of feeling disappointed when his dream is seen to be an illusion, he
determines to take the fact of the bird's joy, not as a call to present
happiness, but as a promise of future raptures.

21. "thou would'st be loth to be such a traveller as I."—This
expression suffers from some confusion, it probably means that the lark
would not willingly plod as he must, but the concessive clause before
clashes with the meaning.

TO THE SAME.—Page 91.

In Palgrave's *Golden Treasury* this poem stands immediately before
The Skylark, by Shelley. This juxtaposition suggests the likeness and
the unlikeness of the poems and the poets.
Wordsworth's lines reveal a great joy in contemplating the bird of
morning ; his sober imagination thinks out the bird's thoughts, feels its
emotions with tender insight and poetic freshness, endows the gentle
creature with a soul and makes it the emblem of lofty spiritual aspiration : the romantic nightingale suffers by comparison with this bird of
light and truth : the moralist cannot conclude this perfect lyric without
a homely reference to the instincts of wisdom. The moral is worthy
and apposite, but a trifle prosy, in as much as readers who enjoy the
first sixteen lines would scarcely need the last two. Yet this is Wordsworth's method faithfully adhered to ; no bit of nature is so valuable as
an object of pleasure to the senses and the imagination that it has not a
higher value as a spiritual symbol, or even a moral symbol.

Shelley's *Skylark* is less the voice of a man than the glorious outburst of the bird itself translated into English verse, and scarcely either gaining or losing by the change : it is harmonious madness and upon it logic, to say nothing of morality, has about as much claim as upon the lark's own song : we care no more for the intellectual qualities of it than for the meaning of an Italian song: wherever sound and sense clash, sense stands gracefully aside, and beautiful sound prevails. A well known critic, the Professor of Logic in the University of Aberdeen, finds the poem wild and lacking in precision of thought ; This would seem to be its great charm, would it not, when one considers the harmony of style and subject matter. Critics have been found with so little feeling for poetic effects as to find fault with *The Cloud* on account of its cease-less changing of comparisons ; but no doubt they would think badly of nature herself for the fickleness of *her* clouds. What has a poet to do with profound lessons when writing an inspired ode to a skylark? Those who answer—nothing, he should give himself up to an intoxicating beauty, are disciples of Shelley : but whoever replies, beauty finds its perfect work only as the hand-maiden of right living, are Words-worthians.

8. **"the last point of vision."**—The lark wheels upward in a diminishing spiral curve, as if climbing to heaven by a circular stair case : on the top of this imaginary conical tower the bird pauses to flood the morning earth with song : frequently the bird is invisible, (having passed the point where it subtends the necessary angle for visibility) while its strong melodious voice is easily audible.

10. **" a never-failing bond."**—This bird appears to have forgotten mundane concerns in its ecstasy of worship, but in fact he is no mere ascetic, for on the ground far below is a little nest, (often in the imprint of a horse's hoof or a similar depression) containing his little feathered offspring, usually four or five in number. It is his love for these as much as his gratitude for sunlight and glorious skies that prompts his music, though one might fancy him to disregard the leafy earth and all therein.

15. **" A privacy of glorious light is thine."**—This fine paradox suggests the isolation of great and elevated minds, and strikes one as a trifle subjective.

17. The divine nightingale is described by Keats in just the manner to set forth Wordsworth's meaning. (*Vide* Chapter V.)

" What do the first two stanzas contribute towards bringing out the main idea ? "

ODE TO DUTY.—Page 95.

Being good now not by design but merely through habit, I desire to become able not only to do right but to do nothing that is not right.

Horace's *Ode to Fortune* (*O Diva Gratum, I, 35*), and **Gray's** *Ode to Adversity* are the poems upon which the poet tells us he modelled the *Ode to Duty*. While the three odes have a general resemblance, both in the calm dignity and thoughtful ardour of their matter, and in a corresponding regularity and seriousness of form, the differences are quite marked. The great sane nobility of the polished pagan shows no touch · of levity where levity would be forced, and the seriousness of Horace has the pathos of a cheerful writer, a pathos free from suspicion of mere dramatic effect.

> " Before thee stalks stern Fate, who joys to bear
> In iron hand the wedge—the spikes so dire,"

he says, addressing Fortune. His cynical view appears in the allusion " white-robed Faith, so seldom found," and the ode ends in a prayer for the success of Roman arms, embittered by despair of Roman virtue and religion: ·

> " Our iron age, well worthy of the name,
> What has it left undared !—when made a pause in guilt !
> Whose altar spared, by piety restrained ! "

The *Ode to Adversity* is a link between the other two ; there is hardly a sentiment that Horace might not have felt ; even the language is more classical than modern, the opening line,

> " Daughter of Jove, relentless power,"

being a keynote of the style ; yet, as will be best seen from the concluding and most elevated stanza, there is not lacking in this piece a modern spirit of love and forgiveness rarely met with in the ancient writings. In versification the resemblance between the two English poems will be observed:

> " Thy form benign, Oh goddess, wear,
> Thy milder influence impart,
> Thy philosophic train be there
> To soften, not to wound my heart.
> The generous spark extinct revive,
> Teach me to love, and to forgive,
> Exact my own defects to scan,
> What others are to feel, and know myself a Man. "

To praise the *Ode to Duty* is as needless as to praise Shakespeare's plays. Yet there is a danger that one may overlook some of its great qualities through enthusiasm over the others. The acuteness and comprehensiveness of intellect, which draws a clear line between freedom and mere license, and finds perfect liberty in a proud submission, the goodness of heart and will which accepts the implied restrictions with enthusiastic cheerfulness, the vigour of imagination which sees the universal law at work among those young-eyed cherubs the stars of heaven, the poetry that personifies the abstraction and clothes it with magnetic beauty, and withal the humility, the sweetness and light, the virility of this poem give it a rank that seems to us unassailable from even the most remote and dissimilar points of view, so that one can imagine Shakespeare, Horace or Plato reading it with as great pleasure as Lowell or Matthew Arnold.

2. "**Stern Daughter of the Voice of God.**"—Compare from the *Ode to Adversity* "daughter of Jove" and "stern, rugged nurse." The appropriateness of the expression " of the *voice* of God " will be seen when one reflects that the Christian view of the Deity would forbid the expression precisely analogous to Gray's. *Voice* means *expressed will*, *Daughter* is required for personification. Observe the economy of the order which gives us the concrete image in the first line and the abstract interpretation in the second.

16. "**kindly impulse.**"—Coming from inborn virtue.

24. "**this creed.**"—That right instincts are sufficient guides.

38. "**unchartered freedom.**"—Boys are happier under rational discipline than unrestrained.

48. "**the stars.**"—If a star were to violate a physical law it would produce untold disaster ; the comparison is not meant to be strictly scientific, of course. A law is merely a generalized statement of facts, not an edict that may be disobeyed. Whether or not man has free-will, the stars have none.

49. "**fresh and strong.**"—The notion that perpetual youth is the reward of right living is common in poetry, and, though discouraging perhaps to virtuous age, is pleasing and romantic. How often good old men call themselves boys. Read Oliver Wendell Holmes on " *The Boys.*"

55. "**the spirit of self-sacrifice.**"—The feeling that by not claiming his rights he was rewarded by greater rights. It has been said that no man has a right to claim all his rights.

ODE ON INTIMATIONS OF IMMORTALITY. —Page 97.

"To the attentive and competent reader the whole sufficiently explains itself," says Wordsworth in speaking of this famous *Ode*. There
is a general inclination among commentators to accept this saying and
to consider all readers attentive and competent. Coleridge (quoted by
Mr. Rolfe) says "The ode was intended for such readers only as had
been accustomed to watch the flux and reflux of their inmost nature, to
venture at times into the twilight realms of consciousness, and to feel a
deep interest in the modes of inmost being, to which they know that
the attributes of time and space are inapplicable and alien, but which
yet cannot be conveyed, save in symbols of time and space." So that
if any youthful reader should find that the piece does not "sufficiently
explain itself" he may justly conclude that his incompetency arises
from an insufficient watching of the flux and reflux of his inmost nature,
and an ignorance of metaphysics in general, or, to speak more clearly,
instead of being discouraged in proportion as he is befogged, he may
rest assured that the years that bring the philosophic mind will bring
as well his competency to grasp the meaning of this philosophical ode.

The estimate of Matthew Arnold will be found on page 24 of this book
and deserves careful reading. It is on the whole an adverse verdict :
that is to say it tends to lower the general opinion of great men as to
the rank of the poem. It has great weight as coming from a man of
great ability who was a devoted admirer of Wordsworth ; still even
Matthew Arnold errs sometimes and we should rather enquire as to the
truth of his views than accept them because they are his, especially
since Emerson, whom Arnold revered, takes a view quite opposed to his.

First of all one should observe that Arnold objects not to the poetry,
but to the philosophy of life, which he finds in the ode. Wordsworth
expressly states the objections of Arnold in language not less forcible:

"To that dream-like vividness and splendour which invest objects of
sight in childhood, every one, I believe, if he would look back, could bear
testimony, and I need not dwell upon it here ; but having in the poem
regarded it as presumptive evidence of a prior state of existence, I think
it right to protest against a conclusion, which has given pain to some
good and pious persons, that I meant to inculcate such a belief. *It is
far too shadowy a notion to be recommended to faith, as more than an
element in our instincts of immortality.* But let us bear in mind that,
though the idea is not advanced in revelation, there is nothing there
to contradict it, and the fall of man presents an analogy in its favour,
Accordingly, a pre-existent state has entered into the popular creeds of

many nations, and, among all persons acquainted with classic literature, is known as an ingredient in Platonic philosophy. Archimedes said that he could move the world if he had a point whereon to rest his machine. Who has not felt the same aspirations as regards the world of his own mind ? Having to wield some of its elements when I was impelled to write this poem on the 'Immortality of the Soul,' *I took hold of the notion of pre-existence as having sufficient foundation in humanity for authorizing me to make for my purpose the best use of it I could as a poet.*"

The italics are ours, and the last three words are especially emphatic. Of course the fact that the poet acknowledges the notion of pre-existence to be a mere speculation does not answer Arnold's criticism, but to remember the fact is to be in a better position for treating the author fairly. Arnold is a terrible critic, he brings the form of a poem into comparison with the chaste perfection of Greek art and the substance of it into comparison with what he conceives to be absolute and eternal truth. He judges this piece to be beautiful but to be lacking in that absolute and established truthfulness which would make it a poem of the highest order. It is not expedient here to argue this judgment, but in order to account for the strange differences of opinion among the ablest judges as to the value of its didactic import, it is only necessary to say that Matthew Arnold's views of truth were, in the respects that make this ode important, so far from those of many other critics, that agreement was out of the question : and it may be confidently asserted that if no work can stand as great poetry which is founded on beliefs concerning other states of life not held by Matthew Arnold, some very famous poems must lose ground.

The line of thought in the poem is somewhat as follows : (1) The poet laments his loss of "that dream-like vividness and splendour" with which children see things about them : (2) Of course he *sees* that a rainbow or a rose, the moon, water by starlight, sunshine, are beautiful, but their *magic* loveliness he cannot realize any more : (3) Under the influence of a perfectly lovely day he shakes off the grief caused by the loss of his childhood gift of perceiving beauty intensely : (4) He almost convinces himself that he has as deep a sense of the beauty of things as he ever had, but he has to confess again that the visionary gleam is gone : (5) The fifth stanza (written two years later than the preceding four) begins to account for the loss of the "dream-like vividness and splendour" of childhood eyes ; it states that in passing from birth to manhood, heaven largely dies out of the soul and the world takes its place : (6) The world is at enmity with our heavenly nature and seduces us to lower pleasures and interests : (7) The poet shows how wordly affairs engross the being of the growing child, but declares that he only acts his parts—in the soul of his soul he is allied to divinity still : (8 He apostrophizes the child and asks him why he seeks to know the world when it would be true wisdom to rest content with the beautiful soul he brought from heaven : (9) He expresses deep joy that even the most seducing wordly interests can never quite destroy the divine nature in a man, and that every man has at times intimations of his heavenly origin : (10) He again surrenders himself to the influence of a perfectly lovely day, (stanza 3) and says that though he cannot feel the pure joy in beauty that he could before the world had claimed so much of him, yet he feels that the centre of his soul is in sympathy with that pure joy, and what he has lost of it is to some extent compensated by a deep human sympathy, (which he could never have had without being to some degree worldly) and by a faith that when the world at last loses it power, he will return to perfect bliss : (11) In conclusion, the poet weighs his gains and losses since childhood ; he has lost the glory and the freshness of his childhood perceptions ; he has retained a great love of beauty and a profound sympathy with heaven-born childhood and nature ; he has gained through worldly experience, love, human sympathy, thoughtfulness, sad perhaps, but a divine sort of melancholy, such as Milton loved : he does not strike a balance, but concludes in a tone of cultured repose.

The comprehension of this line of thought depends chiefly upon the clearness with which one conceives the "celestial light" in which children behold the common objects around them : and how this magic way of seeing disappears as years advance. It is probably one of those graces of nature that most fear to mention for fear of missing a sympathetic ear : yet in Wordsworth it was so positively developed that he wrote of it as freely as if it had been the commonest faculty.

5. "The earth."—Probably meaning the soil itself—since grass, trees, water, and common sights, are species of the same genus as *earth*.

9. "hath been."—What is the regular use of the present perfect tense ?

12. "I now can see no more."—See *Tintern Abbey*, line, 85.

26. "the tabor."—A small drum used as an accompaniment to a fife.

33. "the fields of sleep."—This much-disputed phrase may mean "sleeping fields," "the regions of sleep, the early dawn." It may,

however, mean the happy, drowsy meadows where the sheep are browsing and resting.

37. "**with the heart of May.**"—With springtime joy and life.

40. "**Shepherd-boy.**"—Who may be supposed to be quite Arcadian and unworldly.

53. "**In a thousand valleys.**"—A strong bit of imaginative sympathy.

57. "**a Tree.**"—Who cannot recall a tree that is dear because it was seen through the golden mists of childhood ?

63. "**the visionary gleam.**"—The magic light which makes that tree different from others.

74. "**Shades of the prison-house.**"—Claims of the world.

77. "**the East.**"—Stars rise in the East ; hence the metaphor, where the soul is a star the time of birth is the east.

78. "**Priest.**"—Worshipper and exponent.

89. "**foster-child.**"—Of noble origin, the child has earth for a foster-mother.

96. "**Mother's.**"—Has no reference to foster-mother Earth.

110. "**Actor.**"—Compare the following speech from Shakespeare's *As You Like It* :

> "All the world's a stage,
> And all the men and women merely players :
> They have their exits and their entrances ;
> And one man in his time plays many parts,
> His acts being seven ages.   At first the infant,
> Mewling and puking in the nurse's arms.
> And then the whining school-boy, with his satchel
> And shining morning face, creeping like snail
> Unwillingly to school.   And then the lover,
> Sighing like furnace, with a woeful ballad
> Made to his mistress' eyebrow.   Then a soldier,
> Full of strange oaths and bearded like a pard,
> Jealous in humor, sudden and quick in quarrel,
> Seeking the bubble reputation
> Even in the cannon's mouth.   And then the justice,
> In fair round belly with good capon lined,
> With eyes severe and beard of formal cut,
> Full of wise saws and modern instances ;

19

And so he plays his part.   The sixth age shifts
To the lean and slippered pantaloon,
With spectacles on nose and pouch on side,
His youthful hose, well saved, a world too wide
For his shrunk shank ; and his big manly voice,
Turning again toward childish treble, pipes
And whistles in his sound.   Last scene of all,
That ends this strange, eventful history,
In second childishness and mere oblivion,
Sans teeth, sans eyes, sans taste, sans everything."

112. **"persons."**—Derived from L. *per*, through, and *sonare*, to sound ; *persona* means a mask, used by an actor, then actor, then any-one on the stage of life.   Here, of course, *persons* means *actors*.

117. **"whose exterior semblance doth belie thy soul's im-mensity."**—Whose infant clay gives no indication of its high origin and endowments.

120. **"thou Eye among the blind."**—Read *Earth's Preference*, chap. V.

139-142. I rejoice that in what is left of us after the world has de-graded us there is something of divine vitality ; I rejoice that nature yet remembers what was so fleeting, that is our heavenly instincts.

146-150. In first mastering this stanza, bracket these lines, "Delight and liberty......thanks and praise," and read

" Not indeed
For that which is most worthy to be blest

.   .   .   .

But for those obstinate questionings," etc.

Then in line 158 change *but* to *and*, so as to co-ordinate lines 151 and 158, thus :

" But for those obstinate questionings

.   .   .   .   .

And for those first affections."

153. **"Fallings from us, vanishings."**—Wordsworth explains this satisfactorily ; he speaks of the opening stanza of *We Are Seven*, and adds: " But it was not so much from feelings of animal vivacity that *my* difficulty came as from a sense of the indomitableness of the spirit within me.   I used to brood over the stories of Enoch and Elijah, and almost to persuade myself that, whatever might become of others, I should be translated, in something of the same way, to heaven.   With

a feeling congenial to this, I was often unable to think of external things as having external existence, and I communed with all that I saw as something not apart from, but inherent in, my own immaterial nature. Many times while going to school have I grasped at a wall or tree to recall myself from this abyss of idealism to the reality. At that time I was afraid of such processes. In later periods of life I have deplored, as we have all reason to do, a subjugation of an opposite character, and have rejoiced over the remembrances, as is expressed in the lines—

> 'Obstinate questionings
> Of sense and outward things,
> Fallings from us, vanishings ;' etc."

156. Emphasize *mortal.* The *material* nature seemed humiliated in the presence of this high-born *soul.*

173. "**that immortal sea.**"—The soul comes, like a star, from the east. It reaches the continent of human life and journeys westward on that land. To be far inland is to be at once far from birth, or old, and far from heaven, or worldly.

175. "**travel thither.**"—In imagination the soul of the worldly man may in a moment of supreme elevation have glimpses of his childhood and see the shore from which he started inland, and from which children are now starting inland.

177. Worthy of Swinburne in fullness of harmony : read slowly, and with impressive orotund voice.

182. Notice the metrical changes in this passage.

197. "**years that bring the philosophic mind.**"—When thought takes the place of the divine, but unconscious, harmony of the infant soul.

201. "**Yet.**"—Still.

202. "**one delight.**"—Glorious perceptions of sensuous beauty.

203. "**To live beneath your more habitual sway.**"—This line is not in apposition with *one delight*, but in contrast, and means—in order to live under the calming and ennobling influence of nature, not as the source of rapturous joy, but of serene and supporting strength.

211. "**Another race hath been, and other palms are won.**"— He had grown up with his generation ; some had died, some were successful : this experience had sobered his vision and destroyed the celestial light, but had brought him another kind of vision, the melancholy light of perfect culture.

CHARACTER OF THE HAPPY WARRIOR.—Page 103.

Great thoughts tending to improve our knowledge of right living have
a beauty of their own : aside from that beauty this poem is rather
homely : yet it is dignified and even sublime.

Nelson was in the poet's mind as he wrote, and where Nelson's
character fell short of his ideal he thought instead, of his own brother
John, who was also a sea-captain, though not in the naval service.

Mrs. Jameson said that if one were to read *woman* for *warrior* throughout this piece, it would make truth and sense in nearly every line.

The poem is worth memorizing on account of its delineation of real
greatness from the English point of view.

8. "**bright.**"—Clear rather than joyous.

18. "**bereaves.**"—Suggest another word for this.

42. Compare Tennyson's patriotic lays.

60. "**master-bias.**"—A harsh but effective temporary compound.

LINES WRITTEN ABOVE TINTERN ABBEY.—Page 109.

In the Fifth *Royal Canadian Reader* may be found this passage :
"With Wordsworth, Nature is no mere machine. There is, he
affirms, a soul in all the world—

> " A presence that disturbs me with the joy
> Of elevated thoughts ; a sense sublime
> Of something far more deeply interfused,
> Whose dwelling is the light of setting suns,
> And the round ocean and the living air,
> And the blue sky, and in the mind of man :
> A motion and a spirit that impels
> All thinking things, all objects of all thought,
> And rolls through all things."

This presence he identifies with the living spirit of God. According
to Professor Shairp's interpretation of his meaning, Nature, though mani-
festing itself in various forms, is pervaded by a unity of life and power,
binding it together into one living whole, and possessing an influence
which streams through and stimulates man's life—a spirit itself invisible, though it speaks through visible forms. Its calmness stills and
refreshes man ; its sublimity raises his spirit to noble and energetic

thoughts, and its tenderness, striving in the largest and loftiest things condescends to the lowest, and is in the humblest worm and weed as in the great movements of the elements and of the stars. Its stability and order, too, satisfy his intellect and calm his soul. Our mind, receiving these impressions, adds to them its own thoughts and feelings, and this union produces the harmony he conceives to exist between Nature and mankind."

Myers regards the poem as the "consecrated formulary of the Words-worthian faith." All that has been said of his relation to Nature is found in this poem, which is the very gospel of his mission.

Turner gives the following careful abstract of the piece :

"After five long years the poet once more looks upon the sylvan Wye. Nor, during that absence among far other scenes, has the memory of a spot so beautiful and quiet ever left him. Nay, more, it may be that to the unconscious influence of those beauteous forms he owes the highest of his poetic moods –that mood in which the soul transcends the world of sense, and views the world of being and the mysterious harmony of the universe. He believes that this is so ; at least he knows how often the memory of this quiet beauty has cheered the dreariness of life and soothed its fever.

"And now he once more stands beside the real scene of his dreams, and his present sensations mingle with his past, not without a painful feeling that the past has in a measure faded and belongs to his former self, yet feeling that the joy of the present moment will recur through years to come.

"For although he is no longer his former self, no longer feels the same all-sufficing passion for the mere external forms and colours of nature, is no longer filled with the same gladness of mere animal life, yet Nature has not forsaken, but only fulfilled her kindly purpose towards her worshipper. Taught by her, he has reached a more serene and higher region ; higher because more human in its interest, more thoughtful in its nature, more moral in its object.

"And even if he had not reached this higher mood, none the less by sympathy with his sister could he feel the full joys of his former self. That she should now be as he was then is his wish and prayer ; for doubtless she too will be led by Nature, who never leaves her task incomplete, to the higher and more tranquil mood which is the ripe fruit of former flowers. And so, whatever sorrows might befall her in after times, both he and she could with joy remember that Nature by such scenes and by his aid had wrought in her an unfailing source of comfort."

20. "**hedgerows.**"—Rows of shrubs or trees planted for inclosure or separation of fields.

23-27. Turner says, "The silence is made noticeable by the human life implied by the smoke, but of which there is no other sign." Is this the force one should assign to the word *uncertain* ?

40. These acts have a subtle cause in forgotten sensations of natural beauty.

41-55. The calm repose of such a scene soothes the spirit and leads to communion with the very springs of life.

70. From such repose and spiritual light comes the best preparation for duty.

82-90. This sounds like the language of a lover concerning the glories of love or of Sir Galahad concerning religious transports. To Wordsworth this passion for Nature was what love and religion are to many—the passion that seizes and vehemently controls all the faculties. This is the best note we have on the " celestial light " of his great *Ode*.

98. Compare Rossetti, " And oh, the song the sea sings, is dark everlastingly."

127. "**wild eyes.**"—Quick and imaginative.

129. "**Sister.**"—Dorothy Wordsworth.

136. "**evil tongues.**"—Compare that passage of sublime pride in Milton (P. L. vii, l. 24), where the aged and unfortunate poet says :

> " Though fall'n on evil days,
> On evil days though fall'n, and evil tongues ;
> In darkness, and with dangers compass'd round,
> And solitude."

151. His sister Dorothy ended her days in mental darkness.

THE FOUNTAIN.—Page 114.

Even in this simple dialogue we recognize the superiority of the dramatic form in the portrayal of character. Those who believe with Wordsworth that much true poetry is to be found in the language of peasants when under the excitement of deep feeling will find poetry in *The Fountain.*

If this character is the Matthew of the poem of that name he is a schoolmaster of some village school ; and probably from what we can learn he resembles more or less closely some master known by the poet. He tells us in one place that the characteristics of Matthew are drawn from more than one man.

3, 4. Be careful to read the first two lines with one eye on the punctuation.

5. "**Friends**."—What had they in common?

9. Why does this detail give its name to the poem?

21. "**dear old man**."—Evidently not a Squeers.

35-38. Discuss Tennyson's saying that "a sorrow's crown of sorrows is remembering happier things."

43-46. Compare *Earth's Preference*, Chapter V.

47. "**But we are pressed upon by heavy laws**."—"The days of our strength are three score years and ten, and if by reason of strength they be four score years yet is their strength labour and sorrow."

50. "**Because we have been glad before**."—Because we live in the past.

54. "**It is the man of mirth**."—He has the most to regret.

61. "**I**."—With playful emphasis.

66. "**that cannot be**."—His heart was past new ties, though warm and grateful.

71. "**Leonard's rock**."—Some local land-mark.

PEELE CASTLE.—Page 117.

"Written soon after the death, by shipwreck, of Wordsworth's brother John. This poem may be profitably compared with Shelley's following it (in the *Golden Treasury*). Each is the most complete expression of the innermost spirit of his art given by these great poets :—of that idea which, as in the case of the true painter (to quote the words of Reynold's), subsists only in the mind : the sight never beheld it, nor has the hand expressed it : it is an idea residing in the breast of the artist, which he is always labouring to impart, and which he dies at last without imparting."

Shelley's poem, to which Palgrave in this remarkable note alludes, is:

THE POET'S DREAM.

On a poet's lips I slept
Dreaming like a love-adept
In the sound his breathing kept ;
Nor seeks nor finds he mortal blisses,
But feeds on the aerial kisses
Of shapes that haunt thought's wildernesses.

He will watch from dawn to gloom
The lake-reflected sun illume
The yellow bees in the ivy-bloom,
Nor heed nor see what things may be—
But from these create he can
Forms more real than living man,
Nurslings of Immortality.

16-19. In this immortal stanza the poet seems to come very near the impossible, he all but enables us to grasp the indefinable halo that genius alone discerns about the objects it contemplates—that golden illusion that flits away from common sense to perfect wisdom. That which Ariel was in the Tempest, that which Coleridge felt and often tried to tell us

"A light, a fair luminous cloud
Enveloping the Earth,"

and again,

" This light, this glory, this fair luminous mist,
This beautiful and beauty-making power,"

in another place " A swimming phantom light," and in a fourth " A magic light," all these point to the same mystery. Other expressions of it occur in Wordsworth, notably in the *Ode on Immortality* : and of course it is what Sir Joshua tries to say in the note above ; but no one can say it—so that it may be generally known.

41. "Him whom I deplore."—His brother John.

53. "the Kind."—Men.

FRENCH REVOLUTION.—Page 119.

There is a wonderful charm about this poem. It is as, if one who had been a glorious idealist, but no mere dreamer, had awaked from an illusion and had told his dream ; the reasonableness, the nobility, the romance, the God-like enthusiasm for the best the world aspires to, are told with a poetic grace and a persuasive logic that go far to convert the reader, against his knowledge, into a Revolutionist of the year '89. The astounding skill of this as a defence of what he regards perhaps as a youthful error, is greatly enhanced by his own attitude in the poem, not the least hint of retraction or apology is evinced, but rather he would say, " Had I resisted the glamour of it, would I not have been less a man ? " Compare Coleridge's *Ode to France* where he says, " O forgive those dreams ! "

4. "**auxiliars.**"—Liberals everywhere.

6. "**that dawn.**"—Of freedom.

7-10. See Burke's *Reflections on the French Revolution.*

38. "**Utopia.**"— A work by Thomas More, describing an Ideal Republic.

38. "**subterranean Fields.**"—Alludes to the Happy Valley of *Rasselas ;* and reminds one of Lytton's *The Coming Race.* See note on *Michael,* line 53. •

39. "**secreted Island.**"—Recalling Bacon's *The New Atlantis.* The works mentioned are a few of the numerous "Ideal Commonwealths" outlined by eminent men ; others are Plato's *Republic,* Plutarch's *Lycargus,* Campanella's *City of the Sun,* Hall's *Mundus Altes et Idem.* Montaigne deals with the same subject in his famous *Essays.*

41-42. The sound statesmanlike tone of the last lines, shows that he has fundamentally right views of social reform. Compare Shakespeare's allusion to ideal republics in *The Tempest,* Act II, Sc. 1.

A POET'S EPITAPH.—Page 120.

In this defence of the poet, Wordsworth represents the statesman, the lawyer, the doctor of divinity, the soldier, the doctor of medicine, the student of natural philosophy, and the student of moral philosophy, as approaching the poet's grave ; each in turn is dismissed as unworthy of the right even to pay his respects to the hallowed poetic dust : finally a poet approaches the resting-place of his brother bard, and is warmly welcomed and bid to come, go, and remain at will.

In his enthusiasm to express the central idea—that the poet is the noblest of mankind—the author has neglected to lend grace to the form of his work, hence its stiffness and monotony, not to say narrowness, of tone : in these respects it does not bear comparison with Burns' *Bard's Epitaph,* upon which it is modelled : it is difficult to defend an inferior imitation.

THE BARD'S EPITAPH.

Is there a whim-inspired fool,
Owre fast for thought, owre hot for rule,
Owre blate to seek, owre prood to snool,
    Let him draw near ;
And owre this grassy heap sing dool,
    And drap a tear.

Is there a Bard of rustic song,
Who, noteless, steals the crowds among
That weekly this area throng,
　　　　O, pass not by !
But, with a frater-feeling strong,
　　　　Here, heave a sigh.

Is there a man whose judgment clear,
Can others teach the course to steer,
Yet runs, himself, life's mad career
　　　　Wild as the wave ;
Here pause—and, thro' the starting tear,
　　　　Survey this grave.

The poor Inhabitant below
Was quick to learn, and wise to know,
And keenly felt the friendly glow,
　　　　And softer flame ;
But thoughtless follies laid him low,
　　　　And stain'd his name !

Reader, attend—whether thy soul
Soars fancy's flights beyond the pole,
Or darkling grubs this earthly hole,
　　　　In low pursuit ;
Know, prudent, cautious, *self-control*
　　　　Is wisdom's root.

10. Compare the following passage from Thomson's *Seasons* (*Autumn*, line 565) :

" Perhaps some doctor, of tremendous paunch,
Awful and deep, a black abyss of drink,
Outlives them all ; and from his buried flock
Retiring, full of rumination sad,
Laments the weakness of these latter times."

This passage describes a fox-hunting parson at a hunt dinner, drinking the gentlemen of his parish under the table. Wordsworth's doctor lived after the Evangelical movement, we may presume, and was a degenerate successor of the other.

25. "abject."—Materialist.

33. "All-in-all."—Not recognizing the inadequacy of his philosophy.

38. " with modest looks, and clad in homely russet brown."—
Aldrich, in a pretty little tribute to Shakespeare, describes him in nearly the same words:

> " The doublet's modest gray or brown,
> The slender sword-hilt's plain device,
> What sign had these for prince or clown ?
> Few turned, or none, to scan him twice."

44-45. Highly subjective.

46-53. The poetic function as described here reminds one of Shakespeare's often-quoted lines on the same subject.

SONNETS.—Page 125.

Wordsworth published between three and four hundred sonnets,
Shakespeare one hundred and fifty-four, Milton only twenty-three, of
which six are Italian.   The chief subjects of Wordsworth's sonnets are
Liberty, Church History, and thoughts suggested by *Nature* ; many,
however, have other subjects.   His mastery over this form of verse is so
complete that it may be compared to an instrument which he commanded so entirely as to make it express his mind perfectly.   It is well
known that as a versifier he was very unequal : it would be absurd to
say that the poet who wrote *Yarrow Revisited* and the *Ode on Immortality* was not a versifier, yet from wrong theories or other causes his
poetry is often crude in form and unmusical : it may have been on account of his limitations as an inventor of forms that he used the sonnet
so often.   Still, it was natural that a writer of profound reflective
power should seize upon this simple conventional form as a ready mould
for his thoughts.

The word sonnet (a little strain) once applied to any short song,
especially a love-song. It became limited, however, to poems of fourteen lines, and eventually to these, only under certain other conditions
as to form and rhyme.

The name is now applied to two principal forms, which may for con-
venience be called the *Shakespearean* and the *recent*. These classes
have two characteristics in common—both require that the subject-matter shall consist of *one* complete thought or sentiment,
and both require that the form should be fourteen iambic
pentameters.   The Shakespearean sonnet differed from recent sonnets in rhyme-arrangement, Shakespeare's sonnets having the ar-

rangement *a b a b c d c d e f e f g g*, while recent sonnets follow the arrangement *a b b a a b b a c d c d c d* (allowing, however, some latitude in the arrangement of the *c d* rhymes). There is another important difference also, not so easy to define. The *Shakesperean* sonnet usually consists of some poetical symbol and the application of it to the main thought: the symbol occupies the twelve lines of alternate rhyme, and the application the rhyming couplet at the end, so that one may usually get the main thought by merely reading this concluding couplet. The *recent* sonnets are different in this respect, the division between the symbol and the application (when these occur) usually being at the end of the *octave*. Frequently, however, the *octave* explains the whole thought, while the *sestet* is used for some quiet reflection upon that thought. The *recent* sonnets are modelled upon the Italian sonnet used by Milton. The examples chosen to illustrate these truths are chosen as striking examples of their classes, and as likely to illustrate in a pointed manner the changes already described.

SHAKESPEARE'S THIRTIETH SONNET.

When to the sessions of sweet silent thought
I summon up remembrance of things past,
I sigh the lack of many a thing I sought,
And with old woes new wail my dear time's waste :
Then can I drown an eye, unused to flow,
For precious friends hid in death's dateless night.
And weep afresh love's long-since-cancelled woe,
And moan the expense of many a vanish'd sight :
Then can I grieve at grievances foregone,
And heavily from woe to woe tell o'er
The sad account of fore-bemoaned moan,
Which I new pay as if not paid before.
    But if the while I think on thee, dear friend,
    All losses are restored, and sorrows end.

SHAKESPEARE'S NINETIETH SONNET.

Then hate me when thou wilt ; if ever, now ;
Now while the world is bent my deeds to cross,
Join with the spite of fortune, make me bow,
And do not drop in for an after-loss :
Ah ! do not, when my heart hath scaped this sorrow,
Come in the rearward of a conquer'd woe

Give not a windy night a rainy morrow,
To linger out a purposed overthrow.
If thou wilt leave me, do not leave me last,
When other petty griefs have done their spite,
But in the onset come ; so shall I taste
At first the very worst of fortune's might ;
 And other strains of woe, which now seem woe,
 Compared with loss of thee will not seem so.

MILTON'S EIGHTEENTH SONNET.

ON THE LATE MASSACRE IN PIEDMONT.

Avenge, O Lord, Thy slaughter'd saints, whose bones
 Lie scatter'd on the Alpine mountains cold ;
 Even them who kept Thy truth so pure of old,
When all our fathers worshipp'd stocks and stones,
Forget not : in Thy book record their groans
 Who were Thy sheep, and in their ancient fold
 Slain by the bloody Piedmontese, that roll'd
Mother with infant down the rocks.   Their moans
 The vales redoubled to the hills, and they
To heaven.   Their martyr'd blood and ashes sow
 O'er all the Italian fields, where still doth sway,
The triple tyrant ; that from these may grow
 A hundred fold, who, having learn'd Thy way,
Early may fly the Babylonian woe.

MILTON'S NINETEENTH SONNET.

ON HIS BLINDNESS.

When I consider how my light is spent
 Ere half my days, in this dark world and wide,
 And that one talent which is death to hide,
Lodged with me useless, though my soul more bent
To serve therewith my Maker, and present
 My true account, lest He, returning, chide ;
 " Doth God exact day-labour, light denied ? "
I fondly ask : but Patience, to prevent
 That murmur, soon replies, "God doth not need
Either man's work, or His own gifts ; who best

Bear His mild yoke, they serve Him best ; His state
Is kingly: thousands at His bidding speed,
And post o'er land and ocean without rest ;
    They also serve who only stand and wait."

ROSSETTI'S *BEAUTY AND THE BIRD.*

SHE fluted with her mouth as when one sips,
    And gently waved her golden head, inclin'd
    Outside his cage close to the window-blind:
Till her fond bird, with little turns and dips,
Piped low to her of sweet companionships.
    And when he made an end, some seed took she
    And fed him from her tongue, which rosily
Peeped as a piercing bud between her lips.

And like the child in Chaucer, on whose tongue
    The Blessed Mary laid, when he was dead,
A grain,—who straightway praised her name in song :
    Even so, when she, a little lightly red,
Now turned on me and laughed, I heard the throng
    Of inner voices praise her golden head.

MATTHEW ARNOLD'S *SHAKESPEARE.*

OTHERS abide our question.   Thou art free.
We ask and ask.   Thou smilest, and art still,
Out-topping knowledge.   For the loftiest hill,
Who to the stars uncrowns his majesty,

Planting his steadfast footsteps in the sea,
Making the heaven of heavens his dwelling-place,
Spares but the cloudy border of his base
To the foiled searching of mortality ;

And thou, who didst the stars and sunbeams know,
Self-schooled, self-scanned, self-honored, self-secure,
Didst tread on earth unguessed at.—Better so !

All pains the immortal spirit must endure,
All weakness which impairs, all griefs which bow,
Find their sole speech in that victorious brow.

It will be observed that even Milton does not show so marked a turn at the ninth line as the later poets. It has been said that Milton's sonnets shoot rapidly off like a rocket, and then fall, breaking in a shower of brightness ; some of them, however, have been more aptly described as a trumpet call to duty. The *recent* sonnets have been well compared to a waving rising (in the *octave*) and gently subsiding as the thought spends itself in beauty. One of the most perfect of the latter class is the sonnet *To Night*, in chapter V.

Wordsworth's sonnets stand somewhere between Milton's and Matthew Arnold's in form and manner ; though those who know Wordsworth only by his other works will be surprised at the grace and sweetness of such sonnets as that *To Lady Beaumont*, which Hutton so justly praises.

III.—On the Extinction of the Venetian Republic.

3-4. "Since the first dominion of man was asserted over the ocean, three thrones of mark beyond all others have been set upon its sands, the thrones of Tyre, Venice, and England."

6. **"Eldest Child of Liberty."**—"Founded by Christians" in "the year 421." Read Ruskin's *Stones of Venice*, first appendix to Vol I.

10. **"espouse the everlasting Sea."**—There was a ceremony called the Bridal of the Sea, in which Venice figured as the bride.

15. **"even the Shade."**—In 1797, by the Peace of Campo Formio, Venice was given to Austria. Encyc. Brit., Vol. XIII, page 485.

VI.—Thought of a Briton on the Subjugation of Switzerland.

7. **"a Tyrant."**—Napoleon.

12. **"that which still is left."**—"And ocean mid his uproar wild speaks safety to his island-child." Read Coleridge's *Ode to the Departing Year*.

XVII.—To Clarkson.

4. **"Clarkson."**—Thomas Clarkson, 1760-1846, wrote and worked against slavery. In 1794 his health broke down from overwork, also at one time he lost his sight, but he recovered health and sight and died at eighty-six.

9. **"Voice."**—See line 12.

The activity and energy of the octave, and the peace and calm of the sestet remind one of the third stanza of Shelley's *Cloud*.

XIX.—SCORN NOT THE SONNET.

4. "**unlocked his heart.**"—His plays are objective, his sonnets subjective. See Browning's *House.*

5. "**Petrarch's wound.**"—Francesco Petrarca, 1504-1574, one of four great Italian poets, and the first true reviver of learning in mediæval Europe. He had a sad but romantic attachment to a lady whom he writes of as Laura.

6. "**Camoens.**"—The Portuguese epic poet. His masterpiece is the *Lusiad.* He died in great poverty and was called "*the great.*" The Portuguese accent his name on the second, the English on the first.

6. "**Tasso.**"—1544-1595. One of the four great Italian poets. Tasso was a great though ill-balanced genius : a master of love-lyrics.

8-9. "**myrtle, cypress.**"—The myrtle, sacred to Venus, was the wreath of bloodless victors ; the cypress is emblematic of grief and death.

10. "**visionary.**"—Alludes to the visions of Hell, Purgatory, and Heaven.

11. "**from Faery-land.**"—An allusion to Spenser's great poem, and to a sonnet (the 80th) referring to the sonnet.

14. "**a trumpet.**"—Milton's sonnet to Cromwell will explain this term.

XX.—NUNS FRET NOT.

7. "**Furness Fells.**"—Fells are moors.

8. "**foxglove.**"—A purple (or white or rose-colour) flower common in England.

XXIII.—PERSONAL TALK.

13. "**forms with chalk.**"—For dance-figures.

20. "**undersong.**"—Refrain or accompaniment.

XXIV.—CONTINUED.

14. "**Lady.**"—Desdemona.

15. "**Una.**"—In the *Faery Queen.*

XXV.—CONCLUDED.

2. "**Nor can I not.**"—What figure of speech ?

6. "**genial seasons.**"—Genial is a pet word of Wordsworth's.

13. "**heavenly lays.**"—Specify.

XXVI.—To Sleep.

9. "First Cuckoo's melancholy cry." This bird of spring has a plaintive "two-fold" song.

15. "blessed barrier."—Compare Shakespeare and other poets on the same subject.

XXIX.—Composed Upon Westminster Bridge.

13. "a calm so deep."—What makes this a paradox ?

15. Account for this invocation.

FINIS.

www.ingramcontent.com/pod-product-compliance
Lightning Source LLC
Chambersburg PA
CBHW060557030726
47498CB00005B/1431